THE
WAY-OUT
WILD
WEST

Lyn McConchie

Hadrosaur Productions, Mesilla Park, NM

The Way-Out Wild West
Hadrosaur Productions
First Edition: January 2022

ISBN-10: 1-885093-99-3
ISBN-13: 978-1-885093-99-8

Hadrosaur Productions
P.O. Box 2194
Mesilla Park, NM 88047-2194
www.hadrosaur.com

Dedicated to Matt Fletcher who sneaked into a story, and to Sprocket, every cat should get their name into at least one book in their lifetime.

CONTENTS

THE
WAY-OUT
WILD
WEST

FOR LOVE OF MAXIE

My daughter came past me, walking towards the stable with a determined look on her face. I cleared my throat.

"Where are you going?"

"Riding, daddy."

I looked her over. Annie's only eight, but she grew up out here and she knows the rough country and horses. And she's a sensible child, not one to take foolish chances, but despite that I wasn't happy about her going out just now.

"I don't like the look of the weather, sweetheart. Which way are you going?"

"Towards Verdis Canyon, daddy. I'll be back in a couple of hours, I promise."

It sounded all right, and her pony, Maxie, is elderly, smart, very sure-footed, and devoted to Annie. He belonged to my wife before she died and he's spent his whole life being ridden by one or the other of the Landis women. I nodded and Annie broke into a run towards the stable. I looked back ten minutes later to see them heading west, Annie with her long brown hair lifted by the wind, and Maxie, loping along, his dun hide blending quickly into the landscape as they got further away.

I went back to the ranch's bank statements I'd been working on and it was hours later that I simultaneously realized three things. That it was now almost dark, it was raining solidly, and that I'd never seen or heard Annie come back.

I came to my feet in one jump, and in another couple of seconds I was out the door heading for the stable. Maxie's stall was empty. It felt like all the breath had left my body, and I froze, then I started looking about me. Maxie's saddle and bridle weren't there, and in the mud-room Annie's riding coat wasn't hung up, nor were her riding boots on the boot rack.

1

No, they hadn't come back. I won't say that the area around Bodie in the year of our Lord 1891 is filled with danger, but I've never known a time anywhere when something can't go wrong. And if Annie and Maxie were still out there then something had gone badly wrong, and it was up to me to find them.

I made myself move slowly, considering each step; panic would only slow me down or make me miss something vital. I headed inside, reached for the small steam-powered engine that turned on the house's requirements, hooked up the phone and cranked it. Then I called Jack. He's a nearby neighbor, a mad inventor, and an all-around good man who's an honorary uncle to my daughter. He came on the line and I told him about Annie.

"Not good to hear. I guess she's in some sort of trouble, and we'd better find her. I'll ride over on Dobbin."

Dobbin is his steam-powered horse, Jack's been building those for some years and he's got pretty good at it. Dobbin can go all day on a tank of water, and he's dual-control, he can work off either ordinary horse commands with reins and heels, or work from voice orders. I donned my oilskins, and went out to saddle my mare. I was just leading her out of the stable when Jack came riding up.

"What do you know about where Annie was going?"

"Towards Verdis Canyon, she said. Reckoned she'd be back in a couple of hours, you know Annie, if she says something like that, she'll do it."

Jack pursed his lips. "An' she knows how long it takes to ride there an' back. So we go west about two hours ride."

"Why two?"

"She could always gallop back," was Jack's reply and I thought it a good one. Yes, Maxie was more than twenty, but he could still shift when he was asked, Annie was a light weight, and then too, she could have gone just a little further than she meant to, assuming she could make up the time it'd take to come home by pushing him along.

We found them in a clump of brush half an hour from home. Jack had the big lantern that took power off Dobbin, shining out, and Annie saw us coming. She came scooting out of the brush calling to me, and it wasn't just the rain on her face – or on mine for that matter. I swung down and held her while she cried against my shoulder and I knew from the heaving sobs that there was more wrong that I hadn't heard about as yet.

It was Jack who cut to the chase. "Where's Maxie, honey?"

She jerked her head to indicate the brush. "It was my fault. I was hurrying to get back home, and he put his foot in a hole…"

Jack moved the lantern and I saw what I hadn't noticed before, that Annie had mud all down one side of her clothes and a bruise on her cheek.

"He fell, daddy, he did his best, honestly, he tried not to fall on me, and he sort of twisted so he wouldn't … and … and…," She dissolved in tears again.

I put an arm around her while Jack detached the lantern and walked ahead. We found Maxie lying there. Yes, he'd saved Annie from being crushed under him when he fell, although the Lord only knows how, but in doing so he'd broken his neck and the leg that had gone into the hole. There was no way he could be saved, and I understood that was why Annie had stayed with him. Her horse was dying. He had no more than a few more minutes left to go now and she wouldn't leave him to die alone.

I took my oilskins off and draped them about her as she slumped to sit beside him. She put her arms about his neck, moved his head into her lap and began talking, using the murmurings and sounds, with here and there single words or phrases, with which a horse person communicates with a mount that knows what their rider means. Maxie did. His ears swiveled to listen and his eyes focused on her where she was crouched over him, her gaze fixed on his. And very slowly, so slowly I could never quite see the final moment when it happened, the light faded from his eyes.

A long minute after that Annie let his head slide from her lap and stood up, swaying. I went to lead her away but she paused, working to take something from her pocket. I saw a knife blade glint in the lantern-light as she stooped and carefully cut off a lock of his mane. Then, at last, she let us lead her away, mount her on Dobbin in front of Jack and slowly, silently, we rode home.

I let her sleep in late the next day and when she joined me she never mentioned Maxie. I made her something to eat, told her I'd be gone for a while and left her. Jack joined me as agreed around midday and we salvaged the horse tack before burning Maxie's body. The land hereabout is rocky and it would have been impossible to dig a hole large enough – and unthinkable to leave him to the scavengers – so we stacked brush all around him, fired it and added more and more as time went on until there was nothing left of the body but a scattering of the larger bones.

I went back the next day to bury those and darned if something hadn't already got to one, it had gnawed the end so that it was splintered, and I cursed as I gathered up the chips and bagged them into an old sack that I hauled down to a dip, which I dug deeper and buried them there, adding a cairn of the biggest stones I could carry to top off the grave against other foragers.

Annie didn't mention Maxie for almost a year, and when she did that was Jack's doing. For her ninth birthday he came riding up on Dobbin leading the most nondescript steamer horse you ever saw. It was just under fourteen hands in height; narrow in width, with thick legs, big hooves, and a slightly ro-man nose. It was a dun, not the flashier variation with black mane, tail, and stockings, but a plain dun all over. Jack dismounted and walked it over to Annie.

"Happy Birthday, honey. This is for you. He's got real strong legs so they won't break easily, and big hooves to keep him sure-footed. He's been trained to the usual commands, and he'll carry you all your life if you want to keep him."

There were a few seconds when it hung in the balance then her hands went out to stroke him, and the steamer swung his head to bump her with his nose. I caught Jack's eye at that and he nodded. Yes, he'd taught the steamer a few tricks to make it seem more life-like and it worked because Annie was hugging the thing, and then Jack and me.

"Oh, I love him Uncle Jack, what's his name?"

Well, I doubted the "his". Machines don't have a sex but I wasn't going to say so and Annie was laughing in a way I hadn't heard for too long.

Jack beamed at her. "He doesn't have one yet. That's up to you."

Annie laid a hand on the steamer's shoulder and smiled at us. "His name is Maxie," she said, and that was that.

She rode Maxie everywhere just as she had the original Maxie, except that she was much safer on this one. He had a few features that Jack had been developing. One was a sort of holster where a section of his shoulder opened if the rider pressed on the right place and you could keep a spare loaded handgun or a sawn-off in there, right close to hand. The other shoulder, the off one, had a tiny section that opened as well, just big enough to hold a few coins and notes, or something of that size. That one only opened to a voice command, and it had to be a voice the steamer had registered.

I never tried to open it. Annie kept young girl stuff in there and it would have been unforgivably intrusive had I demanded to know what was in there. It was as well she had a gun to hand as it was; she was thirteen when some lowlife came out of the trees where she took a shortcut home and tried to grab her. She dropped the reins, hit the panel with one hand and snatched the gun out with the other as Maxie pivoted. Then she fired, and the lowlife hit the ground. Jack and I went out in a group when she got home and told us, and we found her target, buckshot in one shoulder, and a broken knee as he tried to ride away while his horse plunged and sidled at the scent of blood and a rider that was all over the saddle. We hung him of course, and Annie praised Maxie.

"He kicked that man. And he lined him up just right for me to shoot too."

I nodded agreeably. Steamers have no volition, they obey commands and Maxie would have interpreted the shift of her body as she turned in the saddle, as a command to pivot, that was all. As for the kick, the man must have touched him, or some movement Annie made was interpreted as an order to kick. It could have been nothing more, and Jack agreed when I asked him.

But it was the event when Annie turned sixteen that made me rethink a good many of my assumptions. The railroad had come through the year before, and steam-trains ran up

and down the line, making getting cattle to market and bringing goods back to our ranches, easier by far, a lot faster – and
often cheaper too, although not always. There were points
that turned a train off into the town siding and I have to say
that there's times when progress is right useful.

It'd rained a lot that week and I took the buckboard to the
township to shop. Annie rode Maxie and it was a very pleasant day. Until we started for home, that was, and the weather
turned to a light drizzle again making the road slippery. I had
a new horse in the shafts. I still often preferred a live animal to
a steamer, and this animal was young, and a little flighty. The
journey hadn't been long enough to tire him since he'd had a
rest while we shopped and he was feeling his oats. It happened
as we neared the rails and a snake broke out of the grass right
by my horse's front hooves. He reared, squealed in panic and
leapt into a run.

Seconds later the buckboard wheels hit the rails and the
buckboard overturned tossing me out across the rails. Neither
of us knew it at the time but as I tried to roll over and stand,
my old buckskin coat caught under one of the cross-rails where
the points were, and there I was, immoveable. Annie was out
of the saddle almost before I hit the metal, and she was hauling
at me. It made no never-mind, I was there to stay and then, in
the distance, I felt the vibration in the rails that says a train is
on its way.

I breathed deep and spoke, keeping my voice calm. "Get
back, sweetheart, a train's coming."

I should have known better. She set her mouth and hauled
again. I saw sweat break out on her forehead with the effort she
was putting into moving me – and for all that she was strong I
didn't move an inch.

"Sweetheart, get back from the rails."

She didn't speak to me but to Maxie. "Here, Maxie." He
came and took hold of my collar in his teeth, but even his
strength only tore away the collar and I was still pinned.

"Annie," I said keeping my voice quiet. "If you stay on the
rails you'll be killed too, I'd rather that didn't happen." But
I saw her eyes and I knew she wasn't leaving me. We'd live
or die together and I couldn't bear it. And maybe something

else couldn't either because Maxie turned, his head cocked towards where the train was coming and all at once he was galloping away, vanishing into the trees that hid us from the train-driver's sight.

Annie stared after him briefly before turning back to put her arms around me. "I love you, daddy."

"I love you too, sweetheart," I told her as she made a final effort to drag me free – and failed. I could hear the train, the chuffing of the pistons and the clickety-clack of wheels on rails, as it neared us.

"Look at me," I said gently, "Don't look at the train, Annie; keep your eyes on me."

And from up the rails we heard it then. The shriek of vented steam as a whistle blew and blew, then a screaming of brakes, followed by a crash, the sound of metal on metal, and a bang like the end of the world. I knew that sound, I'd heard it before when Jack experimented. It was the sound of a boiler stressed to explosion point. Maxie?

They came in a while, found what the thing was that trapped me and I was freed while they told us the story. "Come galloping up the line to us, it did," said the driver. "Rearing up, right on the line, I blew the whistle over and over and it wouldn't move. Just stayed there until I slammed on the brakes but by then it was too late, and still it wouldn't get off the line. My fireman, Lee here, said as how maybe there was something we should look at on the line up aways. So we walked on an' there you were, sir. Reckon that was a very well programmed steamer."

"Yes," I said absently. "My friend Jack builds them."

"Lucky that, sir. Well we'd best be getting back to check that the train will still start, and you'd maybe like to get what's left of your steamer off the line."

With his and his fireman's aid we did that. The train started and moved off and Annie and I were left standing by Maxie's smashed body.

"I'll get him taken home tomorrow," I told her," and she nodded. Neither of us saying what was in our minds, that no one had given any orders, and what order could we have given? Jack hadn't coded anything into Maxie about stopping trains.

Well, we had what was left of Maxie carried home to the ranch, and Jack rebuilt him completely for Annie, until he was as good as new. Before he did that though, I went over the steamer and found that the terrible blow the train had given him had sprung the tiny pocket in his off-shoulder, and within that I found a rolled-up handkerchief. I opened it and wrapped in the material was a chip of bone, and a braided length of horsehair. I stared at them for a long time, then, very carefully, I rolled them up in the handkerchief again, stowed it back in the pocket, and closed the hide.

Did something of the original Maxie come to save Annie that day? Did his hair and bone carry his love for her and at the last impel his deputy to her rescue? Or could something man had created have become so much more than a machine, and had it only needed love for that change? I didn't know then and I still don't, but thirty years later I look out at Annie's three-year-old grandchild riding Maxie and I marvel. Because it doesn't matter how or why, only *that* it happened and like the bard said, I guess that there's more things on heaven and earth than poor fools like me will ever understand.

POLLY AND JOHNNY

"You're a narrow-minded stubborn idiot!"

"Nope, just sensible," I retorted.

"Sensible?" Jack's voice almost cracked, he was so mad. "Look, I built a steam-powered horse, a pack animal that won't tire, won't cost a fortune to feed, can guard you at night, carry twice the load, and doesn't have to be hobbled."

I sighed. "Jack, you make some wonderful gadgets, but they aren't practical for a desert prospector."

He snorted. "Remember John Henry? The song says that he won, but really we all know that he beat that steam-drill once, then he died and steam took over. It's the thing now, it's what everyone uses."

I made another attempt to explain. "Jack, John Henry lost in the end because a man can't beat a machine where no brains are involved. The brute power and endurance of a machine will beat a man, but where the job involves intelligence as well, then machines lose out to people – or even animals sometimes."

I left him thinking about that and stepped up my walking pace. I wanted to get a couple of good drinks inside before he started on me again. Ever since he'd built a couple of steam-powered horses he'd wanted me to take them on trial but I'd been riding Polly, my mare, for more than ten years now. I'd bought Johnny the jack donkey two years after that and he'd been my pack donkey ever since, they understood me an' I understood them. They were company out in the desert too, which is more than a couple of steam-driven rust-buckets would be.

Jack caught up with me next morning at breakfast. "Are you going out today?"

"Yup, as soon as I've saddled Polly and Johnny an' bought my supplies. Gonna try along the foothills towards

Chaco Canyon. Never tried there before an' I think it's about time I did."

Jack laid a palm flat on the table, his round face earnest. "I tell you what, you take my steam-horses with you and I'll pay for your supplies this trip? You can use Polly and Johnny, but take my two as well, see how they go. I bet after you see what they can do you'll take them on their own next time." His tone on that last sentence was confident and I wavered. He continued his persuasion. "They have saddles, I'll saddle one with a riding saddle, the other one with a pack saddle, and I'll put more supplies in that pack for you too. Come on, Hank. What do you say?"

I thought about it while Jack was smart enough to wait. After four or five minutes I nodded. "Okay, I'll take your two but I'll use mine to ride and pack, your pair can just follow along. Can you have them ready by nine?"

"You can't go this morning, I have to teach you the commands that activate them, and you'll have to talk to them an hour or so until they know your voice and understand what you're saying."

I was a mite annoyed about that but I was getting two packs of supplies for nothing and it was worth waiting. I followed along to his place and talked myself hoarse until his steam-powered critters were doing as I told them.

"All you have to do," Jack said, demonstrating, "is pour water in here until the tank is full. Or you give orders and they'll drink. They go twenty-four to thirty hours on a tank. The time difference depends on the land being flat or not, and how fast you run them."

"How big is the tank?"

"Takes ten gallons."

I could have pointed out a few things right there but I didn't. I'd wait until we got back and then I'd have examples I could hit him with.

I left at daybreak next morning, me on Polly, Johnny trailing along, his nose at her flank, and the two steamers ambling along to one side of us. Neither Polly nor Johnny liked them much but once they saw the things wouldn't harm them they quieted down and we went on our way.

That night we stopped at the Washbourne seep. It's in a cluster of rocks and was a damn nuisance. The steamers couldn't climb into the rocks as Polly and Johnny could, so I had to carry bucket after bucket of water to fill the tanks, but I managed and three days later I was at Chaco Canyon setting up camp. I took a day's rest and then started fossicking about, digging in likely places, checking a couple of dry stream-beds, and chipping chunks of any likely-looking rock. The stream by the camp was small and slow moving but there was enough water to do us all so I wasn't worried.

But the steamers stayed a nuisance. I had them under orders to drink when they needed to refill their tanks, and I had them on guard too, but I hadn't thought about that last. Old Standing Bear dropped in and one of the steamers darn near got him before I could call it off. You had to introduce people to them, and they had to be there to be introduced. Standing Bear had just come walking into the camp not knowing any better. He learned though and I wouldn't a' thought the old man could move that quickly.

"What *is* that thing, my friend Hank?"

"Steam-powered horse," I told him. "My friend Jack's making them and this pair is his experimental models. I got them out here to see how they go."

"Go bloody fast."

I had to agree with him there. Standing Bear stayed the night and went off around noon the next day while I went back to chipping and digging, and prying some of the boulders out of a dry streambed. Over two months I found a few pockets of color, washed out a little gold, found one small nugget, and was thinking about starting back when I walked up-stream by the water, spotted a tiny path leading between two boulders and followed it.

It came out in a cirque up against a cliff, and looking up I could see that when it rained hard the water would come down the cliff-face and fill the path so that it was a small river. Not that it mattered, any water would trickle before it gushed, and it wasn't much distance between the valley and lower ground where any water would spread out. I took a look around and liked what I saw. I started digging right below the cliff where the water had washed a sort of deep trough over the years, and once I had a few sacks of earth I took them back down to the stream and washed them pan by pan.

Johnny came over to put his nose on my shoulder when I whistled softly, running a forefinger through the bright grains of gold. "Yeah, look at that, you old jackass. That's the best color I've ever seen. Grains are rough, means it wasn't washed far before it landed here. Could be only a pocket, but even if it is, I could take out enough to pay for a retirement just in case. An an-ui-ty for me, an' a stable an' paddock for you two."

I stopped digging and panning for the day, moved most of my gear up to the valley and settled in. I'd pan until the supplies ran out, and then I'd go back to town, show the usual few pinches of gold, sigh, and say I was sure I'd find more sometime and re-supply. Town was used to it, they wouldn't think anything about it and what I'd washed out so far I could stash at my place and come back here again. I'd give Jack a report on his steamers at the same time.

I was close to finishing up the supplies an' thinking about leaving, so to be on the safe side I sewed that gold – and there was a fairish amount by then – into the hem of my old moleskin waistcoat, and in pockets in the lining, an' cleared up my camp. I got everythin' packed an' all I'd have to do in the morning would be to saddle Polly and Johnny and the steamers and get going.

"Reckon we're just about gone," I said to Polly and she snuffled at me affectionately. At least that was the program I planned. What is it some poet said about the best-laid plans a' mice an' men going ugly? I'm here to tell you they went some ugly all right.

I had the steamers on watch, supposed to stop anything living that came near me while I slept, but maybe they hadn't learned about rattlers. I woke up bright 'n early, ready to get a good day's ridin' in, jumped outa' my bed-roll and there was this almighty sound like stones in a tin and a savage stab in my calf just above my boot-top. I yelled in fright and pain and Jack come busting into camp. He took that rattler in his big yellow teeth, flung it to the ground and jumped on it a time or two. Then he stood watching in case it moved again. It didn't.

I was moving though. I got the blood flowing, and managed to screw my body around far enough to suck a lot of the poison out, but looking at that snake, I knew I was going to be real sick, real soon. It'd taken four fairly easy days to get here, if it took much more than half that long to get back I'd not make it. So it was the nearest steamer I straddled, and the other one that carried the camp gear. I ordered my mount into a slow rocking canter and sat there while its fellow rocked along beside us. Polly and Johnny fell behind over the day despite carrying nothing but their saddles. We camped at a small hollow where rainwater collects in the rock and there was just sufficient there for all of us with the critters catching up an hour after the steamers stopped. I slept a few hours and took off again soon as the moon was up.

By now my leg was twice its normal size and I was starting to feel giddy. I gave us a rest around noon; started off again and kept moving until late afternoon, then the steamer I was on made a strange grating sound and stopped dead. I was too light-headed to think about that much. I got onto the other one and ordered it into motion. At nightfall it stopped too, no sound, it just appeared to have run out of steam – literally. I was scared, and that gave me enough energy to try ordering it, I yelled, hit the thing, grabbed a water-skin from Johnny when he came up with us and poured water into the tank. It ran right out again, damn tank was still full.

I was having trouble staying on my feet but Polly was nudging me, worried I guess. She knew I was in trouble. I gave her the water-skin and she took it in her teeth as they knew how to do, and drank, I passed it on and Johnny finished the last of the water. I clung to her stirrup, and somehow I hauled myself onto her back and told them, Johnny standing there beside her and watching me, listening with his big ears pointed my way.

"Fellers, take me home, don't break up the old team now."

Polly started walking, Johnny at her heels, and that steamer stood there as we left it behind us. I estimated that two days riding the steamers had been three an' a half days on normal horseback, so if we didn't stop I might just make it, but there weren't no guarantees. I dug out a length of rawhide from a pants pocket an' lashed my hands to the saddle-horn, hooked my boots deep into the stirrups, and prayed. I don't know what happened after that. Jack told me that we came walking into town, Polly and that jackass almost on their knees but still moving forward.

It took more than a week before I was on my feet again an' when I was, I had a word or two for Jack.

"Steamers is useless, I guessed they would be, but now I'm not guessing, dunno why they stopped but they both did. And they didn't do much of a job guarding neither." Jack looked incredulous, until I told him the whole story.

"I'll ride out and get them," he said, his face set in determined lines. "I want to know what went wrong, why they quit."

I went back to sleep, and only woke up when he brought in breakfast next morning. He was a bit down in the mouth.

"I know why they stopped. Sand in the gears with the first one, the other one had algae."

"Algy? Who's..."

"Algae, that green scum that you see around the edges of stagnant water. The steamer kept drinking, water where it drank must have been pooled, and it took in more and more algae and with water in the tank too, and it being warm, the algae grew even faster. In the end it filled the tank. I'll have to go back to my drawing board, you were right. Steamers aren't any good for the desert."

I said nothing about how a smart horse wouldn't be drinking algy. Polly and Johnny always drank from the cleaner faster moving water. "How soon before you could get that pair up and working?" I asked.

"Before you're fit to go anywhere, why?"

"If I can borrow them again I've got a couple of ideas we can try."

We talked it over. He's a trustworthy cuss, Jack. Once I was back on my feet, we gave out that we were experimenting with the steamers and took off. That gold turned out to be only a pocket as I'd thought, but it was a fair size. I've got a small ranch on the desert side a' town now, and Jack's got a workshop and a cottage there. The steamers, with a few modifications make good packhorses for the army, or emergency short-term-pursuit mounts. I go out in spring or fall and do a bit of prospecting still, and now and again I take a dig at Jack.

"Something else steamers can't do," I tell him, as we watch Polly's fourth foal by Johnny kicking up his heels.

"Yeah. Like that song in a way."

"Huh?"

He grinned at me. "You and ole Polly and Johnny beating the steamers. And none of you had to die to do it."

I nodded. "That's true, an' maybe always will be because a machine's brute strength, but me and Johnny and Polly, we're *smart*."

"A'course," Jack said thoughtfully. "If I built a machine that could think..."

I could think of nothing safe to say – an' I said it.

TREASURE

Joe Tremain was a man of mostly average description. He was medium height, medium build, medium coloring, medium circumstances, and middle-aged. His father died young, and after that it was just Joe and his mother, who had left him a house that had one official bedroom, a loft that had been Joe's bedroom, and around ten acres of land, (a mere nothing in a land where ranches were measured in square miles,) but Joe got along well enough doing part time work for a number of locals. He lived alone – unless you counted the black cat that spent half its time mouse-hunting, and the other half asleep on Joe's bed. The cat's name – given with Joe's tendency to be practical – was Blackie.

Joe lived in Bodie, he'd been just a bit too young to ride in the war and his widowed mother had needed him, which made him useful locally since a number of those who had gone away came back damaged, while quite a few others never came back at all. So, while Joe wasn't the brightest crystal in the saloon's chandelier, he was bright enough, and he worked hard. What no one knew was that he was also an optimist. He dreamed, hoped that one day something would happen to take him out of his small dusty western town and off to the bright lights. Blackie could go to live with Old Mrs. Mariner if that happened. Joe knew the old lady liked cats and she'd be good to Blackie.

As I said, Joe was an optimist, and severely practical – in his own way – so that when Blackie came in that October night with a live mouse, and the mouse spoke to him, Joe wasn't unduly surprised; and he listened as many others wouldn't have. Blackie carried the mouse over, set it down by Joe, and placed a paw on it. The mouse looked up at Joe and its tiny black eyes widened imploringly.

16

"I don't want to die."

Joe considered that and found it reasonable. "I guess not."

"Save me."

"Why?" Joe was still reasonable. "You mice eat my food. I only put a flapjack to one side while I fetched my socks this morning and when I come back one of you were already eating it, nibbled all around the edge it were. That's what Blackie's for, does a fine job, he does."

The mouse fell briefly silent. "I could give you something?"

"What?"

"I have a treasure. Part of it has come down from my earliest ancestors. If you let me go I'll give it to you."

"How'd I know you'll come back at all if I let you go?"

The mouse pondered. "I could swear…"

"I kin swear too. Don't mean nothing."

"I mean I could give you my word. I could promise on the fertility of my line. That's an oath no mouse would break." The tiny form tensed as it waited for the human to reply.

Joe thought about it. Not a lot to lose really. "All right. I let you go and by tomorrow morning, you'll bring me your treasure. Put it on the shelf by my bed, right where I can see it when I wake." And to the cat. "And you let him. He isn't for you again 'til he's left the treasure and gone to his hole. Then when he comes out of that again it's back to the usual way of things."

He received a disgusted look from the cat, which rose, strolled leisurely from the small house and went to nap in the sunshine. Joe picked up the mouse.

"Guess I'll just make sure he leaves you be.

Placed by the woodpile the mouse dived between the logs and vanished. Joe looked after him. "You remember what's riding on this for you, mouse. Forget and you'll be the last of your line that ever lives."

Joe went to bed that night and slept well as always. He woke at first light, turning over sleepily, and his gaze fell on the bedside shelf. What? He remembered the mouse, the promise, the treasure, and slowly he sat up, his eyes fixed on the items heaped on the shelf; nineteen kernels of corn, two bacon rinds, and a small very moldy, crust of bread. Joe sighed, the thought slowly percolating in his brain. He'd bargained for the mouse's great treasure – the mouse had delivered as promised. What he hadn't bargained for was that what was treasure to a human wasn't necessarily treasure to a mouse.

* * *

Joe dumped the rinds and bread in the fire, the pretty red-striped corn kernels in his mother's vase on the mantelpiece, and went to work. Blackie continued to catch mice – although never that one again. Joe continued to work, sleep in on Sundays, and then, come the right time of the year he planted the corn. Waste not, want not, his mother had always said. The corn came up, a small sea of bright corn. A group of Indians passed by late one night the winter after that. Joe never saw them. They saw the flourishing patch of corn in the moonlight, looked at it, and rode on by, struck at a farmhouse some miles away, killed everyone, looted the place and vanished into the night.

Joe ate corn all that year and found it good, he preferred this not-so-sweet type, and he liked the red striping. It was pretty. The elderly widow Mariner liked it too when he dropped off a small sack of it for her.

"Thank you, Joe."

"T'isn't nothing. Just thought you might like some to make cornmeal. Don't say nothing around. You know how it is. I give you some an' next thing ever'body's expecting their share and getting in a twist 'cos I ain't handing it over."

"I thank you kindly, Joe, and I'll say nothing." She used it as intended and never noticed when her arthritis disappeared.

Blackie the cat tried a kernel one night when the hunting had been poor, and found it good. Thereafter while he caught just as many mice still, fewer were eaten. He relished the lighter spicy taste of the corn more and somehow while cats are not herbivores, he did very well on it, and Joe had no objection so long as the mice weren't a nuisance. Time slipped by, the widow Mariner died at the startling age of a hundred and nine. The local law thinking that her birth certificate must have been her mother's of the same name, so that the lady was noted in the cemetery records – by the undertaker – as having been eighty-nine when she died.

No one noticed, and Joe never cared, that Blackie was, by normal standards, an incredible age, nor did it occur to anyone to recall Joe's years. He was just Joe, the man that fixed things – fences, gates, pig pens, and who now and again, did a little gardening. He had a green thumb everyone agreed. It was a winter's evening in nineteen-forty-six when Joe saw the mouse again. It entered, slipping around the half-open door and sat on its haunches considering the man.

"I kept my promise," it said.

Joe nodded. "You did. Not much use to me your treasure wasn't, but you done what you said."

The mouse stared. "Not much use? Tell me, human, what year were you born?"

"Eighteen-forty-six," Joe said automatically.

"And the cat?"

"Got him when I were thirty-seven. He'd have bin around six when he caught you."

"And," the mouse held his gaze with small black eyes. "What year is it now?"

Joe paused. The truth was that time had never mattered to him. He didn't count the years, just the seasons – four of them, winter, spring, summer, and fall again. But he'd seen changes. Town were gone now, just ranches around, he went with one of his occasional employers to a different town maybe twice a year for the things he didn't grow and couldn't swap.

"I dunno, long time gone, I guess," he said slowly, reckoning it up, remembering. His gaze met that of his interrogator. "Long, long, time. Were that you?"

"The corn."

"Oh, so the widow and Blackie too…"

"Yes."

"So why're you here? Want it back?"

"No. I've taken my share over the years. I just wanted to say goodbye."

Joe blinked down. "You leaving?"

"No, you and Blackie are. The treasure only works on anything living for so long, and that time will be up tomorrow."

"Oh." Joe pondered. "Well. I guess there's some things I should do then, and thank you, mouse, guess it were a pretty good treasure after all."

"Yes." And there was a grey-brown ripple that slipped past the door again going the other way, and gone.

Joe picked up the drowsing cat and stroked him slowly. "Bin a good life, cat, an' you bin a good companion." He laid the cat down on his bed and reached for pen and paper. That's something his mother would have liked, that her son had finally learned to read and write. Nothing much, just the basics, but he could. He wrote for a few minutes, before blotting the ink, and laying the letter aside.

Then he went out to his land, the small patch of corn was growing well, and he sighed, pulling it up piece-by-piece, taking the almost ripe corn inside and placing it on the fire until the last of it was gone. He checked, found a few kernels about the house here and there – he wasn't always as tidy as he should be – but they too burned, and at last he straightened, walking over to stand in his doorway.

He considered the sky, the bright stars, the half-moon that left soft shadows on the land, and very slowly, a smile lit his face. "'S bin a good life, I guess. Friends, never out 'a work, a home of my own, and Blackie allus here so I weren't never alone." He walked to the bedroom where the old cat lay, breath barely moving his body. "We'll go now, I reckon. Tomorrow he said, and it'll be that real soon." He lay down, cradled the cat in one arm, and began to remember. His mother, his childhood, the widow Mariner who'd been a friend, all the employers over the years, some good, some bad, some indifferent. And the town he'd been born near, the town that they called a 'ghost town' these-days – would those ghosts come for him now?

And somewhere as the moon moved quietly across the sky, Joe and Blackie slipped from dreaming into another place. The bodies were found two days later, and buried together by Joe's friends – the cat being added surreptitiously to Joe's coffin by the undertaker who'd owed his client a few favors over the years. The house and the few acres it sat on were taken over by the local authorities, sold as he had asked and the money given to the A.S.P.C.A. The only thing left from Joe's time was a mouse that remembered, and the red-striped kernels that it still held deep in a mouse-sized tunnel. Treasure that was never to be despised; despite what some humans might think.

LONESOME TRAVELER

I came to the hills at dawn of the bright new day. I'd always loved the wild lands. My people condemned me for what they saw as aberrations, so I turned to the hills like a man in love. A man? Not quite. I had looked at sufficient instruments in my vehicle, *Timeline Traveler* to know the truth. This was the furthest of the outer timelines and one where man had risen later, travelled less far. My people here were not those of the confederation in that other world who had gone to the stars generations ago and returned – changed.

However, I was close enough to pass for human here and my other abilities were not those that their medicine men would easily recognize. I brought the ship in to a landing in a fold of the hills and removed my carry-pack. It struck me to the heart to destroy the ship but from here, there was no turning back. I've always wondered why no one was able to devise a ship that could cross the far timelines and return. But two or three is the furthest. After that, the traveler is bound where he is. He can go further and further out – to the very edge of the timelines where people have become beasts again, but he can never return and there is no way that continuing on will allow a complete circle.

My carry-pack was light and my hopes high as I wandered along, smiling at the grass, the trees, and pausing to drink now and again from a mountain stream, the water wonderful in its clarity and sweetness. That night I found shelter in the home of an elderly man who wanted only to talk endlessly of bygone days and to have a listener in return for his roof and the food that he offered.

I listened to him far into the night. There were many things my instruments could not tell me and it might be death not to learn; so I took in every word. I had to bite back a cry of joy when I found that they loved music here. Not just this one half-crazy man, but the whole land, he assured me, loved to hear music, and I knew his words as honest. From the carry-sack, I produced my tarkona and began to play softly. It was clear he had spoken truth, as he sat, eyes filmed over in content and he listened in silence as long as I would play. When I stopped, he spoke. I would not attempt to reproduce his accent but his words sank into my mind.

"You should go into the hills to the East. My kin live there and there's not one of them wouldn't rejoice to host a man who can play and sing like that, one who knows the old songs. You could stay with one and another of them as long as you've a mind to, maybe build there and settle. They always welcome one with music and you have the gift."

In the morning, I took his advice. He had been right and I played and sang my way along from home to home. Finding that word of my coming ran before me and I was always looked for and welcomed. My muscles filled out with the exercise and I could feel myself relaxing under their appreciation and the peace of the high hills.

My own timeline had regarded my hobby of learning the old songs as an aberration. There had been no place for the plaintive minor keys and archaic words there. No place for me who loved to play and sing them, who loved the land and sorrowed at their destruction of it until only infertile scraps of it remained beside the huge ant hills we called our 'Fair' cities.

Now and again, I took the small packet of seeds from my carry-sack and studied it sadly. Iolana. It had been both the bane and salvation of my people but not here. Where I came from it had been a great marvel and an aid to our exploration of space and the spreading timelines, but it was also mostly responsible for the ruination of the wild lands of my world and for that, I could not love it. When few men had to die from aging they lived on and on and the cities swelled.

We moved out to our timeline's stars and made of them the same roiling anthills that had spoiled our own world. Nor could I have brought myself to the utter cruelties needed for the seeds to germinate. There, only criminals had been used, but here? How was I to judge, and who was I to render such a sentence?

I had passed through many places when at last I came
to a place where a sickly remnant of my people still dwelt on
what the ruling people called a *reservation*. I made my home
for a while above them in the clean hills and the people welcomed me as ever. I discovered that if one had money, one
could buy parts of these hills from the government of the land
and I smiled to myself. Money could be arranged once at least
– and was, so that I became the joyous owner of several square
miles of mountain land; that the seller honestly warned me was
completely useless for any sort of cultivation. Not to me! All I
wished was a home and the land to watch, to enjoy its own
wildness, untouched. I had no desire to plow it under or to
'use' it in any way.

I have always had the gift of communicating with the
beasts. I suppose that is why I could not face the Iolana or use
it in the way that would give me its gift. I put the small seeds
away in the back of a cupboard and forgot them. It was a nuisance not having enough of this land's money since there were
taxes to pay and for those I turned to teaching below in the
place where the last of my blood here huddled in squalor.

They accepted me as a music teacher, and my students
taught me as much as I taught them, and soon by ones and
twos, they came to my home to watch the animals that lived
unafraid upon my land. I encouraged them to talk as I listened;
finding the places where this world had taken a different path.
A strong world and a good one, but it was a grief to me that
this, my kin, should have so little portion of it, so little part in
its destiny. It amused me sadly that I was kin and they had no
recognition of it.

On our timeline, the races blended so that I am tall and
lean with blue eyes and an olive skin. My far kin here had still
the untouched look of the pureblood's short powerful build
with a reddish hue to the skin and black hair and eyes. Yet
they were mine, and I wished I might help but I had no time.
In a hundred years, and if I moved quietly, I might change
things here for them, in three hundred I might bring them
back to a complete equality again, but I would have none of
that time. Without the Iolana I would have another thirty or
forty years perhaps. Then they could lay me here in the land I

loved and I would lie in the peace they did not, would never, have.

The beasts in these mountains fascinated me too, so many were gone in my time and I found myself writing down observations, taking photographs, and making small sketches. It was the headman at the school who gave the idea to me. It might solve my tax troubles and I could still work at the school for my pleasure.

It took several years but the publisher he knew purchased my first book, and then another. By the time I had lived here fifteen years, I had sold four books and my friend guided me through the intricacies of their laws in this regard. In this time, the students I had first taught had grown and married, produced children of their own. Soon these also began to climb my path and watch the beasts, learn music from me, and the old songs.

Finally their medicine man came. He studied me quietly through one whole day and then pronounced, "You are not of us and yet you are. There is no evil in you, your medicine is good, and it is strong for us."

I bowed my head humbly. So the old power still lived in this remnant of my kin. We talked as brothers and I shared songs that made him weep with joy. He visited me every so often after that and we became friends, finally I told him the story of my flight and he accepted it serenely.

But the years slipped past until I had lived here twenty years and while my age did not show to others, I knew that it was starting to slow me, as time bit deeper into my body. In another few years, even the Iolana would be too late and I would have only a normal span to live out. Still I refused to consider planting the seeds. I was not that cruel, never that cruel and I would make no judgments.

My first true student had been a boy. I had rejoiced when he loved my music and when he went out into the world and became a success. I was happy for him. Like his own kin, my sorrow was great when, at the height of his fame he was killed and left two small children to the care of my friend, the head of the school, who was his cousin. In turn, they had become my pupils, the best I had.

They called them Hobie and Dawn, and the girl was my special delight, for she could sing like a mountain lark and the beasts trusted her as they did me. I suppose that my reputation as an author protected me in the township, and my isolation in the mountains protected me there. In the area, there was drunkenness but little crime of the sort that springs from real evil rather than simple stupidity.

But in my twenty-second year, it came to my high and lonely hills. My friend had taken the two children to a larger town to see the doctor there to be vaccinated against some disease. Before that, he dropped into the bank to withdraw the money to pay for their treatment and it was while he was there with the children that evil fell upon them. Men with guns burst into the building and took hostages, they also took the money but that was little besides my Dawn. The robbers rode hard, and the men of the law lost the trail near the edge of our mountains and when they caught several of the robbers three days later, the leader, the money, and Dawn had gone.

My friend came to me with Hobie. It was clear to them that the life of a girl was little compared to the tremendous sum of money taken which could result in the bank's destruction. The lawmen would risk the girl, if they could take the money back. Not that they would deliberately put her in danger but perhaps they would not be as careful as they might be with the bank urging them on, and the governor offering rewards. I thought him wrong, those who upheld justice here had never seemed to me to be so callous but I did agree with his distress and their desire to recover Dawn unharmed.

"I had an odd feeling of recognition when I saw the man's face for a moment," my friend said softly.

"How is it that he allowed you to see?"

"They tied us all. I wriggled across to look under the partition and his mask slipped a second. I gave the police a description but said nothing of any feelings."

I listened to his story and remembered, reminding him of something he'd told me many years ago. That once there was a man married to one of the people here. His son had married in turn and moved, but word had come back that he had fathered a son. My friend had known the old man and the son. If the young man who had taken Dawn had looked like the old man's son. Perhaps he was the grandson?

If that was so, then he would be familiar with these hills. It was known that his mother had lived through his childhood on the edge of them, near where the old man still had his musty cabin. The thief might even have made his way to that place as a refuge, which few knew or could find. But I could, since once I had been there for a night and where I had been, the paths I had walked, I never forgot. Many years ago, I had told my friend about that night, it had shaped the years that followed when I found how prized my music was. Now it would lead me back to where the child I loved might be.

I set out the following day, my carry-sack full of food and articles that I might need. When, that night, I rested, I dug into it to find the notebook I always carried, only to find that the tiny pouch of the Iolana seeds was still in its place. I shrugged, they had no weight but if I had to discard the carry-sack I might lose them. I placed them in my buttoned shirt pocket for safety and forgot them again. I would not use them, yet in a way they were a memory of my own place and I kept them as such.

I came upon the cabin four days later. The old man tottered out around midday to sit in the sun. There was still movement inside, behind the filthy sacking curtain. Then Dawn appeared, a bruised-faced, girl with defiance in every line. I could guess what had happened to her by the swagger with which the thief joined her, and I hated him as I had hated nothing since I had fled my timeline.

She would have run, but from somewhere he had obtained a chain and padlocks. Hobbled, barely able to stagger, she had no chance of escape and too much sense to attempt it. I studied the things that held her. If I could have a few minutes alone with her, she would be free, but the man gave me no opportunities. He may have sensed that eyes watched and she was never out of his sight for long enough.

I lay in the scrub and watched the cabin, turning over plans in my mind. Once I had an odd feeling that someone watched me but I must have been mistaken. No one was there when I looked about. He had dragged her back into the cabin by then, and there had been no sign of either for at least an hour although the old man still sat vacantly on the rotting porch. I stood slowly and carefully, reached for the carry-sack and a voice spoke from behind me.

"Leave that where it is, friend." No friend to me, I knew. I turned slightly to see his face and I was right.

"What'cha doing here?"

I talked now for my life – and Dawn's. "I'm a writer; I study the animals in these hills and write books about them. "You must know my name?" I told him and to my delight, he nodded. So far so good!

"I'm tramping this section to see if I can find new plants to draw for my next book. I stayed at the cabin once a long time back, years! I thought I'd drop in and see the old boy but I saw that he had guests. Sorry if I'm trespassing on your land, I suppose you're his kin. I was figuring on a sketch of the cabin and checking up on any animals that might come near it. Part of the book is on inter-reactions between animals and long established houses." Now if only he would believe me. I waited. He grunted and I saw he was suspicious but perhaps...

"Anyone know where you are?"

I looked surprised. "Certainly. I told friends where I was going. Some remembered the old man who lives here. After all, my publisher wants this book. I said he could call me on Sunday at the telegraph office and we'd discuss it, I said I'd be home by then unless something had gone wrong."

That might hold him back. The idea of a publisher beating the hills in search of a lost author would give him pause. He'd guess how fast the media would jump on a story like that and just how many people might head out to scour the hills to assist in the search. He grunted again and his eyes flickered across my carry-sack.

"What's in that?"

"Supplies."

I suddenly remembered that my sketchbook was there and that I had passed the beginning hours in sketching the cabin before Dawn was allowed out. I dug it out and showed him the sketch with a smile. It was evidence that I had indeed been here innocently. There was something in his eyes as he looked it over that bothered me, but he merely nodded, picked up the carry-sack and invited me down to share a meal, a bed for the night too if I wanted. Thinking it best to agree I strolled along with him until we reached the cabin door. His manner changed then and like a snake, he turned on me, flung me sprawling inside and pointed the snatched-up rifle into my face.

I attempted to act the injured innocent. "What? How dare you?"

"Can it! I knew you were a liar when I saw that cute artwork. That was done right in the early morning, I could tell by the shadows. You saw the girl and ten to one you can make a few guesses. I don't need anyone making them and walking off to talk elsewhere."

I cursed myself silently. Poor Dawn. Some rescuer I was turning out to be! "What are you going to do with us?"

He looked slightly surprised. "Kill you both, of course. The old man won't remember you were ever here and there's old mine shafts all through these hills. Snap your necks, drop you down one, and you won't be found in a thousand years."

He dragged Dawn out from the inner room and set her to work on a meal. She glanced at me and said nothing. Suddenly her head came up and she staggered sideways, falling to the floor as the chains caught. He swore, kicked her casually and bent to drag her to her feet again as he beat her. I heard the sounds and wept inside for the girl who loved music and the animals, who'd never known a blow or unjust word. I saw her eyes, black and wicked with hate as a rattler's. She spat out a mouthful of blood and returned to work silently. I moved in the ropes where he had bound me, and in my shirt pocket, something shifted. The seeds! We might have a chance yet.

I began to talk quietly, interesting him despite himself in the life of these mountains as I saw it. Gradually as he ate, I led the talk to the medicine roots and herbs of these hills, of lost knowledge. He listened intently as I described a bush near here. The seeds, I claimed, were a hallucinogen, one with the power almost to allow the taker to read minds. Of course, it had to be studied carefully. It would be fatal if word got out and fools used it wrongly.

He was no fool and at first, he could not believe me, but I used technical words that caught him until at last I saw him beginning to accept the possibility. I insisted that the seeds would not make you telepathic, no, I was very careful to assure him of that. But they made you empathic. You could read another's emotions.

I could see the greed starting to gleam in his eyes. Were there any of the bushes here now? I was quick to inform him that I had only ever found one. That I had taken the seeds from that and cultivated it in cooperation with the Government who wanted it for the military. That I had found silver inhibited the effect. This last explained why I wore a silver band about my throat, and he nodded. I allowed him to drag from me the further information that because of different hormones, women could not use the seeds. That they did not work for them. But for males of any age, the ability appeared within minutes of their being swallowed.

Then I permitted him the final answer, yes. I had some on me as I had intended to make a test of the possibilities of animal empathy. Could I read their emotions as well as those of humans? I prayed that he would not wonder why that had not already been tested, I had an answer ready for him that was weak, but he did not ask. Instead, he demanded the seeds. He would try one on me and if I spoke the truth, I might be permitted to live.

With a steady hand, I withdrew the Iolana seeds from my pocket and handed them over after the ropes were removed from my hands. Equally steadily, I removed the silver band from my throat – and the emotions of the three crashed in on me. I had barely enough strength to cover my reactions to the impact as I was assaulted by hate, pain, rage, and madness.

Still holding the frail shield of my purpose before me, I took up one seed. I flipped it into my mouth and while I held it safe on my tongue, I pretended to chew and swallow. He checked my mouth carefully to make sure it was gone but was unaware that the light covering of the seed is black and easily rubbed off by the tongue. That I had safely swallowed, however the seed itself, still in the harder layer beneath, I had wedged into a gap between two back teeth, edge on. It was white without the black coating and he missed seeing it. He sat for long minutes watching me grimly and I was terrified that he would watch too long.

A spark jumped from the stove and for a second his eyes flickered away so that I was able to spit the seed hard into the corner where it vanished into the dust. Then I permitted my face to show that something was about to happen. I twisted my mouth, twitched the corner of one eye and looked up at him.

"Has it happened?"

"Yes, the seed's working now. I can tell just what you're feeling."

He tested me over several hours using his own, and Dawn's emotions. I was honest, it was our only chance and he merely laughed when I assured him of her hatred. He tied us and left the cabin while he experimented with distance to find that I could still read him accurately a good mile away. I knew he would think of this ability first as a tool for crime and he did. When he returned, I could see that he was jubilant, already he could see himself as the head of a criminal empire in some far city where he could live in luxury.

"How long does it take to wear off?"

"One seed? About half a day, but if you take them twice a day they'll give you the ability permanently after you've taken them for a few weeks, or so we think. So far, we haven't had enough to spare to try. They're hard to germinate. That's also why you have to chew them at first or they just go through without working. The outer layer is almost waterproof. They take hours in your stomach to break down."

He studied the black seeds in the small packet of paper and nodded again, his eyes avid. I could guess his thoughts. There would be enough there to start a tiny plot, enough to use one now and then to commit bigger and better crimes. Would he try one now? I watched as he came to a decision and strode over to check our bonds. Then he tossed one seed into his mouth, bit down several times and swallowed.

I turned my head away. At first, he sat waiting for the miracle to occur. Then a startled look came onto his face and he retched violently. His gun came up but the spasms became convulsions and the pain began. It took him a long time to die and his voice was gone before he did. Once he had stopped moving, I was able to inch past him towards the stove. The ropes

came under my feet to hold my hands at the front of my body
and I could burn through them on the stovetop edge. Then I
freed Dawn.

The Iolana had used all of the body that it needed and I
lifted him in safety. Away to the far side of a long slope, I dug
a hole, dropped in the body and marked the site. I would have
the time now to change the way my people lived. The Iolana
would bear the fruit that would give me a very long life, and
some could be left to turn to seed. Dawn came up to hold my
hand and I closed my fingers about hers. She would be with
me. The emotions I had read with the silver damper band removed from my throat had told me that.

I would remember what had happened to my own timeline when my people forgot the ways of the land, but now there
was a hope for these children of my blood. I gathered up the
seeds that had been scattered when the bank-robber fell. There
would be more out there like him. If I needed Iolana again,
well, I had learned my lesson, they would come to me; if the
bait was right, and thieves and savages would take their doom
into their own hands.

The old man still sat rocking vacantly on the porch. We
fed him and he mumbled thanks, the violence and death had
not touched him, he would recall nothing. The money stolen
from the bank was in the bedroom at the back of the cabin and
I picked it up. Dawn could tell a tale I had already planned, and
the return of the money would quiet the hunters. The robber
would be sought, but never found.

With my free hand, I gathered in the old carry-sack and
slung it over one shoulder then took her small hand in mine.
We were better out of this place, to camp the night in the clean
land. One day I would explain it all to her, I would have to, our
children would almost certainly inherit my in-born ability as an
empath. From her they would inherit the strength to fight on
when all seemed hopeless. They might also inherit the ruthless-
ness of our ancestors – so much closer in this time to her.

I had seen that even as I turned my face away from his
death, she had watched, eyes flat and unblinking, as her enemy
died – her lips curving in approval. I smiled down at her and
her fingers squeezed mine. An Apache renaissance could take

them to the stars in time. And I would do all I could to see that this world did not repeat the mistakes of my time-line. Dawn's hand lay warm in mine and I knew that now and at last, I was a lonesome traveler no more.

HOUNDED

She'd been running a long time and she was tired almost to her death of it. The sheriff had promised a lot, she thought as she boarded the stage. For all his promises, he'd done damn little and for all theirs, the lawyers hadn't done much more.

"How far, marm?"

"Nairnville, please." It was the end of the line, deep into the mountains and about as far from her old life as she could get. He'd find her there, she feared. It was only a matter of time. She'd broken her trail over and over. Maybe she'd have longer free – and maybe she wouldn't, her mind added grimly. Big Mick Islay didn't like to lose.

In the seat in front of her, two elderly women dressed like rancher's wives were chatting. From their conversation, they were neighbors on their way home from visiting kin in the city. Her ears pricked up as the subject changed.

"…cottage going begging and at a rent that low."

"Humph!" the snort was emphatic. "Middle of the forest an' mountains. You need a good horse to get there an' your neighbors'll be uneducated mountain folk. So he did it up nice. Who'd want to live out there?"

"Oh, I dunno. 'S lonely, that I grant you, but the forest's nice in summer." There was a pause. "Anyway, ole Bas never come to no harm, did he? Lived there fer nigh on forty years and he always said he never saw nor heard nothing. Reckoned the mountains was peaceful like."

"Peaceful, I suppose so. Mind you, the Ellices aren't the type to notice if anything was goin' on and the old man wasn't one to see anything he didn't want to."

"Mebbe not. But Bas, he liked living there." There was a short chuckle. "He used to say anyone comes by the main trail,

an' not knowing the short cuts, it took ages. Put them off. Not
to mention having to pass the Langly and the Merrin outfits
and them not being friendly to anyone they don't know."

The stage halted for the women to leave, calling out cheer-
ful goodbyes to most of the passengers. Chris peered ahead.
On one side of the road trees crowded. Tall, ancient but strong.
Oak, ash and thorn, something at the back of her mind listed.
Thorn? she queried back. Hawthorn, recalled her old memories. When she was very young, they'd lived in the country.
Dimly she recalled the scent of hawthorn in bloom and the
croaking of frogs on the pond. Her father had moved to this
country for work when she was just four. She'd married in the
city – her mind shied away from that thought hastily.

The stage rumbled to a halt in the center of an all dusty
town; a shop, a church, a hotel, a school, barbers, and that building on the very outskirts could well be a brothel. She looked
again and a small weary smile fought its way to her face. Not a
big hotel, it would likely have three rooms upstairs. Two single
and one double bedroom, all served by the one bathroom. But
the rooms would be clean, the bath water would be carried up
hot, and the food would be simple but good; or so she judged.

"Nairnville, marm. You getting out here or you wanna
come back to Knoxville?" She controlled an instinctive flinch-
ing at the driver's closeness. He meant no harm. A small elderly man with kind blue eyes and a broad smile, reaching for
her small trunk. He lifted it down from the stage luggage rack,
turning to look at her. "Want me to carry it for you, marm? 'S
a fair weight."

Despite herself, her voice was flat. "Thank you, sir. I can
carry it."

He nodded, stepping back to allow her to take it up. Chris
dragged it up the boardwalk steps towards the shabby hotel.
For a moment, she stood watching as the stage doors closed,
the driver lifted his hand to a couple of passers-by, then the
horses moved out, turning in a half-circle; and the stage rolled
off along the trail by which it had come.

Chris picked up her trunk again, blessing strong muscles
honed by years of hard work. She hefted it across the road,
dumping it by the reception desk. A tall man came from the

chattering bar to attend her.

"Single room, is it? For one night or a bit longer?"

"Single room and," she hesitated. "I'm not sure how long. Is it all right if I just say one night and stay on once I know?"

"Of course. Sign the register. Anything I can help you with?"

The women's gossip flashed into her mind. Without volition, she found she was asking, "Are there any places to rent hereabouts?"

He leaned against the desk thinking. "Weeell, there's Braslington House." He grinned. "Huge old place on the far side of the Douglas River. The owner died, the new chap's yet to arrive and they want to let it until he does. It'd do fine if you've a fancy for twenty bedrooms and a kitchen bigger'n Jim Hooson's hay barn." Chris shook her head smiling.

"Didn't think so. Then there's the old cabin on Barkwell's land. It isn't bad but it depends on how much company you want. Effie Barkwell'd talk the hind leg off a donkey and the cottage is right by the house. She mostly lets that to the teacher when she gets here for the school year."

He took in the frown. "Not that one, then? Only one other I can call to mind. It's a long way from here, a good day's ride, an' it's been empty a while now but the old man's son wants someone living there. He'd let it go cheap but it wouldn't be suitable for a lady." Chris felt her pulse quicken. The women in the bus had said some of the same things.

"It belonged to an old fellow. Bas Ellice. He must have built it morn'n fifty years back. He died last month."

He eyed her doubtfully. "It's isolated. The nearest proper trail's a good two miles away. There's just tracks after that. Bas used to ride his old mule down here every two, three months to buy at the store but he made nothing of that. You might feel different."

"I'd like to see it." Something about the place attracted her every time it was mentioned. Maybe the isolation. Mick couldn't just come driving up with his fancy carriage and his hard men at his back. They'd have to walk and with a number of tracks, they could even get themselves lost. She smiled a little inside herself at the idea. Hitting the trees wouldn't do him any good.

They wouldn't bleed, and cry, and do whatever he demanded.

The hotel owner was deliberating. "Miles Harman could show you over the place. He told me the lawyer said he should have the keys since Bas left him all his personal gear. Likely Miles will stop here for a drink later. I can let him know you'd like to ride out there if you'd like me to?"

"If you would do that, please. I'd like to see it tomorrow if it's convenient."

"I'll do that. Now Miss –" he glanced down at the register, "Miss Ross, you'll be tired being on that stage. I can do you a meal in the dining room or I can send my wife up with a tray in an hour if that'd suit you better?" He saw the relief on her face. "All right then. Do you fancy a hearty meal or something lighter?"

"Light please." Heaven to have the choice. Not to be told what she must do, the order emphasized with an upraised fist if she hesitated.

"Leave it to me."

She left it to him with gratitude. A feeling justified by the tray that appeared an hour later; minutes after Chris returned from a long hot bath in a cast-iron bathtub. The tray was borne by a large smiling woman who announced herself.

"I'm Mrs. Moorhouse. My husband owns the hotel. Where do you want the tray, my dear?" Chris indicated the bedside table.

"It's very kind of you. It looks wonderful."

"You just eat up, dearie. You could do with something. You look as if you've been ill."

"I was in hospital." She heard her words and hastily added to them. "Appendicitis. I was quite ill for a while."

"Ah," said Mrs. Moorhouse. "Nasty, that is. But I mustn't keep you talking while the food gets cold." She left, quietly shutting the door behind her. Chris was left to consider the food.

Light meal or not it didn't look as if she'd go hungry. The scrambled eggs were light and fluffy, the teapot full, and there was a stack of hot buttered toast. Chris ate, then lay back on the bed sipping her tea. Mick didn't like tea. She'd been expected to make his powerfully strong coffee at all hours, then be blamed when he couldn't sleep.

Outside the moon was rising. She heard the men downstairs in the bar laughing. Now and again, someone sang something. Overhead from the clear crisp sky there came a long drawn-out yelping. Chris recognized the cry of wild geese. In the bar below all sound ceased briefly. Then the rumble of voices began again. When Chris did sleep, it was to jerk awake from a dream in which Mick moved towards her cursing.

"Useless cow. Can't even give me a son without mucking it up. God knows I waited long enough."

For once in her dream, she defied him with the bitter truth. "It was your fault. Couldn't even stop hitting me for a few months. *You* killed your baby."

She lay awake then until dawn, falling asleep again with first light, only waking mid-morning. She stretched. Sun streamed in through the curtains, warming the room as it lifted her mood. She'd dodged for weeks changing names and rooms, using the money her mother had left her and that she'd managed to get from the lawyer without her husband finding out. At last, just before she fled, she'd met the lawyer dealing with her mother's estate, making arrangements where they could send the bulk of the money. After that, she'd picked it up and run again. She knew Mick would have an eye out, what was his he kept; and he'd be furious if he found out about the money too.

But she'd broken her trail so long and so often, surely she could stay here safely a while. Mick was a man of the city for all he owned a ranch. He wouldn't think to look for her deep in mountain country, and if he did – she smiled briefly. He'd stand out like a fox in a hen house; then too, people so far west might not be willing to let him bully them. They carried guns. She'd seen them.

Chris studied herself as she dressed. She'd changed her hair color and style. Lost so much weight as she crisscrossed the country, missing meals, endlessly driving herself on, that she looked younger than the late twenties she was. At nine that morning she descended the stairs to eat a hearty belated breakfast. Mr. Moorhouse was waiting once she was finished.

"I talked to Miles last night. He said if you'd like to see the cabin he'll be here at seven tomorrow morning with the buckboard if that'd suit you?" She nodded agreement. "I'll let him know then."

"Thank you for your help." All her gratitude for unexpected kindness was in her voice and he looked surprised.

"Nothing to it. Have a pleasant day."

Chris did. She wandered out to the shop first to see what she could discover. There was a stack of thin, poorly printed pamphlets on a shelf by the door; written so it was said, by a local teacher. The town was just another tiny place, more off the beaten track than most. It had a history with few events of interest according to the leaflets.

There were the usual legends; the Tennessee Mountains hereabouts were supposed to be the haunt of a spirit which hunted evil men with horse and hounds. Chris frowned then shrugged. Somewhere she'd heard that Scots-Irish peasants had originally settled here. The tale was likely a corruption of one of their legends from the old country. (The country that had once been hers.) It was all nonsense, probably some old tradition. In a way, she found that a pleasant thought though, that traditional tales still lingered.

They'd lingered in Mick's family as well. A fist for any man who defied you, the back of your hand to any woman. Never forget a debt you owed – or that was owed to you. She owed Mick a life, the son she'd lost him as he saw it. Chris shivered suddenly although the day was warm. She'd told the sheriff and her mother's lawyer once she was safe in hospital. They talked of invoking the law to keep him away from her. She's explained that no piece of paper would keep Mick away and they'd spoken of the law's power.

Believing she'd made a statement, they'd prosecuted, but Mick had good lawyers and a lot of friends, men of his own kind. They'd made her out to be clumsy, a liar, and the jury, which knew nothing of her, had acquitted. Mick went free and for all the legal talk about how she'd be protected they hadn't saved her. A wagon had come out of nowhere to run her down. A stolen wagon with a driver she'd recognized, but his alibi stood up. There was no proof and no safety there, so she fled early from the hospital where the accident had put her.

She shrugged the shadow from her mind. She was away

from him. He wouldn't find her here, deep in the mountains where folk had no time for strangers; and with her mother's money, she could live for the rest of her life without having to find paid work, so long as she didn't waste it. She went back to eat a late lunch and rest on her bed until it was time to come down for dinner. She ate well and slept unusually peacefully. A better sleep than she'd had for almost longer than she could remember. Mrs. Moorhouse came tapping lightly at the door at six the next morning.

"Miles Harman will be here in an hour, Miss Ross. I'll be putting your breakfast on the table this minute."

"I'll be right down." She flung a buckskin jacket about her shoulders. It would be cold under the trees. She ran down the old creaking stairs to eat and wait. It was a little less than the promised hour when a lean old man walked up to her table.

"I'm Miles Harman."

Christine rose to smile at the waiting man. "Thank you for this, Mr. Harman. I'm most interested to see the cabin."

He smiled back gently. Once in the buckboard, he talked about the small cabin they would see.

"It was well-built. Bas knew what he was about. Don't have many amenities as they say, but it's a good solid place. Small, mind. Just a bedroom an' a big kitchen with room for a dining table, no parlor. Water right into the kitchen though. It comes from the roof into tanks, that's why Bas put a real good roof on. You have to be careful though. If it don't rain, the tanks don't fill and you have to go down to the stream an' haul it back."

"What about light and heat and a way to cook?"

Miles Harman grinned. "No problem there, marm. There's a good big flat-topped wood stove with an oven on one side. She'll boil all the water you need an' then some. Ole Bas's son left the lanterns and lamp there as well. There's hooks to hang 'em on in the ceiling 'a both rooms and there's a good table lamp as well."

"I'll need an axe for wood, and a small one for kindling?"

"All there." Miles told her briefly. "The boy didn't take much but his pa's personal gear." After that he was silent until they halted by the side of the trail, the buckboard drawing into a small layby cut into the forest edge. He hitched the horses and helped her down. "We walk from here."

They walked along a narrow track, which wound through great trees until a shape bulked against their background. Chris halted. 'Bas' must have believed in camouflage. The cottage, built of logs with the bark on still, blended almost invisibly into the surroundings. Miles led the way to the door, opened that, and waited for her to enter.

But Chris halted a moment, studying the trees about the house, the sunlight glimmering in patches across the ground; a small expanse of flat ground without obvious boundaries. The trees loomed above it all, sheltering, protecting, holding her safe from brutality and the fear she had lived with so long. Beneath them she would feel and hear little even of a gale. She fell in love as she looked up at the green foliage towering over her. It was as quick and simple as that.

She said nothing but turned, preceding Miles into the cottage. He'd told the truth there. It was well built, dry, and plainly furnished. She cared nothing for any of that. He showed her the two rooms, mentioned the quarterly rent – minute, and added that if she chose to accept the place the rent was to be paid to Mr. Moorhouse at the hotel who would hold it until young Ellice could pick it up. When he finally ran down, she nodded.

"I can move in tomorrow. How much advance rent will they want? I can pay a year."

"Don't you want to think it over?"

"I'll have tonight. If you meet me at nine tomorrow morning I can confirm my decision and pay Mr. Moorhouse."

"Very well, marm. I'll drive you back now. I can tell you anything else you want to know as we drive back."

Chris got out of the buckboard once they were outside the hotel. "Thank you. I'll see you at nine." She waved as he drove away. Now, was the livery stable still open? It was a mixture of a place, odd bits of harness, an old pony trap, and a corral with several horses and ponies standing half-asleep in the last of the sunshine.

She approached the owner. "That pony trap?"

"Aye, marm, belonged to Charlie up at Hooson's ranch. He

built it outa bits. T'aint exactly standard like, but it's good 'n' safe to drive."

"Is it for sale?"

"It is."

"I'll need a pony to go with it, but I want one broken to ride as well."

The man nodded thoughtfully. "I may have one. He's about fourteen hands, broke to ride or drive, an' he wun't be too big fer you, nor too small. But he's ugly."

Chris bit down a smile. She guessed which pony he meant at once. The beast was roman-nosed, an odd shade of grayish-brown and the small skirt of hair above each hoof said that there'd been a draft horse somewhere back in his ancestry. She haggled but closed the deal for both pony and trap and paid cash. She left with instructions that the pony was to be given a decent feed, watered, and groomed. She also bought a sack of oats for him to be left waiting in the trap.

After that, she went shopping at the general store, buying sacks of food, a drum of fuel for the lanterns and lamp, lengths of cloth to make dresses, and a whole list of small items that would make her new life comfortable.

Miles Harman arrived at nine a.m. the next day, took one look at her new possessions and blinked. "That's Bas's pony."

Chris looked up in surprise. "He is? The stableman never said anything?"

"Well, he is, Bas swapped him from one of the mountain folk an' called him Mouse. You could'a done a lot worse than buying him. He's a smart beast, sure-footed, an' he knows all the trails hereabouts." Chris smiled as Miles continued.

"That trap you got, that's a good buy too, you got a fair eye, marm. Couldn't git the buckboard in to the house but if you go the way I'll show you, you kin just about get that there trap to it. Bas has a stable an' a shed where you kin put Mouse an' the trap. I'll ride along behind you with my buckboard an' haul some a' the heavier stuff you bought."

Chris waited only to pay Mr. Moorhouse before mounting the step of her trap and leading off down the trail. They forded the river, plodded up the narrowed trail, and once they reached a turn-off, Miles clicked to his horses and took the lead.

"This way, marm." His beasts pushed through brush onto a trail that had been invisible up until then and Mouse plodded after them. The buckboard halted. "I can't go any further from here, marm. I'll unload where I am and help you pack it in."

Chris aided him to load her trap with about a third of her goods and gear. Mouse moved off obediently, leaning hard into the breeching. It took another fifteen minutes before they came up on the house from the far side and she halted the pony to look. Her house, her land, her refuge now. It took a couple of hours but finally everything was under cover. Miles departed, leaving her with a wealth of good advice and information. Chris didn't even look after him; she was too busy making decisions as to where things should go and listening to the soft shushing of the trees.

In a week, she had settled in. In a month, it was as if she had always lived there. Let it be more than a respite only, she prayed. One day Mick would find her, but her mother had left Chris a lot of money. More than she'd realized until she met the lawyer. Enough to keep her forever if she lived quietly, enough to buy this cottage if she could ever be sure Mick had given up the hunt. A shudder savaged her.

The letter had come to the hospital where she lay after her so-called accident. The woman who'd brought it had known where Chris was and had chosen not to give the letter to Mick. He'd never known his mother-in-law had died – although undoubtedly he knew by now. Still less had he any idea that the woman he'd disliked had left so much. Her first husband, Chris's father, had been well off and it had been saved. Her second husband had enough to keep them all and had never known about the bank account; and in the end that had come to her only child.

Chris had sent a private message to the lawyer from the hospital, instructing them not to approach her husband, but to wait until she contacted them again. Then, barely fit to walk, she'd fled hospital: the law that had failed her, and the husband who wanted her back – or dead if she would not return. She'd left the hospital late that night, made arrangements with her lawyer, who was sympathetic, and run again.

Miles Harman had come back the day after she'd settled in

here. A kind man, and concerned for her.

"Miss Ross? Are you home?"

She jerked upright from her single armchair. "Come in."

He entered, beaming in an almost proprietary way at her. "Wondered if you could use the woodstove an' the lanterns yet. It's fall in another few weeks an' it'll be right chilly soon. I thought I could show you if you liked."

He meant well. Chris let him show her as he wished. She had the stove already lit from the previous night, but it was true she'd half forgotten how to use the lanterns. Mick had put gaslights in their house in the city and it was the servants who lit and used the kitchen stove. After Miles Harman was gone again, she settled back in her armchair. He'd been right, the last few evenings had been chilly, but the lamplight glowed on the wooden walls of her home in a way that delighted her.

Miles returned again and again until he was sure she knew how to bank the fire to stay alive at nights, the best sort of wood to use, and that she could use the axe and safely. Then she had to make it gently clear that she preferred her own company. He stayed away after that – with a half embarrassed anger he did not show. He'd liked the woman. Then she'd made him feel as if he was a bothersome old fool.

To Chris the forest and the mountains were timeless. In the silence and peace of the trees, she relaxed slowly. Finding there was nothing to make her afraid here. She learned the scream of the vixen, the call of a hunting owl, the wild shriek of a cougar and the snuffling of a bear as it passed.

Mouse was turned out each morning in hobbles. He would come for a handful of oats each night and be barred safely within the stable. Chris wanted that to become a custom. There would be starving predators in the mountains in winter. One of her purchases in the store had been a rifle and a goodly stack of ammunition. She used the gun to shoot the rabbits that came to her small patch of garden and had rabbit stew to go with the greens.

For the first time in years Chris could read all she wished. She'd brought books with her, purchased in Knoxville, and she read greedily in the evenings before she sought her bed. On her visits to the town, she purchased magazines and enjoyed those too, using them to light the fire at need. Winter drifted in so slowly it was a while before she realized it had truly arrived.

She knew it the day she drove Mouse to the village and found the stream's ford fringed with ice. That day she also found a book in the general store, traded in by some stage passenger. It was old, bound in shabby green with rubbed gilt lettering. She picked it up, examining the title with interest. *Folktales from England*. Chris bought it along with the food and fuel. She still had ample but if she was snowed in she would do better to have more than enough rather than too little.

She chose the book to read the following night and was soon deep in tales of strange events, a haunted church, the death of a miser, and ... she stared at the title on the next page. "The Legend of the Hunter." She read on with interest. When the story was done, she closed the book to sit thinking. She dimly remembered hearing the name they'd said. And, oddly enough, it was the same name she'd heard muttered in the mountains. Chris snorted. Some twisting of old legends brought with the first settlers here most likely.

She noticed it was colder. The woodpile in the shed by the back door was getting low. She should walk down the track a ways and see what she could collect. It had been a full moon last night. Even if she stayed after dark there'd be light to walk home safely. She could take Mouse to carry any dry wood she found, or to haul a dry tree-trunk back if there was one they could move. There'd been an old dead tree she'd seen last week. Chris bundled herself into warm clothing, haltered Mouse, draped a sack either side of him, and set out, axe in hand.

Leaving the track, she meandered along between the trees, gathering and cutting until she had armloads of dry wood in each sack. She stopped abruptly when she heard a faint whimper. Mick had disliked animals. Chris had wanted a dog but he wouldn't hear of it. Now the forlorn sound called to her. A puppy? Lost, starving, hurt or trapped. She called back, following the answering sounds.

She froze as she came in sight of the beast. No puppy, it was an adult dog, nor was it of any slight breed. Standing, it might reach four feet at the shoulder. The heavy powerful muscles curved in flowing lines under the smooth-coated pelt. It was gray, or to be more exact, Chris thought, a silvery color. The head was massive, narrowing only a little to heavy jaws. A mastiff of some kind? Gold eyes stared at her. Then it whimpered again.

Would it savage her if she tried to help? How was it hurt? Could she leave it here, go for help? But she'd gone wood hunting in the opposite direction. It would take an hour to walk home. Bringing help back would take a day, and what if no one wanted to come? The dog looked at her.

"If I try to help you'll understand, won't you?" It wouldn't but maybe the sound of her voice would help keep it calm. She moved in a little. "Poor boy. What on earth happened to you? Oh!" She could see a foreleg now, swollen twice the normal size, the swelling reaching far up towards the shoulder. "Oh, you poor dog. Don't worry. I'll help you." The swelling seemed to be getting worse almost as she watched. Maybe a snake had bitten the dog. She could deal with that she hoped.

"Just let me get Mouse to you." She was as quick as she could be, leading the placid pony right up to the injured dog. "Now, let's see if we can get you across his back." It was difficult. The dog was not only big but heavy. Still it seemed to appreciate she was helping. Chris forgot in her efforts any fear it might bite. Finally, she had it lying along the pack-sacks. Abandoning her gathered wood to be retrieved another day she moved as quickly as she could along the tracks until they reached her cottage.

By the time she had the dog stretched out on her hearthrug she was exhausted. She offered water, which the beast drank. That was good. Then, very gently, she turned the grossly swollen leg to look at it. Half buried in the paw's pad she saw something protruding. That had to be it. The dog had trodden on something sharp and infection had followed the wound. She patted it.

"I can see the trouble."

It whined softly.

"Don't worry. I'll look after you. I wonder who you belong to, someone who treats you well, I believe." It was so huge but so gentle. It had made no attempt to bite even though she must have hurt, getting it onto Mouse and off at the house again. Odd eyes. She didn't know a dog could have eyes of such a bright gold. She stroked the short fine coat, enjoying the softness.

"Okay, now, keep still." She was using her fingers, trying to get a grip on the thing, which was sunk into the paw. "Ahhh!" Her fingers gripped. "Ouch!" She held up a finger from which blood oozed. The dog leaned forward in one swift movement to lick off the blood. "Don't get ideas." Chris patted him, then took another grip. This time the object slid smoothly from the puffy flesh.

She glared at it. "A quill. Don't you know better than to tease porcupines?"

She tossed the quill to one side, dressed the injury carefully, then made the animal comfortable on the hearthrug with food and water. There went her own dinner she thought ruefully, but tomorrow she could drive Mouse to Nairnville. They might know if a dog like this was missing. If not, she could tell the storekeeper and he'd pass it on to anyone who came asking. If no one claimed the beast, she'd like to keep him herself.

No one did but he stayed only a short time. A few weeks later on a bright moonlit night, she let him out when he was insistent. He never returned and she wept. Winter went by and apart from mourning the loss of the dog, she was happy. Spring is a time of renewal but this spring brought floods, Miles Harman came to see that she'd survived in her isolation and – late one evening, her husband, Big Mick Islay in his buckboard with his gun-slick driving.

Chris saw him first from the shelter of her trees. Dear God, somehow he'd found her, she wondered how he'd done that but none of it mattered now; she had to get away. He hadn't seen her. If she faded back into the forest, she could be home in half an hour, grab a few things, her money, and make a run for it again with Mouse. The pony would take her through the mountains to one of the other small towns on the far side. There she could catch the stage.

Big Mick Islay kept his eyes busy. He'd been told where they'd have to leave the buckboard. After that, they'd have to walk but he had a map. He hitched the horses, pausing with his man to collect a couple of lanterns from the back of the wagon. It'd be dark any minute now. But if he waited, some busybody'd talk. She'd hear and God knows it had taken long enough to find her this time. If it hadn't been for a lawyer's clerk with his hand out, and a man here who resented being sent away, he'd never have found her.

He started walking down the track. At the cottage, Chris had leaped through the door, snatching up her money and other items she couldn't leave behind. Mouse, she must saddle him quickly. She heard footsteps then, stared out of the half-open door and froze in terror. He was here. She thrust the bills into her pocket and dived for the bedroom window in silence. It would take him a few minutes to realize she'd gone. It would have but Mick had left his man to watch. He shouted. Mick replied and as Chris ran, they were after her, deep into the heart of the mountains.

"I don't like this, boss. There's some funny tales about the mountains hereabouts." The hired gun shivered briefly. It was freezing too, and the moonlight bothered him, there was something about that light. He remembered stories his grandda had told him, of great trees back in the country they'd left behind, and tales of the wild lands and who it was that hunted there.

"What are you babbling about," Mick Islay snarled. "She's getting away. After her, if I lose her this time…"

Above their hunt, the moon rose higher, flooding patches of clearer ground with light. But under the trees it was flickering shadows. Chris knew the tracks by now. It was all that was keeping her ahead. She ran weighed down with her fear. She had the speed but they had the stamina. She dodged, twisted and turned but always they came back on her trail. She was tiring. Mick shouted furiously after her flying figure.

"Chris, stop. Stop, wife, or you'll be sorry." He cursed when she continued. Once he laid hands on her … Ahead, her foot caught in a tree root that lay across the path. She stumbled, slowing. He half-caught her arm. She wrenched free, leaping forward in a last gasp of speed and as she ran, she screamed for the first time. A short shrill cry of hopeless terror – and of rage at the man who had taught her that fear.

Above her, a gap in the trees flooded the forest floor with

silvery moonlight and in that flood something appeared. A shape, itself a part of the glimmering moonlight. Chris did not slow. Whatever it was had to be better than the men behind her. It halted to look at her. She fell again, gasping, and it whirled to stand over her as from its throat came a wild belling cry – a summoning. One that was answered by others as Chris flung her arms about the shape.

"Dog!" He lowered massive jaws to lick her gently. From far up the track came a wild thunder of hooves, a horn blowing as it overlaid with savage music the growing clamor of hounds crying the trail. Mick Islay and his man halted. Then came on. Only a dog and they both had pistols. Shoot it and they could get the woman away before the distant hunt reached them.

The dog was looking at him. Mick Islay shot, cursing the moonlight that affected his aim. The horn sounded louder. He stared incredulously as the hunt poured down the track towards him. A giant of a man on a great black horse whose hooves spurned the ground they did not quite touch. A pack of hounds that raced before him, their eyes blazing golden flames. The horn sounded louder, bringing a hot gust of terror to take him by the throat. His man was babbling. Mick seized him by the arm, hitting him across the face.

"What are you babbling about, you superstitious fool?"

"Herne! Oh, Jesus. Me grandda was right. It's Herne the Hunter. She's called the hounds of Herne to save her. *Look!*"

He pointed to where Chris knelt. Before her, protecting, stood the dog. But this was no beast of earth now. Its eyes flamed the same gold fire as those of the pack, moonlight glowed silver fire along the muscled flanks. It shifted, half in and half out of their world. The huntsman's mount reared high. The rider's eyes fixed on the two men. The horn sang as the milling pack turned to look at them too – and with those eyes upon him – Mick Islay broke in that moment. He ran, his man running faster before him. The pack followed, the high wild music of the horn urging them on. The prey was chosen. Let them follow the prey. They did not see the rider turn back.

Chris knelt on the forest floor her arms about the great dog. Hooves sounded beside her and she looked up. The huntsman's face was strong, clean planes of bone framing eyes that blazed down at her. Yet despite the power it was a face without evil, he would always deal justice – yes that was his failing she thought. Little mercy showed in the lines. But the black eyes, which surveyed her, were unexpectedly kind. He nodded once, his gaze holding hers. Into her mind came understanding like a blow.

Perhaps it had first been a test to see if she was fit to share the mountains and forest with he who hunted here. But the beast she had aided, a dog that in the space of a moon had come to love her, had answered her cry. It had licked the blood she had shed for it.

The terror of the hunt could never touch her. Justice was met. Ahead lay justice for those who had dared to hunt her in one of the Hunter's own forests. Hoof-thunder receded.

The dog urged her to her feet and walked beside her as she staggered back to her cottage. Now and again, his tongue came out lovingly to lick her hand. She would not see Mick or his man again. They would run until they reached the buckboard. Then with fear hot behind them, they would drive the horses like madmen until the buckboard crashed and they would be flung off the cliff the horses had swung hard to avoid. They would die, the horn call still sounding its wild scream of justice in their ears.

Chris bought the cottage when the year ran out. She lived there after that, accepted by the mountain folk who knew more than they found it necessary to tell. And if on moonlit nights she met a friend, if she walked and talked with one on two legs, and if one who ran fleetly four-footed now and again returned to stay the night, who was there to speak of it?

But that was all to come. For now, she stood at her door, one hand on the dog's great head as she listened to horn-song fading, riding the sky, the music of hounds singing back to it. The dog was gone when she lowered her eyes; gone to find his pack and the trail they cried. There is a strange reality behind some legends, nor are they always bound to one place, and for that, the widow of Big Mick Islay could only be thankful.

SUCH AN UNFORTUNATE FAMILY

My pa wasn't always the most honest of men, nor the most fortunate for a fair time. In fact, in his younger days he spent too much of his time tip toeing into other people's houses to see what small valuables he could find to leave with. That's how he met ma. She was a widow with a nice ranch – why, people all over the state talked about how she had her outhouse at the end of a little covered walk so's she didn't get wet going out there. She had a herd of good fat cattle, a flock of chickens, and two sows to boot, but she surely needed a man to help her with the work although that wasn't quite what pa saw to start with.

What he saw was the pretty silver dishes she had – real solid silver. And there was talk in the bank once; when pa was in there listening, of how she kept cash money in her desk. She loved animals, did the widow Jennifer Blackson, and she had one of the biggest, friendliest cats a body ever saw. Half lynx they said, but you couldn't tell it from his temper because he loved the whole world and everyone in it.

But pa didn't mind cats, an' he was thinking of all those silver dishes that'd sell down in Mexico for enough money to keep a man drunk for weeks – an' that wasn't counting any cash money that might be in the old rolltop desk. So he found an excuse to be riding over that way, and stopped in for a dip-per-full of water.

Well, the widow she came out, and asked if he wouldn't rather have tea instead and pa allowed as how he could manage that, nor a scone or two with jam and cream wouldn't go amiss … He followed her into the parlor, and that cat came in with him and settled in his lap. He must have weighed

51

twenty pounds or more and he overhung here and there but he purred loud enough to deafen you and the widow smiled approval.

"He likes you."

Now pa was a smart man. He didn't say that from what he'd heard the cat liked everyone he'd ever met, but he praised the animal an' petted him while the cat purred fit to beat the band, an' pa ate a whole plate of scones and thought that the widow could sure as heck cook.

Well, the long and the short of it was that he got a good look about the house and by the time he got up to go he knew where to find the silver dishes; and they was finer than he'd ever heard too, an' he saw where that old desk was. That night he came drifting back into the house real quiet, packed up the dishes, got the desk open and found a whole mess of papers with banknotes mixed in. He didn't want to stand there too long with the lantern so he grabbed all a' the papers and took them to the outhouse to sort through. The door on that was to one side away from the house and he figured that no one would see any light if'n he turned the lantern down, sat there, and worked.

So that's what he did, and he was just sorting out those bank notes when something real heavy and furry landed on his lap. Pa got such a fright he tried to jump up, hold onto the papers and get rid of the intruder off'a his lap, and all of that at once. So instead, he lost his balance, fell sideways, banged his head real hard against the wall and that saw to it that he sort'a lost interest in the proceedings for a while.

When he come to there's the widow standing there with a shotgun trained on him and her cat purring around both sets of their ankles. She looks mighty fetching in her floral sprigged flannel long-johns, and pa he's a man to think fast. Besides which, the likelihood of her telling the whole town how her cat jumped onto his lap in the outhouse and scared him so much he knocked his-self out was the sort of tale that'd make people laugh from the Pecos to the border. So he up and says.

"I shouldn't a done it, but I fell in love with you when I saw you yesterday. I wanted to know if you really was a widow because I'm honorable an' not a man to be courting another man's woman."

And while he's talking he's figuring that she can't have seen her silver dishes are packed up or she'd likely have said a lot more and wouldn't be looking so kindly on him, and if he can get them back in place before she knows then maybe he could be falling into the cream pot.

Well, the widow's eyes light up, and she tells him she really is a widow, and she isn't averse to a new husband, and as her cat likes him too she sees nothing against it and what with one thing an another, he got the silver plates back where they should'a been, and it went on from there. So that's how pa came to marry ma, but I think ma guessed some of that because if pa got a bit casual about her an' started spending too much time in the saloon, she'd smile and ask how his head was, and pat the cat; while mentioning as how pa seemed to worry about misfortune. Pa still didn't want that story getting around and he'd come to heel. The cat, he lived to a very old age and he jumped on a lot of laps before he died, although I don't think he ever got a husband for but one widow.

That seemed to of changed our family's luck that'd always been bad up to then; or so pa allus claimed. We was fortunate all the years until ma died and pa started worrying about his own health. There's an old cowboy remedy that they used to say would guarantee a long healthy life and danged if pa didn't take it up. Every morning he put a teaspoon a' gunpowder on his porridge, and when I switched us to some new-fangled breakfast stuff that I liked better he kept a'using it on that too. Maybe it worked because he was near a hundred when he died and a month before that happened some young reporter from our local newspaper interviewed him.

I was the oldest an' inherited ma's original farm so I was around when that reporter come by again a week after the funeral, an' five days after pa's coffin went to the place he'd picked to dispose of him proper. The young man was wanting details of the funeral and then about pa's descendants an' I told him.

"Ma's been dead a good while now, but although they wasn't so young when they wed her and pa ended with a fair-sized family. When he died he left me and my five brothers, he left nineteen grandchildren, twenty-six great-grandchildren – and," I paused, "a fifteen foot hole in Mr. Parker's crematorium wall." Pa would have said we were still an unfortunate family, but Mr. Parker ain't a relative and the rest of us have been doing fine.

THE FAST GUN

Joe Deshanes was a fast gun. Not that you'd think it to look at him. He stood five feet seven inches in his socked feet. His hair receded slightly. He wore glasses, and while wiry and strong enough, he was lightly built, and looked all of his thirty-seven years. His Pomeranian dog, a feisty little animal named Dusty, usually accompanied him everywhere but to work. Joe worked in Albuquerque as an accountant for Hemmings, Fisher, and Watson. In fact, he was head of their forensic accounting division and valued by his employers who approved of Joe's devotion to duty, hard work, and his quiet solid stubbornness that kept him digging away at something until it came out the way he thought that it should.

It was those qualities that had made him a fast gun as well. Every Saturday he went out to the range with Dusty and competed against cops, bank tellers, two local lawyers, and several dozen other workers who loved reenacting the Old West. There was a sprinkling of women who competed, some almost as good as Joe, but he was top gun, and everyone knew it – although here and there some sneered.

"Joe? Yeah, yeah, he's good, but it's all fake."

"Whadya mean, fake? You mean he cheats?"

"No, far as that goes, he's honest." The speaker was an aging, overweight cop who'd lost matches against Joe for the past ten years. "I mean he's the fastest gun in the club against targets, is all. S'easy to win like that. Be a different story if he was having to hit targets while dodging bullets."

The fireman he was addressing nodded slowly. "Yeah, guess so. Out on the street it's different, civilians never get that."

The gossip turned to a recent spate of minor arsons and neither heard the retreating footsteps. Joe stopped once he was

out of earshot and stood looking down at Dusty. Was what
they'd said true? He shrugged after a couple of minutes, how
would he ever know? He checked the lying accounts of failed
businesses to determine if there was anything that could be
salvaged from the wreckage they'd left. If he met a mugger one
night he might get a chance to find out. He did carry a small
pistol to and from work after dark.

Joe's lips curved up in a thin smile. It was unlikely though,
and frankly he'd rather it didn't happen. Denizens of the Old
West might have congratulated him on ridding them of just
another thief; slapped him on the back and bought him a drink
– somehow he doubted that the police here and now would be
quite so casual. And maybe Sergeant Hack was right; maybe
Joe wouldn't be so good against targets if the targets shot back.

It never occurred to either of them that the sergeant was
wrong. Joe had the ability to discard everything but the job in
hand and concentrate on that ferociously. It was what made
him so good at his job. He also had a very good eye, steady
nerves, and reflexes that had begun as fast and had been honed
over years of practice to a speed that could have startled Wyatt
Earp.

Of course, Joe knew that he was fast – he'd won club com-
petitions for years and even the State Competition twice – but
he discounted his speed against that of the famous fast guns of
legend. He couldn't be faster than they had been, not genuine-
ly. His speed was a product of better equipment, the better nu-
trition that improved reflexes, and the money to buy thousands
of rounds each year and burn them all in practice – something
that most men of the Old West couldn't have afforded.

He went home to his wife who loved her husband and
approved his hobby. "How'd you do tonight, dear?"

"Not bad. I beat Hack anyhow."

Lavinia Deshanes, who'd met and disliked the sergeant,
smiled. "Good. I bet he didn't like that either."

Joe met her affectionate gaze and found himself telling her
what he'd overheard. "What do you think?"

Lavinia snorted. "Did it occur to you that everything you
heard was a load of sour grapes? *Sergeant* Hack! Sergeant of
what, Joe, tell me? No, I mean it, tell me!"

"He works the desk."

"Exactly, when he was a rookie he had a couple of years on the beat. That was thirty years ago when the streets were a lot easier too, and did he ever shoot anyone?"

"Not that I know of," Joe said slowly.

"No, I bet he didn't, I bet he was never even shot at." Lavinia snorted. "And if someone *had* shot at him he isn't a target they could miss, the fat walrus. He just thinks that because he's a cop he should be better than you. But does he put in the hours, spend the money on ammunition, and buy the very best of everything? No, he doesn't," she answered before Joe could. "He's cheap, he's all mouth, and you're better than him any day." She looked at her husband. "Didn't you tell me once that your people were ranchers back in those days?"

Joe nodded. His ma knew a lot more about that than he did. She had all the family letters, photos, old deeds, and maps. But he knew some of it. "Yes, my great-great-great-great-grandparents had a ranch, it wasn't huge but when it was sold three generations ago it made a real profit. My grandfather invested the money and his investments did well. When he died, Grandma put all the money into a trust."

They'd never been a prolific family so far as children went. Joe had two cousins, and that was it for his generation. For the next, he and Lavinia had no kids, one of his cousins was gay and didn't want kids, and the other cousin had a little girl. The trust was split between everyone in direct descent from their grandparents. With only Joe's mother and the cousins' parents left, that made a total of six adult beneficiaries to collect the trust interest each year. It was a solid little sum, not quite enough for a person to live on but it supplemented pensions or salaries very nicely.

"So your great-etc. grandparents were real ranchers in the Old West?"

"Yes."

"Which makes you a genuine descendant of the time; I wonder what the sergeant's family was doing then?"

Joe grinned at her. "Don't ask him."

That, he thought, was the thing about women, if they took a dislike to a man he couldn't do anything right. If he was lucky enough to be loved – and he knew he was and knew how lucky that made him – then they'd overlook almost anything. Including a man being short, skinny, needing glasses and starting to lose his hair. He hugged his wife hard enough to make her squeak.

"I love you."

Lavinia hugged him back. "I love you too. Now go and wash up, dinner will be ready in ten minutes."

She looked after him as he headed for the bathroom, Dusty at his heels. Joe was a dear, good, kind man. There wasn't a mean bone in his body and she could kick that Hack. She smiled suddenly. Of course, Hack didn't know that the core of Joe's heart was the thing that his mother had taught her son his entire life that women were to be respected, loved, cherished and protected. Why, she'd bet that if the chips were down and she was in danger, Joe would do far more than that fat cop ever would to protect her.

They ate the excellent roast – a slice for Dusty found its way to his plate – and enjoyed the ice cream and peaches that followed. After the dishes were done, Lavinia watched a TV program with the dog in her lap while Joe worked at the small table behind the couch. There was this firm that had gone bankrupt owing millions. He thought that some of those millions weren't quite as unrecoverable as the firm's owner kept insisting they were. Now and again as he paused to think, Hack's words came into his mind and it was an effort to force them away.

It reminded him too of the family history. He should go see ma in a day or two. She had everything, knew all the old family history and the stories they'd told. They talked on SKYPE and via Facebook often, but it was almost four weeks since he'd last visited. He'd maybe cut the club this weekend and go then. Lavinia and ma got along very well and they'd be happy to see each other too. He went back to the figures. He thought that he saw an anomaly there and his eyes narrowed.

The weather forecast in the morning was for continued bad weather. Joe wore his overcoat out to the car, and arrived at work to find that the firm had a problem.

"Can you work from home?"

"Of course, but..."

"The damn roofs sprang a leak; wind brought a chunk of debris down on it. Must have happened right after everyone left, and the water's been coming in all night. Ceiling upstairs was soaked; one section gave way and dumped a ton of water into the next floor down, that's starting to weaken. We're two floors under it but the experts want us out just in case. It'll be a week before we can get back in safely." Mr. Fisher told him tersely. "Can you manage?"

Joe nodded, thinking of the various jobs he was doing. "Yes, I keep backup files of all my work on encrypted flash-drives at home. I was working on the Saminson file last night as a matter of fact."

The firm's partner was momentarily diverted. "Find anything?"

"I think so, there's a note on a file that just might be a bank account, no indication where, but I have some ideas."

"Good man, if anyone can find it you can. But be careful, word has it that Saminson has some odd associates. If you do find that account and we can retrieve some of the money there could be people who won't appreciate it."

Joe smiled. "I've got a pretty good safe."

He headed back to his car, briefcase and notebook computer in hand, thinking that Fisher was exaggerating. The directors of the firm he was investigating were ordinary American businessmen, not the mafia. He drove towards his suburb anticipating a peaceful morning at home. If he were going to be working at home all week, he'd do something he rarely did and take today off. Lavinia would be at the library where she volunteered. She'd be done after lunch, and he could maybe collect her from there and they could go see ma today. This morning he'd go to the club with Dusty and practice.

Joe entered his house. Being neither large nor heavy and naturally light-footed, the men working on his safe didn't hear him until he reached the door. It was then that several coincidences came together. Elsewhere in time and distance, someone was praying for a miracle. The intruders' watcher had returned to ask a question so missed Joe's silent arrival and his minutes in the bedroom. The safecracker they were using

wasn't as experienced as he liked to think, and in the rush –
they'd only learned the previous day who had the firm's files
– he'd taken more plastique than he'd have normally used. He
was being rushed here too and he'd made the mistake of using
all the plastique, adding the detonator, connecting everything
up, and only then realizing how much of the plastique he really
had here and starting to pinch off the excess amount.

"Come on, hurry it up."

"Shut up, I'm trying to concentrate." He regretted that the
moment he said it. His payment was a stunning blow across the
back of his head.

"Tell *me* to shut up? I'll…"

Joe appeared in the lounge doorway, Dusty on his leash,
Joe wearing cross-draw pistols under a black-stitched, white,
knee-length duster, belts filled with ammunition, and his Stet-
son in one hand. "Hey!"

Several people moved incautiously – and there was an explosion. It took out most of the lounge, the three men before
the safe, and the safe door fell off to reveal that it had been
empty. Joe never kept his work in the safe. He preferred to
keep it in a cavity in the wardrobe floor in his bedroom but no
one apart from him and Lavinia knew that. The blast threw Joe
backwards.

He landed on soft earth and blinked. What…? He stared
around, at the grass, the trees, patches of scrub and mountains
in the distance. How…? A small work-hardened hand grabbed
him by the arm. His still bemused mind completed the trium-
virate. Who…?

"He's coming. Do something!"

Joe staggered to his feet, automatically settling the gun
belts comfortably into place. He found that the person clutching his arm was a girl. She was white-faced with fear or she'd
have had a healthy tan. Dusty barked at her and she glanced
down incredulously.

"You brought a *dog* with you? Oh, never mind, there isn't
time. He'll be here any minute."

"Who?" Joe asked reasonably.

"Ed Baker. He's working for the man who wants our
ranches. He's driving out all us small landholders so he can have

everything. Baker's a fast gun. My husband left to find a man who was as good who might fight for us. I didn't know he was back until I walked out of the house and you were here, but Baker's coming. He's killed people, they say he doesn't care who if the money's good enough, you, me, Michael ... where *is* Michael?"

"*Who* is Michael?"

"My husband of course, you must have met him when you were hired." She called, "Michael, Mich..." Her body jolted around as the hoof-beats caught their attention. Joe realized that there was a rider approaching fast on a nondescript bay.

"That's Baker." Her face and voice calmed in resignation. "He'll kill us, and then his boss will have another ranch."

The bay horse stopped in the center of the yard, and Dusty perked up. He'd seen a horse before. They could be spooked and the resulting excitement was fun. He charged barking, circled the horse, nipped at a heel, dived between the animal's legs, nipped again, and leaped away. The bay horse rose into the air and its rider, while he remained in the saddle had a hectic few seconds. His eyes narrowed, a hand flicked down, the gun flowed into his hand and he shot. Dusty's shrill barking became a squeal of fright as the bullet parted his thick fur.

And Joe's reflexes kicked in. His hands flashed down in a cross-draw so fast that it momentarily froze Ed Baker. Before he could line his gun on the true danger, two bullets slammed into his heart and he was dead before his feet left the stirrups. The bay horse sidled away from the body, reins trailing. Joe might have been horrified – he was an accountant not a killer – but for the arrival of Baker's boss and close to a dozen hands. They saw the body and came in already shooting. Dusty wisely went to cover behind the water trough by the corral fence.

Joe wasn't just a club fast-draw champion. He'd also competed a number of times for his own amusement in the type of competition that requires the competitor to shoot while being shoved, pushed, and knocked off balance. He went flat and shot back, while the girl had gone flat behind him. That got Joe's dander up. They were shooting at a girl – an *unarmed* girl. Where was the spirit of the Old West that said no decent man harmed a woman?

He shot, rolled into cover of a leaky trough, yanked the girl behind that too, and fired again. There was a hideous sound, a jarring sound that went on and on. Must have hit a cow or something, he thought vaguely and shot again. He didn't notice the man half sitting to one side against a post. Joe's bullet had struck the saddle-horn, ripped upward spinning sideways like a buzz saw and opened the hand up the belly as a hunter guts a deer. The pain was everything it was said to be, and the hand half-lay staring at his entrails and shrieking his agony in a series of squalls that sounded less and less human as the minutes passed.

The sounds unnerved his leader. Wayne Cullen had killed men, seen men die, but he'd never seen or heard a gut-shot man before and without thinking, he spun and fired once. The squalling stopped as he turned back to fight. Joe shot again. The target had been moving and while the shot was a hit, it wasn't a clean kill. Cullen staggered and turned, his face a bloody ruin of smashed teeth, cheek blown off, tongue in shreds and one eye hanging down his cheek. He gave a groaning guttural scream and collapsed. His men broke. Their hired gun had been defeated, the man who paid them was dead or dying, and with him gone there'd be no one to keep this story quiet – or pay them. Horses galloped away, their riders urging them on and Joe was left, with only the girl, the dying rancher, and a small prancing dog, as living witnesses.

Dusty was triumphant. He bounced between the dead gunman, the other two hands Joe had shot, and the rancher – who's rasping breaths were slowing … slowing … stopped …

"Come away from him," Joe ordered the dog, which obeyed reluctantly.

The girl was hanging on his arm again. "Thank you, thank you. Whatever my husband promised you, we'll pay, I swear. Thank God you came, I prayed so hard." She was leading him around the house and pointing. "Washroom's there. I'll make coffee. Come in when you're ready."

Joe went to sit on a log outside once he'd wiped his face and hands with a piece of towel using water he found in an enamel basin. Dusty sat panting at his feet. Joe absent-mindedly reached down, clasped Dusty's leash – and, they were standing in his hall by the lounge door. Through the open door, he could see a thoroughly dead safecracker, two men staggering to their feet and he stepped hastily aside as they charged for the door – or for him. He had no way of knowing.

They passed him, and still confused, he followed. They reached the edge of the property and one spun, snarling words Joe barely caught – something about finishing the job? The man's hand went under his jacket, Dusty charged at him barking, and Joe's reflexes kicked in for the second time as a gun came out. His opponent shot once and missed. Joe shot once and didn't. Two police cars pulled up, fourteen neighbors who'd been watching from various vantage points converged on them. The remaining – unarmed – intruder made a run for it and was brought down by Mr. Dawson who'd been scouted for football – but rejected – in 1989, and had never forgotten it.

Joe had wisely dropped his guns back into his holsters, and let everyone see that his hands were empty. The cops who'd arrived were local men who knew him. They listened, examined the dead man – and his gun – separated out fourteen pop-eyed neighbor's excited tales, patted Dusty, and agreed that Joe had acted in self-defense, but they'd have to take him and his guns into temporary custody. From which he was released in a couple of hours. Too many people had seen him drawn on and were willing to swear he'd done no more than save his own life.

There was quite an aftermath to events however. Mr. Saminson – he of the failed firm and missing cash – took an abrupt holiday in Italy and decided to make his home there permanently. His half-uncle was annoyed at the loss of two men, and far more irked by the default of a third – in custody and singing like the proverbial bird. Nothing could be conclusively tied to the uncle but life was uncomfortable for quite a while. It was also shorter than it would otherwise have been for the singer the first time he was careless.

Dusty got a bone that was almost as big as he was. Joe, who wasn't certain about some of the events he'd survived and couldn't make up his mind if it had all been a dream, sat down that night to cuddle his dog and found a singed path through the long thick reddish fur. He regarded that very thoughtfully.

He was happy when he received a raise the next week –

and noted the increase in respect from colleagues at his firm. It isn't every accountancy firm that can boast a fast gun on the payroll. Only Lavinia was told about the gunman and the rancher and Joe's defense of the girl while he showed her the furrow through Dusty's fur. And Lavinia, who turned out not to have been at the library that morning, had news for Joe.

"The doctor confirmed it. We're having a little cowboy or cowgirl in six and a half months. We have to tell your mother."

The drive out to where Mary Deshanes lived took a couple of hours during which they talked and Dusty slept in the back seat.

"Do you think it was real?" Joe kept his eyes on the road as he asked.

Lavinia nodded slowly. "I think I do. I saw Dusty's fur, and Joe, you aren't a liar. I don't know how or why it happened, but I believe that it did. You said that the girl told you she'd prayed for someone to save the ranch." Her smile lit up Joe's heart. "It looks as if you really were an answer to prayer, my love."

Mary Deshanes was overjoyed at their news. "Sit down. Drink your coffee while I get some of the old records down to show you. And Joe, this will amuse you, great-Uncle Trevor died last year and I've finally had time to read through his family papers. Did you know that he had several letters and photos dating right back to the Peterson ranch?"

She was laying out a faded sepia photo and letters cross-written in crabbed handwriting as she spoke.

"Look, this was Judith, she wrote several of the letters. I didn't know but apparently some big rancher in their area not long after she and Michael were married tried to take their ranch."

Joe looked down at the photo of a girl. Last time he'd seen her she was thanking him and offering coffee. His mother was reading one of the letters.

"She used to write to Uncle Trevor's grandmother's grandmother. Apparently they'd been at school together. Listen to this, she says, 'Michael had gone to find a man who might fight for us. I came out of the house when I heard something and I knew Michael had succeeded because the man was standing in the yard. He wore cross-draw holsters – odd-looking guns,

I've never seen anything quite like them before or since – but he was about the fastest I've ever seen. Ed Baker went for his gun and this man outdrew him. Put two shots into Ed and Ed went down.

"'Then Wayne Cullen and his hands came galloping in, started shooting and our man shot back. He killed Cullen and three of his hands and the rest ran. I asked our man if he'd like a wash and then to kindly come in and have a mite of coffee until Mike arrived and we could pay him. He never did come in, never asked for his money and we never saw him again. We kept the ranch because of what he did, and likely he saved other small ranches here too. He didn't take the money we'd have paid him so I pray for him every night and will so long as I live. I'll never forget him. He was no more than five foot seven, a slender man, wearing glasses and a fancy duster, and – you won't believe this – he had a little dog with him, fluffy with a fox face, and so sweet. Whoever would think of a fast gun with a lapdog?'"

Mary Deshanes folded the letter and smiled tolerantly. "An interesting story. Although I'm sure this hired gun can't have been quite like that."

Joe's gaze met that of his wife. They both knew that Judith's fast gun had been *exactly* like that, fluffy fox-faced dog and all, and it was nice to know the girl had prayed for him for all those years. Next time he went to the club, he could ignore Hack's comments about what Joe might do if he met real trouble. Joe smiled at his wife, and she smiled back, both of them knowing. A man handled trouble when he met it – and Joe was a man.

THE LOST

It was the year after the Great War ended, and in small-town Arizona that the initial conversation took place. "Have you heard," I asked my friend, "that your old house is on the market *again*?"

Shari swallowed the last piece of her cake and shook her head. "No, I hadn't."

"It's weird though, don't you think. I mean, your family lived there for three generations. Then once your mum sold it no one's ever stayed there for much more than a year." I counted back, muttering to myself. "That has to be right. Your mother sold five years ago, and since then there's been three – no, four – owners."

"I know, it was a bad year." Shari leaned back sipping her hot cocoa. "My brother was killed, Mum had that fall and couldn't stay in the house any longer and Tigger died."

I gave her a sympathetic look. I'd never liked Shari's brother: an over-bearing self-righteous man, but her mother was fine and she liked the home for old ladies in which she lived now. Tigger, however, had been a real loss. He'd been – as Shari often described him – sixteen pounds of bone and muscle, and a cat that knew his own mind. He'd liked most of Shari's women friends, a few of her male friends – and no dog he'd ever known.

"Have you ever thought of buying the place back?" I asked.

Shari sighed. "I'd like to, but I don't have the cash. I want a proper house of my own for sure, but house prices keep going up, and fast as I can save something out of what I get from the trust I can't ever quite catch up."

"Even if you sell your little place?"

She made a wry face. "Even if I got more than it's worth."

66

I caught the waitress's eye and signaled for more hot cocoa. "You'll just have to sell a book or something." Then I switched the subject.

Later when I was driving home, I remembered Tigger again. He'd always unbent towards me too from the day Shari found a kitten shivering by the side of the road where someone who'd decided they didn't want him had tossed him away. But he was Shari's cat – or she was his person. She'd even dumped a guy she'd been keen on because of the cat. When he'd gone to pat Tigger, she'd warned him not to, he'd done so anyway and been bitten – and he'd taken a swipe at the cat, who'd dodged, having clearly expected it.

As Shari said, any man who hit an animal for no good reason was the sort of man who'd hit women and children too. I didn't disagree although it occurred to me that as Shari had no intention of having children or possibly even marrying, she didn't really have to worry.

(Her father had inherited a trust, he'd left it to Shari and her brother, and she now got all the income since her brother had died at the start of the war. The amount had dropped; wars do not improve most investments, but she did own a small apartment over a local fabric shop, and the trust income meant she didn't have to work unless she wanted to.)

I met her that weekend and we spent most of the day lazing in the park at the fringe of our small town, talking casually.

"How's the new scheme going?" she asked.

I shrugged. "Okay, but all Bob can do is fiddle with it. The company knows just what they want. Talk about a scorched-earth policy. He's trying to save some of the better trees, and making sure that they'll replant as soon as they've contoured, but in my opinion it's still going to look like hell."

My husband is a well-known architect, and the only reasons he'd taken on this job were that it paid *very* well, and he might be able to save some of what would otherwise be discarded, since this company was known for their habit of not starting to build new houses until the land they'd be built on was nothing but bare earth with all greenery gone. The market for moderately-priced three-bedroom houses had skyrocketed since the war ended fourteen months ago.

"Oh, and oddly enough, the daughter of the chap who's doing this sub-division is the one who just bought your house. She was waiting for her father after Bob's meeting and saying they'll move in once they're back from visiting family. So that's it."

Shari chuckled. "Not if you're right. Let's see, four owners in about five years. At that rate it should be for sale again in around eighteen months."

"Fat chance. These ones will probably be the ones who stick to it."

"Maybe. Anyway, do you want to go see the play here to-night?"

I did and said so. There's nothing like watching a play in a cool park on a hot night.

* * *

Three years passed, but not uneventfully. Josie moved into Shari's old home. The sub-division was finished. Bob was paid a bonus and we had a holiday. Shari's writing suddenly took off. She resigned from her part-time job in the fabric shop and she turned thirty-six. I threw her a great party and when she called the following day, I initially assumed it was to talk about that. It wasn't.

"Jan, I've just had wonderful news." I waited. "I can't quite believe it, but you know *Wolves*?" I did. It was the first in a series of mysteries she'd hoped to sell. She wrote them under a man's name and while she'd sold other singletons to small or even medium-sized publishers; this would be her first series. '*Wolves*' was the primary book and a large publisher had been interested. (The main character was a soldier who'd returned to being a policeman after the war, and he was the archetypical 'wounded hero.')

"Don't tell me...?"

"Okay I won't."

"*Tell me!*"

"I spent three days in our capitol and..." here she named a firm I'd knew to be major players – " have offered me a con-tract, not just for *Wolves* but for the other two books completed as well. They'll bring them out over the next two and a half years, and they asked if I have more planned."

I cracked up. Shari hadn't just written the first three, she had plot ideas and outlines for another six. "What are they paying you?" The amount she told me wasn't that much, and I said so.

"That's the advance on the first book. But I'm not getting excited. Not yet. It'll depend on how the books sell, if the publisher stays with the series, and if readers really like it."

I'd read the books in manuscript and I'd liked them, so I hoped this was her big break. Then I had a thought. "You know, it really is time you bought a proper house. You need more room for your books and writing."

"Same problem applies as it did last time we talked about that. And banks don't like giving loans to female self-employed writers even if they do have extra income from a trust and an apartment they could sell."

"True. Anyway, once you have a signed contract bring it over and we can gloat."

"I will." She brought it over a week later and I swept her out to lunch to celebrate.

"How's the fourth book coming along?"

"Like an express train on a downhill run. I'm calling it, *With a Bear Behind.*"

I choked on my salad. "How will the publishers feel about that?"

"They like it. They said it's just risqué enough to be appealing."

I grinned. "With luck like yours you should take a raffle ticket."

And on the way out of the restaurant I stopped at the counter where they had tickets for sale. Giggling, we bought one each, but put both our names on them, with my address and phone number on one and hers on the other.

"Twice the numbers, twice the luck," I said, patting the tickets. It must have been, because I was at Shari's apartment the next month when her newly installed phone rang. She had the window open and was transplanting seedlings into her window box.

"Get that will you, Jan. My hands are filthy. Tell them

you're me."

I reached out lazily. "Hello, Shari Aarlton here."

The phone spoke briefly and to the point. I put it on hold, and turned to Shari with my face showing disbelieving excitement. She stared at me. "Jan? What is it?"

"The lotto tickets we took, the ones we got because of your book contract. One of them's won a prize. Talk to the man." I held out the phone.

They sorted out who she really was, and then that, yes, I was the other name on the ticket. He rang off once we understood that we'd have to claim our money in person with I.D. and the ticket. Then we grabbed each other and did a wild dance around the room.

Shari sank into an armchair. "Almost five thousand dollars each. Wow, what couldn't we do with that?"

I sat up straight. "I know exactly what *you* can do with it."

"What?"

I reached out for the newspaper that I'd brought with me and that Shari hadn't yet read. "Look at this." I pointed and read out. "For sale, large house, pleasantly situated in cul-de-sac...." Shari was looking at the sketch over my shoulder and squealed.

"Our old house!"

"Yeah, it's on the market yet again. But with the money for your apartment, the lotto cash and the book contracts you might only have to take out a tiny loan, and surely the bank would agree."

The long and the short of it was that we went to see the house that afternoon. I gave Shari instructions – I'm not in the real estate business but with Bob being an architect, I know a fair amount about that sort of thing.

The house was surprisingly run down. It didn't look as if it had been painted since Shari's mum had had that done in nineteen-twelve, ten years ago now. While a few minor renovations seemed to have been started, they'd all been dropped. It was a mess, and as instructed, Shari said nothing while we strolled through. We were just leaving when Josie, the sub-division magnate's daughter came by and I said her name. She stopped.

"Oh, Jan, Jan ... um?"

"Jan Conney."

"Oh yes, nice to see you. What are you doing in the area?"

"We were thinking of looking at a house for sale a street over, "I said smoothly, pointing in the other direction to where we'd been."

She swayed slightly and Shari and I realized simultaneously that dear Josie was a bit under the weather.

"Why are *you* in the area?" Shari asked.

"Trying to sell a damned white elephant," Josie promptly informed us in tones that could have etched glass as she pointed in the opposite direction to the one I'd indicated. "I don't suppose you'd like to buy a dump. Guaranteed to give you nightmares and sell for less than you paid for it as soon as you've had enough."

I caught Shari's eye. "Come and have a drink and tell us all about it. You poor kid, you shouldn't have to put up with stuff like that."

Since Josie agreed with my opinion, she came with us to Shari's apartment and while she was soaking up more alcohol, we got the full story. How no one could live in the house. After a few months it would be up for sale again, and between neighbors talking, friends and family who'd heard something, and local gossip about the place in this rotten town, fewer and fewer people would consider buying so that each time the price slipped further down the list.

"But what's wrong with it?" Shari asked.

"What's right? There are odd noises, and sometimes you feel something brush past you in the dark. Things fall off the top of the furniture and break." She sniffed. "My grandmother gave me a vase that came from China and the second night we were there it fell off the corner shelf and broke. It was valuable, I liked it and it was pretty."

"Maybe the vase fell because of a vibration, and old houses can make odd noises settling at night."

Josie snorted and tipped back the last of her martini. "You don't get vibration in a cul-de-sac. That's trucks and what big truck comes through a dead-end street? And that's not all. What did it for me – and I got straight out of bed, dressed, packed a case and told Alan he could sell the house if he wanted to stay

married – was being asleep in bed when something jumped on
my feet and started moving up the bed." She shivered. "I've
never been so scared in all my life. I turned the light on and
there wasn't anything there but I'll never set foot in that house
again. I don't care if it goes for peanuts, I want away from it
and that's that." She swigged back half her replenished drink
in one gulp.

Shari had an odd look in her eyes. "What room did you
have?"

Josie stared blearily. "Huh? The big room at the back. Why?"

"Just wondering if a squirrel could have got in perhaps?"

"Whatever it was, it was no squirrel. It weighed ten times
what one would, and anyway, Alan searched the whole place,
an' so did dad the next day. There was no way any animal
could have got in – or out again. And I don't care," her voice
rose hysterically. "It's cursed or something. They can sell it, give
it away or tear the place down…"

I made soothing noises, got her up and out to the pave-
ment where Shari and I persuaded her into my husband's little
car and I drove her back to her father's office. We left her in the
receptionist's hands and once we were outside, Shari turned to
me and I could see that she was strung as tight as a bow.

"Did you see who the agents were for the house?" I nodded. "Do you know where their office is?" I nodded again. "Will
you drive me there right now?"

This time I spoke. "Yes. Do I presume you're going to make
an offer for the house?"

"I am." There was confidence in her voice and a bubbling
happiness.

She knew something. What it was I didn't know, but if
she was that sure of herself … "Then let me do the talking. Let
them think Bob and I want it to rebuild."

"Okay."

I knew what money she had, what her apartment would
probably sell for and what moving would cost. We arrived at
the agent's office, and once they knew which house I might be
half-interested in buying I was greeted with panting enthusiasm. They mentioned a price and I kicked Shari's ankle when
she gasped at how low it was.

"Quite," I said, looking at her and then at the agent. "That's ridiculous. There's a massive amount of repair work needs doing. It looks as if every useless renovator in the area has started something inside and got bored partway through. Not to mention the *turnover*." I added significantly.

"The turnover?" The young man faltered.

"That place has had half a dozen owners in a few years. People don't buy a house and sell it a year later if there's nothing wrong. You can tell me. Is it the drains? Or does the roof need replacing? I suppose it's up to code?" I looked disbelieving, as if I was certain that it wasn't but was too polite to say so. "What about the piling? My husband wouldn't consider a house that needed to be re-piled." I was assured that roof, piling and drains were all up to code. "Then why doesn't it stay sold?"

"Um, there's been bad luck. One couple needed to move away to look after her parents, another couple, the husband was offered work out of town."

"Really?" My tone was neutral in a way that said I wasn't swallowing any of it. "I have several other places to see that don't have a dubious history. I'll tell you what. The location isn't bad. I'll give you my best offer, no negotiation. But if the offer isn't accepted within three days I'll assume you don't want the sale and feel free to move on."

I wrote an amount on a piece of paper, passed it over, caught Shari's gaze and swept her out while the agent gaped. I didn't fail to notice however, that his look was already turning thoughtful as we passed through the doorway.

"Do you think...?

"I do."

"I saw what you wrote. It's ridiculous, Jan."

I smiled. "Maybe so, but I think they'll take it. He's legally obliged to put the offer to Josie and her husband, and Josie wants rid of the place at any price. I think you could pay her in washers and she'd take it."

I was right. My offer was accepted the next day – no wasting time. I had Shari pay through her lawyer so Josie's lot never knew until the deal was signed and sealed who'd paid the money. Mr. Sub-division Magnate was suspicious once he knew. He called on Bob and me and mentioned the sale.

"So you were acting for this other woman who used to live there?"

"I was."

I continued to stonewall and while he was sure that somehow there'd been dirty work at the crossroads he couldn't tell what it was and left unsatisfied. Bob grinned at me.

"He thinks there's something funny about it, and so do I. What do you know?"

"Nothing. Shari knows something, but she isn't telling, she said she will once everything is signed and she's moved in."

And that took weeks. But over the past year, her own area had started to gentrify and the price she got for her apartment left her with more money than expected. That together with the lotto cash and the price I'd got her home back for her, meant she was left with a freehold property. It helped that the publishers had seen her fourth book in draft and paid an advance on that one too.

Shari had been in the house a month when I arrived to hear what she had to say. The place was back to its original condition, all the part-renovations removed, the outside painted, the lawn mowed and the bushes neatly trimmed. It looked the way it had when we were kids at school together and I'd come back with her for milk and cookies.

I settled on a chair at the original big old table she'd unearthed from the back of the shed – it having been thought too old-fashioned to use, and too big to bother hauling out and selling or dumping by any of the subsequent owners. Shari looked so happy, but despite what Josie had said and my common sense agreement there had to be trucks causing vibration somewhere, I could hear that faint engine sound.

"Talk!" I instructed her firmly.

"You've had cats all your life." I blinked. I had, but what was that to do with the price of fish? "Just wait. You know something about cats. So tell me, Jan. If your cat is playing with a mouse and loses it, where does he look?"

I laughed. That'd happened last month. "He looks in the second-to-last place he had it. Not always but at least half the time. The other half he does look in the last place, but it's as if sometimes they get lost in time, and forget the last time they had it, they go back one place before that."

"Yes." Jan said. Then she added calmly, "That's what Tigger did."

For a moment, I didn't get it. Then I did. "You mean, he moved from here with you, died elsewhere, then came back here looking for you."

I wasn't sure which one of us was off her trolley; her for suggesting that or me for understanding it.

"Yes, I knew as soon as Josie talked about something jumping on her bed. You know that was my old room." I did. "Remember how Tigger used to come up the tree and climb in through that small circular window. That's why I always kept it open. It was safe because it was too small for any human. He'd jump right down on my bed and it'd feel like an elephant landing. Then he'd come crawling up the bed to snuggle with me while I talked to him."

"But one of the other owners cut the tree down and Josie said her husband checked that the place was locked up," I protested and then felt silly. Of course. If it *had* been Tigger, he was probably climbing the memory of a tree and coming in through a window that – for him – was always open.

Shari grinned.

"All right, I get it. But how sure are you? I mean, I'm not even sure that I *believe* in ghost cats, and…"

She cut me off with a chop of her hand, speaking gently. "Tigger, Tig-Tig, here's your old friend Jan. Say hi to her."

The engine sound increased and I suddenly recognized it – the deep throbbing purr of sixteen pounds of bone and muscle, a cat that had always known his own mind. He'd been misplaced in time. Now he was in his own home with his own human again; where he belonged. The purr swelled until his joy seemed to fill the old house and I sat smiling at my best friend. That which had been lost had found its way back home again.

THE GHOST OF
OSCAR WILDE

I bought six pullets for our small ranch and five grew up to be what they were supposed to be. The sixth turned out to be a rooster that I named Oscar Wilde – the way that very tall men may be nicknamed 'Tiny.' Oscar grew up to be a massive bird, and, unlike the man whose name he bore, my rooster had an obsession for the females of his kind.

For a long time everything was well, until a hungry and penniless outlaw came looking for chicken dinner. We heard the commotion, raced out with lanterns in one hand, guns in the other and saved the hen, but it was too late for Oscar. The man had kicked and stomped him and he died in my arms, while the hens clustered about, as if mourning the loss of the best husband a feathered girl could have. And that was that – for a while.

I was busy come spring but I noticed that two of the hens had gone broody, and to my enormous surprise and despite there being no rooster as yet, one hatched a chick that was the image of Oscar. I named him Oscar Two, and was sorry when he seemed to vanish – a coyote, I thought, and planned to buy my hen another rooster as soon as I could find one for sale or swap.

However I got the full impact of events the night a bandit came; a man from over the river, a fool determined to take whatever he wanted. I ran out with the scattergun but I didn't need it. I stood and gaped as the screeching man tried frantically to fight off something neither of us could see that was ripping at him, and rising above the man's yells, I could hear the furious crowing of a rooster.

The bandit fled. Coyotes and other predators left my chickens severely alone thereafter, and the hens had chicks each year – always girls. Until one spring morning – when a living rooster might be getting very old – and I saw a hen march by with her latest brood, a gap in their center, a space that none of the chicks encroached upon, and I knew. For the final time, the second Oscar had taken care of his hens. I tossed out wheat and watched a small scattering vanish grain by grain. I leaned over, speaking quietly. "You'll be Oscar Three," I told the space, and – something cheeped agreeably at me.

HARRY'S BAD MAN

Icame back from the war and settled in Bodie with my wife. A year later I was asked to be town marshal and agreed. It was no big deal, I thought. I wasn't a fast gun but I'd been a fair soldier, my shooting was accurate and I kept my head. That had been demonstrated while the council was still deciding, when a couple of ex-soldiers made a try for the bank and I saw what was going on. I'd strolled up, untied their horses, led them around the corner, retied them there and waited. The two came slamming out of the bank and found they were horseless.

I spoke quietly. "All right, lads. Time to give up, you haven't killed anyone yet, better a year in jail than hung, and I'm in cover, you aren't."

They glanced at each other, recognised the truth in what I said – and gave up. They did their year, the bank lost nothing, no one was hurt, and it mightily impressed the town's council. So I accepted my star and went home to tell Linda; who wasn't sure she liked it.

"What about the ranch?" We had us a small place, nothing fancy, but there was a spring, a stream that never ran dry from that, and I'd managed to obtain half a dozen lame cows and a young cross-bred bull cheap from a trail herd that'd had some bad luck. I shrugged.

"Linda, love, how much work do I do with what we've got? Another ten years and we'll have a good place. As it is, I can do all the work in a few hours a week. Marshal's pay will help us get on a lot faster, and l can always retire when the time comes."

Linda thought about it and nodded slowly. "Just promise me you'll be careful, Jake. I don't want to be a widow and Harry loves you too."

I grinned. "I swear I'll stay cautious. I don't want to be dead any more than you and Harry want me that way." (Harry

78

was our daughter, never still a minute from 'can see to cain't see,' and just about to turn two.)

I kept my promise for the next three years until the largest ranch was sold to an Easterner, and he got ideas about being the biggest man around. He pushed several small ranchers on his boundary, and they pushed right back. His original crew were all good men and most didn't like what he had in mind. Several quit. His foreman was shot in a fair fight, and Molton leaned on me about it.

"He shot Joe, what are you going to do?"

I stood up slowly and met his glare. "Nothing, Mr. Molton. Joe called Dawson out in the main street in front of witnesses, and Dawson was the better man. Man's got a right to defend himself, and that's it."

Molton stamped off, and the next thing I knew word came that he was expecting a new foreman. No one knew who. Molton referred to him as Alex, and that was all we knew until he rode in. I was standing by the door when I saw a rider in the distance. He headed for town, rode towards me once he was there, and I nodded politely, wondering who he was.

He didn't look to be trouble anyhow; a lean man, not that big or tall, dusty fair hair, clean-shaven, steady grey eyes, and neat well maintained gear. I couldn't tell his age for certain. He looked to be as little as twenty, but he could have been up to ten years older, and he had an air about him that said now and again he'd run into trouble and stood to it. His horse was a plain chestnut, a stocky animal, not tall, I'd guess about fifteen and a half hands, and short-coupled in a way that suggested both speed and power. I noticed he used a snaffle bit and no spurs, and thought the better of him for that.

As the rider passed, he drew rein. "The Molton ranch, Marshal?"

I pointed. "That way, about ten miles, track going off to the right."

"Obliged." He rode on and I gazed thoughtfully after him. If that was the new foreman, I thought we might get along. I kept that opinion for six weeks, until Mike Staund came into town and found me in my office. He was dusty, hard-eyed, and there was a small bloodstain on one sleeve.

"I got trouble, Jake."

"Molton?"

"Yeah." He nodded. "Tree branch took out a section of the fence, or that's what it looked like. Molton's cattle came through and near drank my pond dry, trampled the couple of acres I had shut up for hay, and I chased them out. His foreman came looking for me, said I had no right to move someone else's cattle. I said the tree branch came from their side, so it was up to them to keep the fence fixed."

"And?"

"He said the fence was as much mine as theirs, I said it was a matter of opinion but we could always ask you. One of his men dropped a rope over me and yanked me off my horse when I turned away." His gaze met mine. "I lost my temper I guess. Reached for m'gun and that new guy had one hand up stopping his boys, and the other had a gun in it faster than I've ever seen before." He took in a slow breath. "I gotta say he did stop them shooting me. Just sat there looking, and after a minute, he said I should be careful, a man with a wife an' kids couldn't afford to be reckless."

"But you drew first and he stopped them shooting you?"

"Yeah. But he didn't stop them dropping a rope on me and hauling me a ways. And like I said to him. That tree's on Molton's side. A branch wrecks my fence and it's their responsibility, I gotta right to chase their cows off'a my land and I expect you to back me on that."

I pondered that and it seemed true. But there was something Mike wasn't thinking about. "I normally would," I said slowly. "But with this I can't. Molton's place is outside town limits, I'm marshal here, I can talk to Molton about this, but truth is, Mike, I can't tell him flat out not to start trouble when it's outside my jurisdiction."

Mike went off looking sour, and I went to talk to one of the council. "You see the problem?" I asked.

He did. "We may be able to get you in as county sheriff, but it'll take time."

"If it takes too much time we could have real trouble on our hands," I said flatly. "Molton's been winding up for a while, and he won't wait around for an election." Another thought hit me on that. "And what's to say one of his men can't stand for sheriff anyway?"

It was his turn to look thoughtful and I left him considering on that. Things got worse, Molton found a neighbor with one of the MR-branded cows. Claimed it had been rustled, that the man had shot first – and missed. His foreman hadn't. No one else wanted the small ranch the man had owned, his wife sold it cheap to Molton, left the area, and I wasn't happy.

Harry turned eight. We had a small party for her, I'd got her a larger pony, a good black with some class about him, and she started riding further and being gone longer so Linda worried. I grinned at my wife.

"Leave the kid be. Good rider, sensible, doesn't go too far from home, but I'll mention that again if you think I should." I did and Harry promised.

"I'll stay on our place, dad, or just into the hills a ways where it's no one's land. I promise."

I let things be. A promise is a promise and if I pushed things that'd suggest I was distrustful of that. Besides, the kid was a good rider, and the horse was part-mustang, fast, and smart too.

Then we started getting attacks on the cattle. Not Molton's beasts, but several local ranchers found a dead cow. Looked to have been attacked by a wolf or something, throat torn out, partially eaten, and no matter how often they patrolled, no one saw anything, just another dead animal now and then. Things built up as I'd feared until at last we had everything short of open war. After that, a drummer came to town on the stage. I met him in the saloon, sat to ask him what things were like back in the towns he'd come from and he grinned.

"Better than you have here, Marshal." I raised an eyebrow. He nodded. "Yeah, no town's better off where you have Covac, started losing cows to a wolf yet?"

The name rang a faint bell, and – a wolf? I asked a couple of questions, listened to the answers and went home that night to talk to Linda.

"Killer Covac, that's who Molton's foreman is. Never heard them name him as anything but Alex or I'd have maybe guessed. Funny rumors about him. He really isn't much older than I guessed first time he rode in, only twenty then but there's a fair few miles and a lot of deaths behind him."

"What does a wolf have to do with that?"

"They say that's Covac too." I told her tersely and she snorted.

"Really, Jake?"

I was serious. "That's what they say. Fact is that wherever he stays a while, there's wolf attacks on cattle. And as is also mentioned, the cattle on any ranch where he's working are fine. It's the cows belonging to those who're against his employer that get savaged. Makes it look as if the animal, wolf or whatever, can control itself."

"Or be controlled," Linda added. "What if he has a tame wolf?" We discussed that before heading to bed, and came to no conclusion.

Things came to a head six months later. The council ran an election, two of Molton's men stood against me – a mistake, it split the vote – and I was elected sheriff as well as town marshal. That gave me a right and I went to see Molton and laid down the law.

"No more trouble else I'll be stepping in. And if I have to do that, I'll see there's charges made."

I got a look that should have left me dead on his floor but he nodded. "I don't start trouble Marshal ... er, Sheriff, but if someone else does, I have a right to defend myself, that's what you said when Dawson shot Joe. I guess it still applies?"

I agreed. "It does. Just be *sure* it's self-defense else I'll have something to say, and so will the court."

It was self–defense when Alex Covac shot a small-time rancher. Clear as day that was, and there was nothing I could do. But I pushed Molton harder, and things became nastier, until Molton lost it one day, came to my ranch when I was in town and threatened Linda.

He had come with only Covac and he stood there in our kitchen and spoke his piece. "I'm not a happy man, Missus. You want to be careful, if your husband makes more trouble you could end up as a widow."

Linda said something. He snapped back, and her retort caught him on the raw. He hit her. There was a shot, and he yelled, grabbing his shoulder. Covac caught him as he slumped, and had him out of there, onto his horse and away. I got home half an hour later; heard half the story – and just as she was telling me, there was a yell.

"Hello the house?"

I walked out to the porch. One of Molton's men rode up letting me see he had no gun, and passed over an envelope. I opened that and blinked.

"Linda, did you actually shoot Molton?"

I heard the rest of the story then, and my grin was so wide, you'd have had to move my ears back for it to be any wider. We went to court a week later, me, Linda, Harry, and the other side. That being Molton, Covac, and two of their men. All of us – along with half the town – before Judge Arthur Benson who'd been judge here twenty years and knew everyone around. It was an event I thought Molton wouldn't forget in a hurry. I'd made my preparations.

Benson opened proceedings by having Molton speak. His claim was that he'd been bothered by the dissent between neighbours and had gone to my ranch to talk to me. Linda had met him with insults, and when he demanded to stay and speak to me, she had shot him. He'd been unarmed, made no threats, and no, he hadn't hit her. She'd tripped on the step. The judge nodded, called Covac and asked a single question.

"Did you see Mr. Molton shot by Linda?"

"She had no gun." Covac said flatly, and there was a soft rustle of movement throughout the court.

"Then who shot him?"

Covac shrugged.

Judge Benson looked across at me. "Marshal, you stated you knew who did shoot Mr. Molton, please have this person come to the witness stand."

I spoke quietly to the shooter who stood up, marched down the aisle and moved to the chair, took the oath on the court Bible and sat to await what would come next.

Judge Benson studied the witness briefly. "Did you shoot Mr. Molton."

Harry nodded. "He was a bad man. He hit ma. I had my .22 and I shot him. He fell down. Mr. Covac took him away, and I fixed ma's face where she was bleeding."

Half those there turned to observe the bruise surrounding a cut on Linda's face. The judge frowned. "Did you mean to kill Mr. Molton?"

"No," Harry was serious. "I was scared he was going to hit her again, and there were two of them. So I shot him to make them go away."

The judge nodded. "In other words, you shot in defense of an unarmed woman. Have you anything to say, Mr. Molton?"

Molton took two quick paces towards Harry, and the kid stood up, facing him like a terrier. It was clear to everyone in court at that moment that Molton had been shot by a nine-year-old – who looked ready to do it again if a gun came to hand – and a yell of laughter went up. It rose in waves, until Molton, bright red, stamped out, Benson declared his verdict to be self-defense, and sat back in his own chair grinning at Harriet, my daughter.

Harry looked confused, her pink hair-ribbon matching the dress her aunt had sent for her Sunday-go-to-meeting best that had arrived only last month. She'd worn it for her ninth birthday, it suited her freckled face, and the long pink-ribboned light brown pigtails down her back. I saw Covac slip out, a grin on his face, and I thought that it'd be a long time if ever before Molton lived this day down.

Judge Benson took Harry's hand and shook it. "Good girl."

"Thanks, Uncle Arthur. Can I go home now?"

"Yes." And quietly to me once she and Linda were out of earshot. "Be careful, Jake. Molton's the sort that holds a grudge."

That had been my own thought and I *was* careful. A year went by, and another, we never saw Molton in town. His men came in now and again but never him. Covac ran the Molton ranch, and Harry rode further and longer from home. And then the day came when she didn't return. Being a fair tracker, I went looking, found the old line shack where she was facing Molton. He had her thin wrists in one big hand, and the other came up, tearing her shirt while she fought him.

But as a counterpoint to the ripping cloth there was a sound like thunder, and a beast brushed past me. I'd seen the occasional wolf before, but never one that size. There was an aura about it, of a ferocity like lightning in the air, thunder roared from its throat. Molton shot, and it came on. He dropped Harry, shot again, and went down under the impact as it reached him.

To my shock, Harry grabbed the ruff on either side of its neck and yelled. "*No!* You can't." The wolf hesitated, and she hauled at its fur. "No. Kill him when you don't have to and you'll *change.*"

I had no idea what she meant, but the wolf drew back, still snarling softly. And in those seconds, Molton was on his feet, through the door and running. We heard retreating hoof-beats seconds later and I snarled myself.

"He's getting away."

"No, he isn't," my daughter said calmly. "Where he's going he'll find justice, just not ours."

And that, as I heard a day later had been true. Molton was found dead on the trail from the main road to his ranch. After some confusion, a will was found that left that ranch to Covac, who proved to be an excellent neighbour – and, after the next election – our sheriff. I remained as town marshal.

Covac's pack on his ranch behaved themselves. I'd had no idea Harry had been meeting Alex, no idea she knew the pack, and no idea that Molton in attacking her had violated pack law against attacking cubs. They enacted justice on Molton, and that satisfied them. I worried now and then about it, but I worry less since I'm kin these days. Harry married her Alex three years after Molton died, and they have a son with another child on the way.

Our area is peaceful these days – it's never wise to annoy the pack. We prosper and if, now and again, a cow is found dead, well, they're Alex's cattle only, no one else's. And if too, someone riding through sees a woman on a black horse with a huge dog loping along beside her, we assure them it's all right. The animal only hurts bad men. Information that now and again speeds the visitor on his way, and all that's as it should be – so long as the land endures, wolves run free and love does not die.

THE LOOKING-GLASS GIRL

Edith stared into the mirror. Her saloon-girl frock clung to her exposed shoulders and she felt sick. The saloon's owner had said she didn't have to go upstairs with any clients, as they'd previously agreed. But men didn't always keep their word. She was a good girl, she always had been. And what was her reward? To be left penniless, her only way of survival to work here and pray the owner would give her time to find an option other than selling herself. Her face in the mirror vanished as her eyes blurred with angry memories.

"Don't die, please, ma, don't die." Edward was frantic. Edith took him by the arm.

"Make her a cup of the sagebrush tea, Eddie. It'll give her strength. Bring in firewood an' stoke the fire too. She needs the warmth."

She gently encouraged the nine-year-old to the necessary errands while her mother watched from the bed, all huge dark eyes in a gaunt face. Ma would be another day or so dying and Eddie had to be kept busy. Once he was gone, her mother beckoned her close, speaking in a low halting voice.

"You're a good girl, Edith. Now listen. Edward will be all right when I'm gone. Your father had some savings put by and I sent a letter to the schoolmaster. He came and we talked. He said he'll take your brother in. The money will provide Edward with a home and schooling until he's fourteen. He's a clever boy and by then he should be able to earn himself a living."

Edith bit down a gasp. Five *years* board and schooling? She had no idea her parents had that sort of money tucked away. Where had it come from? She asked the question.

Her mother's head moved on the pillow. "Some from my

grandmother. My mother was her only daughter, an' I was hers. When my grandma was a little girl, she found a strange metal thing in a deep arroyo. She told me stories of it when I was small. There were bones in it, nothing like she'd ever seen and she buried those. She said the thing was like a house with furniture that came from the walls if you touched them in the right places. She used to play in it all that year until the spring floods washed it away. Once she touched something and a small drawer sprung out. There were things inside that she took."

"What sort of things?"

"Jewels, maybe a woman's things. They were odd, nothing that would fit a woman but the fabrics were beautiful."

"What did her parents say?"

The dying woman closed her eyes briefly. "Damn locusts, damn clumsy horse. We'd have been all right of it weren't for the bad luck. Jack dying that way, an' the crop eaten."

"I know, ma. What about the things your grandma found?"

"She never told her kin. She said to me they'd have taken them from her. There were a couple of scarves. She wore those to dances when she was older. They caught the eye of the man she married, an' when he needed money to buy into a business she told him about the necklace she'd found. He got a good price and bought a half-share in the dry-goods store. She gave the scarves an' the other stuff to my ma when she wed. Just in case, she said. It pays for a woman to have a little something put by. The rest of it your pa saved from the last farm. We had to sell, but he got something."

"An' you still got something for me? Cash put away?"

"No, no, I guess there's nothing, not really."

Edith felt the shock of that right down to her bare calloused feet.

"Ma, I'm fourteen. This here's Arizona. I can't go back east an' pa's aunt wouldn't have me if I did. It's a couple a' day's ride or more to Tucson. I can't stay on the farm; we haven't been here long enough to prove up. Soon's you die the government'll be here to take the land away an' toss me out. You mean you've given Eddie everything we got?"

"Mostly."

"That ain't right."

"Maybe not, but he's a little boy. He can't get a job around here. He has to have his chance, a man needs an education, an' a woman can get by without it. You could maybe get work as a maid or something in town."

Edith looked at her mother as the dark eyes closed in weariness and knew bitterly how the decision had been made. Eddie had always been ma's favorite. Edith's dad had loved her best, if he was still here he wouldn't do this but he'd died last year when his horse mis-stepped along the edge of a canyon. Half of what ma had spent on Eddie could save Edith too but she knew she wouldn't be getting that.

A maid or something, ma said. Edith knew what the 'something' would be. There was a saloon in town, and that was the only place she'd find work. But ma didn't care, just so long as Eddie was provided for. Edith walked away from her mother's sleeping form, her mind busy. There was the milk cow, the old pony, her ma's wedding ring an' pearl brooch. There were the furnishings; they'd fetch a dollar here and there. Not much, but maybe enough to give her some kind of chance.

Later that night while Eddie slept she sat up with her mother again, talking, asking questions carefully. She had a feeling there'd been something about that house thing her ma still wasn't telling her.

"You said your grandmother found woman's stuff in the funny cabin? Was scarves an' a necklace all of it?" Her mother was weaker and Edith had to lean close to hear.

"Rest's gone, mostly long gone. Just the looking glass left."

Edith's breath caught. Yes! The oval piece of etched and polished metal and she remembered the one time she'd seen it work. Pa had gone to town to buy supplies when they first came here before they settled the farm they'd subsequently lost to the locusts – and the bank.

Eddie had been only two, and Edith seven. They were camping in the old wagon. Edith had been sent to gather firewood; ma was exhausted and had fallen briefly asleep. With no one to watch him, Eddie had taken the flint and steel Pa had in the wagon for emergencies and lost it somewhere. They might still have been fine but for a snowstorm blowing up.

Edith remembered her mother's reluctance as the afternoon became colder and colder until Eddie was whimpering as he shivered.

"It's devil's work," she'd said. "The devil's mirror, but we'll die without a fire." The mirror had been brought out and angled to catch the fading light. Her mother had touched the etched areas on the back and a narrow beam of light had appeared. It touched the firewood, clung, and the wood burst into flame. Ma had put the mirror away hastily then, and sat looking guilty. "Don't you say nothing to nobody about that, Edith. Tisn't a holy thing to be using but I couldn't let us all freeze an' die."

That had been seven years gone now but Edith remembered. "The looking glass? Where do you have it, ma?"

"Bottom o' the blanket box. But you beware. Bites you first time you hold it, then it's like it knows you. Won't let any but someone of my grandma's blood use it. My pa couldn't make it work, nor could your pa. 'S why it weren't sold." She took a low rasping breath. "All I got to leave you, Edith. Dunno what you can do with it, but it may be good for something besides starting fires."

"How's it work, ma?"

The dying woman was reluctant but the desperate girl was insistent. She cajoled, demanded, nagged, and returned to cajolery until her mother began to whisper weakly again. Edith kept asking until she believed she had heard all her mother knew, then she sat back as her mother's eyes closed and her breathing slowed.

Edith stood then, looking down. "Devil's toy or not, I'll take it – and anything else I can find," she said softly to the unconscious woman. "I'll not be trapped as a whore in some saloon until I'm too old to work an' they throw me out to starve."

She padded silently to the kitchen and considered the pots and dishes she could see. Aunt Bess on the next farm would buy a lot of this to set up her daughter who was about to wed. Mister Jonas down the road would buy the cow an' the pig. Edith could ride the old pony to town an' sell it to the stables there along with its gear. What else was there she could find to turn a dollar on?

She returned to the bedroom and searched quietly but very thoroughly. When she was done, she sat back on her ma's chair and smiled to herself. So? There was nothing left for her, huh? Ma must have planned for Eddie to have this too, well, he wouldn't. He was set for the next five years an' he could go without. She fingered the five gold eagles. The coins had been hidden within a twist of grass in a small carved wooden box that had a trick to its opening. Ma had tied a label to it with Eddie's name on that. Fifty dollars was two month's pay for a cowhand. With everything else she could scavenge and sell she'd have enough to stay in town a while an' look around her.

At the funeral she stood, thinking sad thoughts, allowing the tears to flow down her cheeks. The neighbors would expect to see that and she'd learned long since that it was wise to do as people expected. Edith had been cautious. She'd watched the grave dug herself, and laid her mother within it clad in her best dress, the body wrapped in a good quilt. But her mother's wedding ring and pearl brooch were in Edith's pocket. The naked hand had been hidden under a posy of flowers. Another sheaf of them lay across one shoulder. Too many neighbors knew of the brooch and knew too that her mother was to be buried with it.

She'll keep the ring and brooch hidden until she had no choice but to sell them. Then, if possible, she'd see to it they went to a stranger. Eddie went off, still weeping, with the schoolmaster.

Edith went silently into the house to spend her final night there. Most of the furnishings were gone and the rest would go next day. In the firelight, she counted her coins. The fifty dollars she'd found, then the coins the neighbors had paid for cow, piglet, and items from the house.

Edith had a plan for that money. She turned the mirror over in her hands. Her ma had made a small padded drawstring pouch for it and Edith hadn't seen the mirror since that night of the snow. She loosened the strings and took it out, allowing the etched oval to lie flat on her palm. There was a stinging sensation and she gasped. Ma had said it would bite so's it knew her. Well, now it should.

She moved to the door and stood looking out at the moon.

Then, carefully, she lifted the mirror to catch the moonlight, and pressed the etching on the back in the pattern she'd been told, watching as an almost unnoticeable streak of thin light flickered out to touch the single piece of dry wood she'd tossed as far as she could from the house. It burst into quick flame and she smiled, slowly and thoughtfully. She had two halves of an idea, they didn't match each other but in time, she might fill out both – and together they'd perhaps give her a life beyond a saloon in a small dusty town, growing though that town might be.

She took a room in a boarding house for the first week. Once settled in she walked to the saloon and spoke to the owner. Edith wasn't conventionally pretty, but even at her age she had something more. She was graceful, her movements sensual, and her fine boning gave her an elegant look. Those things she'd keep into old age. The saloonkeeper bargained cheerfully with her when she laid out her idea.

Yes, he'd give her a room at the saloon. She could eat breakfast and an evening meal there each day. In return, she would serve and dance with the customers, but not have to go upstairs with them. He was shrewd enough to know she'd be a draw-card. She had a good singing voice and the saloon had a pianist. And – he smiled to himself – the whole town, or the men in it anyhow, would be taking bets on who could have her and how soon. He'd take their money and make certain if she took a man, it was at the right time for the saloonkeeper.

He reckoned it'd only be six or seven months, a year at most. She'd need more than bed and board, and she'd have only one way to get it. Until then he could afford to keep his word. She was a woman. They were all the same, weak and easily seduced by pretty things. Edith guessed his thoughts and ignored them. She could be seduced – if the right offer was made, but not easily, and not by flashy items. Nor was she weak.

She worked hard and managed to overcome the antagonism in the other girls at her good fortune by being always pleasant and helpful. The day she moved in Edith also called the blacksmith and had him place a lock outside, and a bar of iron in brackets on the door inside, her room. She took only half of her money to the bank and placed that in an account, allowing a number of people to overhear what she did. They would assume all of her meager wealth was safely there, but if her room was plundered, or the bank robbed, she would still have something.

For the next six months, she did well. Men brought her meals and trinkets in the hopes she'd succumb, while the local women waited, eager-eyed for her downfall. All were disappointed. Once every two weeks Edith hired a pony and rode out for half a day. No one cared or followed, which was as well, since she was systematically studying her mirror and what could be done with it. Over the six months, she learned far more than her mother had ever known.

That winter her brother, Edward, died of pneumonia. Two nights later Edith went to the schoolmaster's house that was only a few hundred yards from the saloon.

"My mother paid you for five years bed and board, five years schooling for my brother. It's been six months."

The old man eyed her sourly. He would have given the lad what he'd been paid for but he was giving nothing to some town whore.

"I've spent it, bought the boy books, clothing, a bed an' other truck."

"Sell those then and give me the money."

He grinned at her. "No, and you can't make me. Your mother made the bargain. She said nothing about you getting anything. If you have nothing in writing I'm not legally obliged to give you a dime."

His smirk was triumphant and Edith bowed to the realities. No, he wouldn't give her anything, but as her pa had always said, there were more ways to kill a skunk than choking it with cream. If she acted tonight, he'd have had no time to talk to anyone.

That night she danced and flirted, sang several songs, then said she must refresh herself. She went to her room, poured cold water into the basin and took out her mirror. The moon was full and it took seconds to start a ferocious blaze. The old man's doorway half faced the saloon. She made sure the fire was engulfing the front of the small building before angling the mirror to set fire to the rear of it as well. That should do all that was required. She flicked water over her face and allowed drops to fall on her dress, then ran lightly down the stairs to sing again.

The schoolmaster died in the fire, and Edith quietly put in a claim for what remained of his possessions. She explained it to the sheriff while maintaining a quiet and ladylike pose. The sheriff, a single man with hopes and aware of her agreement with the saloonkeeper, agreed that she should receive the old man's goods remaining.

Edith acquired a good horse and buggy, and – shrewd in the ways in which people hid their treasures – she also made a foray the night after the fire and found the old man's own savings in a small cash box under the half-burned floor. She sold what survived of his other belongings and openly donated the profits of those to the church asking that the preacher pray for her much beloved little brother who'd died only a week earlier. She took all of the old man's gold and hid that, while depositing the silver and coppers in the bank. The horse and buggy she sold at a bargain price to the banker who had long coveted them. It always paid to have those in power thinking kindly of you.

Spring came, then early summer, and with summer a pair of heavily laden wagons. The word went around quickly. A new store was to be built and Matthew Jason who owned the only store in town developed a permanent scowl at the news. There wasn't room in the town for two stores and it looked as if this one would be bigger and better than his own. He talked about it to the saloon singer one evening when he was a little drunk and she nodded.

"It's wrong, him coming into town an' spoiling all your hard work. I mean, you were here first. It's you who's taken the risks. You could have lost everything an' here he comes to help himself."

Matthew agreed. In fact, the more he thought about it the righter she was. "It just ain't fair. Man works all the hours God sends to him, and for what? Some stranger to come in and take it all away. Something's gotta be done about it."

Edith encouraged that line of thinking but in careful generalizations. She wasn't going to have him remember anything she'd said to repeat it where it might cause her problems. Matthew Jason was working very late in the store three nights later. There was a tap at the back door and he opened it cautiously, to find the shadowy figure of a slight young man waiting outside who spoke in a soft hoarse voice.

"I hear you got a problem, storekeeper. Mebbe I can help."

"What...?"

"Reckon it ain't right for a man like you to be done out of all his hard work." Matthew grunted agreement. "What would it be worth if a man found his competition had gone? Mebbe if this here interloper had a fire an' lost ever'thing?"

"I could be blamed. Everyone knows I ain't happy about him coming in."

"Not if'n you knew when it'd happen and was careful to be in sight a' good witnesses. You play poker with the banker, don't you?"

"Every Friday night 'til midnight or later, yeah."

"Then if'n we come to an agreement, you can be playing poker and all surprised."

Matthew Jason made an offer, then a larger one. The third figure was accepted.

"I git half now, half afterwards. An' Jason. Remember something. You don't pay me the other half an' what's done once can be done again. You don't know me but I know you."

Jason shrugged. "Got no reason to cheat you if you do the job. It's worth it to me. Wait there a minute."

He shut the back door, went to the sliding board in the wall that concealed his cash box and opened it. There was just enough to pay the money agreed. He took half, opened the back door and handed it over.

"Friday night then?"

"Yeah, about midnight. Keep the play going until you hear the alarm given."

Matthew Jason was on tenterhooks that night, but it went like clockwork. His competitor lost almost everything, the half-built store, one of the three laden wagons – and his life. He'd been heavily asleep in the wagon nearest the store and the burning store's framing, falling across it, had blocked his exit. Jason acquired the surviving wagons cheaply, and added to his dry goods counter. He paid up promptly too. His conscience bothered him a little but by rights the man had been a thief, trying to take what was another man's livelihood. The town would hang Jason in lieu of the real killer if they knew he'd been involved.

Edith had counted on that. A few drops from a small bottle in the glass of wine she brought him in the saloon that evening, and Jason's rival had slept like a hibernating bear. She smiled in the solitude of her room. He'd been a brute, trying to fondle her and when she refused, he stamped off, saying he'd come back to pay her employer and the saloonkeeper would make her obey. With him dead, not only was Jason too involved to say a word, but also there was no one to make demands on the saloonkeeper concerning an uncooperative girl.

She'd made sure everyone had seen her for some time before the fire began and for a brief while after – until the alarm was given. Matthew Jason had been playing poker for many hours with the banker, the livery-stable owner, and the doctor and no one could accuse him either. She had enough money in the bank and in various hiding places now. It might be time she packed her bags, found a good excuse and left town.

Two fires were reasonable; any more could be too many. The time to get out was well before people became suspicious about those, not after it. She wrote a letter to herself and used the envelope she'd stolen several months ago. It had been addressed in pencil but she erased that and readdressed it to herself in ink. Then she managed to slide it into the mail distributed from the stage a week later.

"Edith Hamilton. There's a letter for Edith Hamilton."

She took it, pasting a look of surprise on her face. "Who can be writing me? There's no family apart from my pa's old aunty in Tucson."

Someone craned over her shoulder. "That's where it come from, see?"

She opened the letter and read, making it slow so others could get a glimpse of the words.

"Lord, if it isn't an invitation. She wants me to come live with her now I've got no one else. Says her older sister didn't like my ma's side of the family but now she's dead Aunty

Maude can make up her own mind an' kin's kin. She says if I don't have the fare to write and tell her but otherwise she'll expect me on the next stage. Well, if that isn't a surprise."

"What'll you do, Edith?"

"Guess I'll go. I got just enough in the bank to buy me a traveling trunk and a decent dress and pay the stagecoach fare." She turned to the sheriff who was listening. "There's nothing here for me, no one's going to forget I worked in a saloon an' no decent man would ever want me even though everyone knows I only worked downstairs. A man needs a wife who's lived respectably with her kin and maybe brings something to the marriage. "

He nodded slowly. He'd been thinking of asking her to marry him but she was right. Small towns didn't forget and they weren't forgiving. Everyone knew women were weak but that just made it more likely they'd succumb to temptation. A sheriff couldn't afford to have a wife that the town was watching and waiting to see fall into the devil's snare.

He still liked her though and he touched her shoulder. "Guess you're right, Edith. It's a piece of good luck for you. You should grab it." And his mind added that John Townsend's daughter was almost fourteen. She was an only child who'd inherit a nice little ranch sometime in the future. A man could marry and settle down, take it easy with less chance of being shot.

Edith, well aware of his thoughts – if not the girl's name – hurried to the saloon. Good, that would keep him from following her to Tucson if he'd been so inclined. She headed for the store to purchase a respectable dress for her trip, a matching bonnet, new stockings and handbag – and an expensive full-length whale-boned corset. The stage would arrive in five days, just long enough for her to do what she needed to do.

In those five days, she neatly removed some of the whalebone from the corset and sewed gold coins in their place. Two hours before the stage arrived, she withdrew her money as banknotes from the bank, paid the fare, gave small presents to the girls and her employer, and boarded the stage when it arrived. Her trunk was tossed up on the luggage rack and, waving goodbye, Edith Hamilton left the small town of North Wells forever.

In a year no one remembered her – or would have known who that was if they'd heard of her being in Tucson. She had another name and other employment. Her occasional disguise, as a young man eager to help those who required it, provided her with several lucrative jobs before she moved on to Phoenix, then to California, making money, most of which she invested wisely. At other times, she was Edith Goodwin, a young lady whose family had all died tragically in the western lands and who had independent means. Not a wealthy woman, but one who was comfortably off.

No one ever noticed the outbreak of fires in a number of cities coincided with the arrivals and departures of a well-dressed young lady. Edith had learned the secrets of her mirror well. In full sunlight, the narrow beam it could send out was invisible, and could stretch – needle-thin – for several blocks. Nor would anyone on earth have recognized a Rannanin trader's light-powered laser from a space life-boat's emergency kit.

In California, Edith met the man she fell unexpectedly in love with and married. He too had made money and she bore him three children, laying the mirror away as they prospered. Her son and daughters never knew the secret – but the mirror appeared in family photos taken in the early years of her marriage, and in a delicate little watercolor sketch done earlier by an artist in Phoenix when Edith was still in her teens.

Her family, who had loved her, buried the mirror with her when she died, as she'd asked. And long after she was dead they and their descendants remembered her from the delicately drawn and finely framed sketch which hung in the family home and which had been titled on an engraved brass plaque affixed to the bottom of the frame as, 'The Looking-Glass Girl'.

GREEN EYES

She was three, with sun-tanned, fatly dimpled little legs and rounded arms. It was summer and the field was hot, the water calling, cool and beckoning with flashes of shade and shadow under the willows where the brook widened to a pond on the ranch where the cattle drank under the line of willows. It wasn't easily seen though, the cows knew where to go but others, passing, might have no idea it existed.

"Jandy, where are you going, darling?"

"Nowhere, mummy."

"Stay near me, dear."

A man's voice. "Don't worry."

"She's only three. They can always find danger at that age."

"What danger. You can see everything around us for miles and the stream's only a couple of inches deep."

It was, where it was only a brook, and the trees hid where it was not. The sun was hot, almost burning small chubby arms and back above the light cotton of the cut-down shirt that served as a dress. The water called enticingly to an overheated child and Jandy answered the call, stamping in the shallow stream, throwing water up, diamond drops in the sunlight as it showered over the small body. Her clear happy giggles shrilled out.

"See, she's fine. We'll have to go soon."

"I'll start packing. You move the buckboard closer. That way we won't have so far to carry everything."

A cane hamper was filled with used plates and mugs. The picnic blanket was gathered up, crumbs shaken out, and slim hands began to fold it as heavier footsteps went towards the vehicle, which had brought them there.

Jandy paddled her way under the trees; the shade was soft on her hot skin. The water slipped over her body, deeper, then deeper. Her foot slid on a stone and she was drifting under the water, almost unafraid, until she tried to breathe. Water filling her mouth, her ears and eyes, choking her. She flailed, unable to swim.

Untaught, she could not float or save herself, until – a hand laid itself in hers. She clutched, despairing; the grip of her small fingers an unspoken plea. *Don't let me die, not die, not yet, oh please?* She could not have formalized the words, but it was all there, in the desperate imploring grasp. It was answered, the hand lifted her, choking and gasping from the water, flipped her belly down across the bank edge, leaving her stranded there.

Her eyes opened as she attempted to find air again, and she stared into leaf-green eyes whose gaze swallowed her until they were all she could see. At last, she had breath, and her outraged howl brought both parents at the run.

"I thought you said she was safe?"

"I didn't know this was here. Dear God, she could have drowned."

"My baby, oh, thank God you managed to get out."

The deeper voice struck in then. "Marcie, how could she? Look at the bank, if she was in that pond there's no way she could have climbed out on her own. She hasn't the strength."

"Don't be silly, there's no one else around. She had to have done it." Jandy was rocked, loved, cradled all the way home. Until she forgot the eyes, the hand, and even the event. At ten, she learned to swim, unafraid of the water, unremembering of a pond where cattle drank under shady willows.

She was almost forty but looked younger. She had a good marriage with an older man she loved, but it kept them moving, sometimes overseas. They were in Mexico, a brief holiday after one of his diplomatic missions was completed, the day she crashed, driving a young, over-excitable horse along a dusty narrow country road, going perhaps a little faster than she should have let him canter, but it was safe. There was no other vehicle in view where the road climbed ahead. She was not to know there was a side road. In the land she traversed, private roads were often without signposts.

Her curricle spun around the bend, to find a large farm cart suddenly turning before it, she hauled the horse aside, his hooves slipping on the surface. He panicked, rearing, leaping forward. The curricle slammed one side into a tree, spun, and toppled.

Hot! It was so hot; the sun was starting to burn her. Jandy's hand went out, groping. Into it, another hand was laid, so gently at first she did not register. Then her eyes flew open. She was trapped. The curricle was poised on the side of a cliff. She couldn't escape although she tried, and it was swaying, a fraction further each time. A few more movements and it would fall.

Her hand clamped down desperately and from the blazing sunshine, a face formed. She could see nothing clearly, only the eyes. Green eyes swallowing her up as her hand gripped tighter, in an unspoken plea. *Don't let me die, not die, not yet, oh, please, not yet?* The hand raised her, seemed to float her through the air until she landed belly down in a swirl of long skirts on the bank beside the curricle even as it slid forward and she could hear it land – a long way down.

She caught her breath; crawled further from the edge until, at last, as staggering footsteps came towards her, she looked up. The man was elderly, brown-eyed, with once black hair now almost completely gray.

"Madonna Mia, señora, you are alive?"

Was she? Jandy moved, stretching her arms, her legs. There were bruises and scratches, yes, but no major damage. She stared up.

"You, señor, are you hurt?"

"By God's grace I am not. It was my entire fault, señora I should have looked, but there is little traffic here. I did not expect you."

"You are alone. There wasn't anyone in the cart with you?"

The elderly man stared. "No, señora. Was anyone with you? If so, I fear…" he broke off as he turned to look far down to what remained of her curricle. Jandy shook her head.

"I was alone. Now, is there anywhere I may obtain another vehicle, or find someone I can send to the police so I may report this?"

As she dealt with the police and the technicalities attendant on the loss of a curricle with all her papers; with the stress of the crash, and the distress of her elderly companion who kept apologizing for his lack of care – the memory of the green eyes, the saving hand, slipped away. She must have crawled free without help. The police themselves assured her of this.

For weeks, she was kept in Mexico with questions involving the accident. Her husband had to return. He had other work, and when, six years later he died, being childless and with everything left to her, and, remembering the peace of the quiet dusty countryside, the warm brown of the hills, and the smiles of the people, she bought a house there with a little land and visited each year. It was there that she finally retired on her sixtieth birthday. From then on, she did good quietly among the local people and was respected by all, even liked by many, but she called no one her close friend.

* * *

Jandy's ninetieth birthday was celebrated alone. She'd out-lived her parents and she had been an only child. Her will would leave all the money she'd garnered from her husband and from them, to the small, poor school some miles from her home, for scholarships to the university in the city.

Her cat had died the previous month, there was no way she would take another and maybe leave the poor beast to be discarded onto the street, or given for euthanasia. After all, it was unlikely she'd outlive another pet. She lingered on, healthy apart from the normal aches and pains of her age. But quietly with only her servants who came in daily; never quite acknowledging the feeling she was a little lonely as if there was someone she had never known, but missed despite that.

It was the early hours of a morning a week after her birthday when the sound came. A soft groaning, rising to a roar of sound. Deafening, paralyzing, and Jandy knew it then for what it was, as the earth below her home heaved and shifted. There was a period of confusion when she was showered with objects, some small, some larger and heavier. When at last the shaking and the bombardment ceased she lay still.

There was no pain but she could not move. Her body felt lighter as the hours passed and over the hills behind what had been her home, dawn-light showed the sky a little paler. There was no sound, only the sudden feeling of presence. She looked up into green eyes; it was as if she'd expected them, her mouth curved into a tiny smile as a hand slipped into her own chill fingers.

And a voice that only she could hear, said, *"Will you deny me again, my once and future love? Come with me, I have no wish to walk alone any longer."*

This time she did not clutch that lifeline. Her hand curled a little, a comradely grip, the sort of grasp with which one holds the hand of an old and very dear friend. Gradually as the light grew, she was seeing more of the face in which those eyes were set. Her body was without pain, in fact she felt comfortable, warm, and secure. The green gaze held her cradled in expectation as all sensations save that of the hand in hers, faded and she who had once been his until she wanted to walk the mortal world just one more time, accepted *that* time was over.

They came from the village to find her at last, and mourned her sincerely. Yet as one old man said, as he tossed over her the vivid multi-colored silk cloth she had used upon the huge mahogany table. "Do not mourn her too greatly, mi compadres. She lived long and long but Lord Death comes for all. Yet she must have died without pain or fear, for look, see how happily she smiles, as if she greets someone beloved."

IN MEMORY OF BENNY

I bit back a cry of pain as the cane landed, closed my eyes and endured as Mother Ames counted to 'ten'. I relaxed – and screamed as another blow savaged my torn skin.

"One extra to remind you of your duties, Thomas."

There was an undercurrent of amusement. She'd been pleased to wring a howl out of me. What she didn't know was that she was beating the wrong person. It had been Benita who should have trimmed the lamps and had forgotten. Benny was a year older than I was but looked younger, and the last beating had almost killed her. So when we were asked who'd failed in their duty, I said that it was me.

I took two more beatings for her that year before Benny vanished, and people gossiped that she'd run away. I was certain she'd have told me if she planned to run and she'd never said a word. Mother Ames shook her head.

"I did my best. She had a good bed, decent food, and lessons, but some orphans are ungrateful."

All that was a lie of course. Not that the townsfolk cared. What the eye doesn't see the heart doesn't grieve over, as my mother always said before she and dad died in a house fire. I'd been spending the night in town with John's family, but they had little money and couldn't keep me.

I grew up in the orphanage just outside of Bodie and my best friend there was Benny. I was twelve when she went missing and I left as soon as I too was thirteen. I went to work at a local ranch and moved on from there. By the time I was twenty-five I was a ranch foreman on a spread a hundred miles away. I called myself Cole Parker – my mother's maiden name – not Thomas Cole Stewart and I never planned to go back but life has a way of changing your mind.

"Cole?"

"Yes, sir?"

"I want one hundred and fifty heifers, all good quality, five bulls that're young an' top studs, and a remuda of twenty-five horses. Pick yourself six of the boys, and you'll be moving the cattle out in two days."

My boss was a grizzled old rancher. He was tough as raw-hide and he'd grown up in this county, but he had a twinkle in his eyes most times.

"Sir, you got it?"

"Sure did, son. 'A course the place has run down since old Johnson died. But it's the land I was after and I got it. Good land, good water, an' I got the cattle to spare. Once you got everything rounded up, you an' the boys drive the cattle over to Bodie – I'll give you a paper to say you speak in my name – and you set up a bank account in my name, get to fixin' the place up an' move the cattle onto the flats near the ranch-house."

"Yes, sir. Mr. Crosset. Are you coming over to live there?"

"Cole, I'm too old a dog to change kennels." He grinned and I laughed. "No, son, the fact is that right now I'm over-stocked on cattle, rich, an' under-stocked on land. But in an-other few years cattle prices will rise, an' ranchers who have them to sell will make a killin'. Reckon I'll get maybe thirty-five dollars a head."

I gasped. Cattle were selling at just over a third of that this year. A man that had the kind of numbers Mr. Crosset was talking about would end up seriously rich.

"Cole, I trust you to run things the way I would myself, and Cole, a man that's a foreman an' twenty-six this year could do worse than think about a wife. Man does not live by bread alone."

So I thought about it.

We made the drive. I started in to run that ranch, and it kept me mighty busy so that I was only in town twice that first year, an' the third time was the kicker. I rode in and saw her, Mother Ames, sitting up in an open carriage, her dress the same thing she'd always worn but this wasn't cheap cloth, it was silk, and the brooch on it shone with a glimmer that said diamonds. The carriage had good horses and a driver sitting up in front. I was with Yance Melville that came from around here and I asked as if I knew nothing.

"Who's that fine lady, Yance?"

He looked where I was looking and tipped his hat to her. "Miz Ames. She runs an orphanage south of here. She's a real decent woman, Cole, takes in them orphans out 'a the kindness of her heart, gives them a bed, feeds them, teaches them to read an' write and then finds them a good boss. Most a' the girls go east to work fer rich women."

"She can't wear silk from being kind to orphans?"

"No, an' that just shows you what sort 'a person she is. My da says that maybe a dozen years back some kin of Miz Ames died and left her money. It gets doled out to her, so much every few months. Word is the banker would kiss her feet did she ask it."

"But she still runs the orphanage?" I kept my voice neutral.

"Sure, and like the town says, that just shows you. Miz Ames says that Bodie needs an orphanage and what'll happen to all the orphans if she shuts the place? I'm telling you, Cole. That there's a wonderful woman."

I looked after Mother Ames, remembering cold and hunger, the crack and bright hurt of a cane across my shoulders, and I remembered Benny's dog.

* * *

She'd found him wandering and taken him in. I'd protested. "Benny, what if she finds out?"

"We'll see she doesn't. I've made him a bed in the far shed, she never goes there."

"And what do we feed him?" I asked in exasperation.

"I'll share with him, an' when I work in the kitchen I can take bones."

She did. Now and again when I wasn't as hungry as usual, I gave her a mouthful or two of my food, and she saved it faithfully for the dog. The people who came out after dark every month or so sometimes tossed away scraps as they left and we picked up those. Benny called the animal Solomon because she said he was a wise dog. He made her happy so I let it be. I knew it was too good to last and it was. When Benny was twelve, she went out one night to feed Solomon and I watched from the window as I always did.

That night I saw Mother Ames, sneaking along after Benny, her face showing white in the moonlight. She was wearing an expression that scared me and without thinking, I dropped over the windowsill and followed her. I heard the voices as I moved up.

"Whose dog is that?"

"Mine. His name is Solomon."

"And how long have you had him?" Her voice sounded reasonable. Benny must have thought that it was going to be all right.

"Two months."

"What are you feeding him?"

"I give him some of my food, and there's bones from the kitchen." Even believing it was okay she wasn't telling about me.

I got to the shed door in time to see without having time to do anything.

"A stray..." Mother Ames moved in a smooth flow then. She produced something from her skirt pocket and struck, Solomon went down silently as blood trickled from the terrible wound that smashed in half his head. Mother Ames rounded on Benny.

"A stray that you've been feeding at my expense. If I've been giving you too much food I can feed you less." Benny was weeping, holding the body of her dog. I stepped back where neither could see me. "And stealing from the kitchen as well. Get to your room. I'll talk to you later."

Benny stumbled past without seeing me in the dark. Mother Ames stayed in the shed where the candle-lantern Benny had brought still gave light. I put my eye to a crack and watched as she wrapped the dog in a tattered old blanket Benny must have found somewhere. Then she picked up the body and, candle-lantern in one hand, she started walking as I followed. She walked a long way to the old dry arroyo. There she rolled Solomon's body down the bank and dropped down to stand over him.

"Damn brats," I heard her mutter. "But there's ways they pay me." She laughed, and it chilled my bones.

She buried Solomon by caving in some of the bank over him, and a few days later, when I could get away I went to see and found that she must have gone back with a spade and done a better job. Benny was given only dry bread and water for a week. I shared my own food as and when I could but for months the light went out of my friend and I hated Mother Ames with all the impotence of a child with no recourse against adults.

* * *

I sat my horse on the edge of Bodie's main street and watched her out of sight.

I went with Yance to the store and bought goods and needed supplies, then Yance made a suggestion.

"Why'nt we eat at the new cafe before we start fer home?"

I agreed – and changed my life.

The cafe was clean, and the tables were pleasantly decked with red and white gingham tablecloths, while the smell of food made my mouth water. I ordered steak and coffee and both were excellent. I noticed the waitress as well, and she was even better. She caught me looking and smiled. I smiled back, heard her mother call her Emma, and next week I found an excuse to take the wagon into town again, and the next week, and the next … We married a year to the day after I first saw her.

Now and again, I saw Miz Ames, as the town called her, riding past in her carriage. She didn't recognize me. How should she? I'd been thirteen with a different name when I left. Now I was a man, tall and broad-shouldered. I was a ranch foreman with cowhands who looked to me for orders. The banker touched his hat to me as I did to Mother Ames when I passed her.

Why not? My ma always said that courtesy cost nothing. Besides it was better she didn't remember me, because I remembered Benny and I had other questions now. Here and there, I asked them, listened to the answers, and moved on.

Emma had a boy, we named him Michael and I loved my

wife and son, but I continued to listen to town gossip, and now and again I dropped a question, casually, as if I only half listened to the answer. Mike was six when Mr. Crosset started to fail. His heart had him gasping for breath and he couldn't walk far. He'd made a fortune when cattle prices rose, and he'd left me in charge of the old Johnson ranch while he stayed where he was. He sent one of his hands to get me. We rode back as fast as I could push the horses.

"Cole, I'm on the way out, lad."

I opened my mouth and found I had nothing to say. He knew though.

"It's all right, boy, I've had a good long life and there's no pain. Listen, my will is filed with lawyer Abbots, but I may as well tell you now. I've left you the Johnson place. I never married, never had children. When I die my ranch here will be sold and the money will go to cousins back east that I don't even remember. It wouldn't be right for that to happen to the ranch where you've worked so hard for so many years now."

"Sir, Mr. Crosset, I – thank you."

He looked at me. "Cole, if you hadn't shaped up you'd have nothing. But when you worked here you worked hard and you were honest. I've kept in touch with things on the Johnson ranch too. I know you've accounted for every penny and I've never got less than what I was owed. You never said, but I reckon you named your boy after me."

I nodded.

"You've done well by me over the years and now I've done right by you. The Johnson ranch is yours. What do you say?"

I'd been thinking and I was ready. It was something a man wanted, to be remembered. He had a namesake, and I could give him another.

"Sir, if I have another son I'll call him Andrew."

Mr. Crosset smiled. "After Michael Andrew Crosset, hey?"

"Yes sir."

"That'll suit me, lad, now go back to your own ranch and you'll hear from me."

We heard a half year later that he'd died. Lawyer Abbots called me in and told me that the Johnson ranch was mine, that the will said I got it all, everything on the place and every penny in the account as it stood the day old Crosset died. And a surprise. Several times, I'd taken Mike with me to see the old man and they'd got on well. He left Mikey his choice of items in or on the ranch where he'd lived to the value of five thousand dollars, said value to be decided by the lawyer.

Mr. Crosset left money in a trust too. If I had a second son and named him Andrew the boy would inherit five thousand dollars when he was twenty-one, however if I'd had no second son within the next twenty years then the money would go back east as well. After that things jogged on as usual save that, the banker was more respectful and Emma was invited to join the ladies circle.

* * *

When Michael was seven, he wanted a dog. Without telling me, Emma found one for him, a puppy that Mike called Jack. I asked him why?

"Gee, dad, one day he'll grow up to protect us all, just like Jack the Giant-Killer."

I looked the pup over. I doubted he'd ever be a big dog, but that was okay, so long as he could bark he'd do well enough.

"You do like him, don't you, dad?"

I rested my hand on the soft warm hide. "Yes, Mike. He'll be a good dog one day when he grows up."

He never did.

Mike and Jack came with me into town six months later. It would be Emma's birthday in a week and we wanted to buy her presents. I left Mike with his dog at the store, carefully choosing from the array of items suitable for a lady while I went to get my horse re-shod at the smithy in the outskirts of town. I was on the way back, cutting through a narrow alleyway shadowed by the back of the old livery stable when I saw everything. Mike told me later that Jack had run off and he'd been hunting for him.

I was unseen in the alley shadows when Mother Ames' carriage came bowling down the road into town. I don't know why the dog acted as he did, maybe she called him without my hearing, maybe he associated women with food, but he went running at the carriage and jumped up to almost touch her. And quick as a snake, her hand came out with that thing she'd used before. The pup fell back with his head broken open, the carriage rolled on and I watched it go.

She was the town's saint, the woman who stayed looking after children when she had the money to go east and live in luxury. It was then that it occurred to me. I'd asked why she stayed. Maybe I should also have asked where the money came from. There was just her word on that. And there was another question too that I'd never thought to ask.

I slipped out from the alleyway and picked up the still-warm limp little body. Mike saw me and came running as I walked towards the store.

"Dad, dad? Is he...?"

I moved the body in my arms so that he could see and watched as he tried to be a man about it.

"Dad? How do you think it happened?"

"Maybe a horse kicked him, Mikey, I can't say." No, I couldn't, because I wanted Mother Ames unaware of what I'd seen – and because no one would believe it of her. "Listen, son, you get Yance from the feed-store, we'll take Jack home and bury him by the corral. He'd like that, you know he always enjoyed being with the horses?"

"Yeah, he did."

I took boy and dog home, we buried his pup by the corral and when Emma suggested that we get another dog, I vetoed it.

"He's still grieving. Let him get over it first."

I had other fish to fry. One of them was a killer pike called Ames. After that, I cultivated a man named Jim Robertson who worked in a branch of our bank in the next-over town. He liked a good drink and a bank clerk isn't overpaid. I supplied the drinks and listened to Jim ramble once he'd had sufficient alcohol to get him started.

"Yeah, she puts money into the bank every so often. A banker's draft? Not likely. She comes in with cash," he tittered. "The snooty cow thinks I don't know where some of it comes from. She's wrong on that."

I filled his glass again and spoke casually. "Of course you do, you're no fool."

"No, I'm not. Last year she came in with a real wad of greenbacks an' I recognized some of them. Old Joseph Collan took a couple of hundred out a week before and I knew the numbers. They were in sequence, see?"

I did. I filled Jim with enough whisky that he'd forget everything we'd talked about, saw him to his room, and rode home thinking hard as I rode. It took time for me to get the answer, during which Emma came to me smiling.

"Cole, you know you promised Mr. Crosset you'd name a second son after him?"

I looked at her and she nodded happily.

So between working my ranch, watching over Emma and looking into Mother Ames I was busy. The ranch prospered and here and there I greased a palm, paid off a man who could tell me things. Gradually I unwound what had been going on. And at dusk on an evening in late October I took a folding shovel, a hand-pickaxe, and rode off to the arroyo where I'd once watched Mother Ames bury Solomon.

I dug slowly, carefully, uncovering the bones of the dog, I continued and they were there, the slender bones of a young girl. It had to be her. I stood looking down. Then I covered everything over again, took my gear and rode home. Now I knew where Benny had gone.

As I rode, I turned all of that over in my mind and it came to me that I might be asking questions the wrong way around. Maybe I shouldn't be asking why Mother Ames stayed, but why she didn't go? Could it be that if she left there would be no more money? And that meant it was something she did, or had, here that brought in the 'great wads of cash' Jim had described.

Yet the only thing she had was the orphanage. Mother Ames sent her orphans away to work in wealthy families – she said. But how did anyone know? Which of them had ever returned to talk about it? I knew what had happened to Benny. She'd been killed and buried like a dog – beside her dog. And where could I go from here?

I could bring people here, show them the bones, but what said that Mother Ames – the town saint – had anything to do with it? I recalled how we'd picked up food-scraps discarded by

Mother Ames' visitors and used those to feed Solomon when we could. It suddenly occurred to me to wonder why the people came to an orphanage after dark and why no one saw their faces. No one but her.

It was as if a great light shone in my mind. I believed I had answers to that question and I thought I knew what to do. I arrived home, slept well that night and the next day I went into town. I knew it was the day that she usually drove in and I waited beside the road. Then I lifted a hand.

"May I speak with you privately?" I saw it then, the flash of greed.

"Certainly, Mr. Parker." She alighted from her carriage nodded to the driver who walked the horses down the road a short distance and then Mother Ames turned to me. "How may I assist you?"

I smiled. "I found Benita's bones," I said softly. "Some people remember when she went missing. If I tell them where she is, they could ask very inconvenient questions."

She caved in on the spot, which surprised me a little. "Don't tell anyone, I can pay."

I didn't want money but I did want to see how much she valued silence. "How much?"

"What do you want?"

"Five thousand dollars."

It was a large sum but she never blinked. "Done."

"And..."

"And what?"

"You close the orphanage and leave."

She stared at me, her eyes sharpened and she knew who I was. "Thomas? Thomas Stewart. So that's it. Been looking for that little tramp and now you've found her."

"Benny was never a tramp, but," I said, watching her, "that was what you sold her for though, wasn't it? To one of the men who came riding in after dark, the men we heard and never saw. What happened? She fought too hard, so you buried her. Then it dawned on you, you could sell them to men who'd take them away. And if anything went wrong you could claim you knew nothing. That the person had come looking for a housemaid, and that was perfectly respectable."

She stared at me, her lips clenched tight.

"You sold children," I accused her. "How many others are there? How many died here before you got smart and sold them away?"

"Five thousand dollars, and I close the orphanage and leave," she said.

I nodded.

"I'll meet you in the livery barn tomorrow once it's dark, the old one that isn't used any more. I'll pay you off and be gone in a week." She turned on her heel, walked to the carriage, stepped into it and was gone.

I must have been dreaming when I assumed she'd give in so easily. I met her on the Day of the Dead at the barn. I came walking in to find her standing by a stall, lantern in one hand, a pocket pistol in the other. In the stall something moved.

She smiled at me, the sort of smile that makes the sweat trickle from a man's brow. "Mr. Cole Parker, rancher, husband, and … oh yes, father. Don't come any closer Mr. Parker. Just listen to me. Yes, I sell children from my orphanage, I get very good money for them and I intend to keep on getting it. Benita was a stupid girl. She could have gone with Mr. Collan and worn silk. Instead, she said she'd tell people, and Mr. Collan decided that he wanted what he'd paid for even if he couldn't take her with him. Silly little fool fought and he was too rough. It happens now and then."

"So you buried her – and how many others?"

She shrugged. "A few, here and there."

"And you think that I won't talk?" I asked incredulously.

"There's no money, but I brought you something much more valuable. All you have to do is get out with him."

She waved one hand at the stall. I moved a step sideways to look. Mike was there, tied up, gagged, and his eyes on me were terrified. Mother Ames smiled again, and tossed the lantern behind her. The old straw flared up and in the stall, Mike began to thrash about. I saw that he was tied to a stanchion and couldn't even roll towards me. She stepped to the wall where a small door led to the outside. I ignored her. If she escaped she escaped, Mike was more important. He'd rubbed his gag loose and now he cried out.

"Dad!" and then…"*Jack, Jackie boy??*" His voice was incredulous and I turned. In front of Mother Ames, the door she'd reached for refused to open, as around Mike the flames died to nothing, and a young dog fell on him, panting, licking, and whimpering in joy. I reached Mike, slashed him free. He yelled in pain and landed on the ground and I saw his ankle was badly swollen. I stooped and he hugged me briefly before taking the dog in his arms. "Jackie, how'd you get here, boy? I missed you so much."

And a soft child's voice answered from the shadows. "I brought him."

I knew who it was before I looked. "Benny!" Mike was engrossed with his dog.

Brown eyes smiled at me. "Tommy. On the Day of the Dead there's a debt to pay." Beside her, a big, ragged dog reared up, his teeth showing in a white snarl. "Solomon wanted to be here too."

Mother Ames moaned and yanked at the door until blood ran down her fingers. Benny nodded to me. "Get out of here, Tommy. You'll have to carry your son. His ankle's broken."

I reached out and my hand was cold with nothing but mist against it. I tried again. "Benny?"

"You can't and Mike doesn't see anything. He'll forget it all as soon as you walk through your door at home."

"What about you?"

"Bury us together, me and Solomon."

"I will," I swore, crossing my fingers in our old promise as she laughed.

"Take Mike and get out now, I can't hold things together much longer."

I looked at her before I scooped up Mike. "I loved you," I said. I walked through the main door that opened for me. Mother Ames dived for it and Benny was there first.

"You told me you were a businesswoman. Stay and talk business with us."

Solomon locked his teeth on her skirt. Puppy Jack had her by the ankle. Mother Ames struck at them again and again with what I now knew to be a cosh. (Ned Buntline had written of them.) She was struggling towards the door. Benny took two paces forward, wrapping her child's arms about the writhing woman, the flames roaring up around them all then – as Mother Ames screamed and screamed in throat-tearing wordless agony. I stepped outside, and, as the doors swung shut behind me, I heard Benny's voice one last time.

"I loved you too, Tommy. Remember me."

* * *

I carried Mike home, he recollected only falling and breaking his ankle somewhere. Once they found Miz Ames' body in the burned-out shell of the old livery stable I spoke to the right people and got an agreement that I should close the orphanage and make the necessary arrangements. It was a lot of work and no one else wanted to do it.

During that time, I'd been wondering what happened to her driver. Interviews with the orphans said that he'd been deeply involved. I kept a watch for him and when, desperate for food and money to get away, he came creeping into the orphanage office, I took him at gun-point far to the desert side of the orphanage's land. There I broke each thigh with a bullet, gut-shot him and left him to the affection of his brothers – the coyotes.

With him gone I 'found' a plan in Mother Ames' desk – I'd drawn it but I didn't tell people that – I simply said that, curious, I'd gone to the place it showed and dug, to find the bodies of over twenty children. I showed the townsfolk the accounts she'd kept of who had bought and where she'd sold. I found homes for those left in her 'care' before she died, and I liquidated hers and her driver's assets and saw that each of her victims that could be found had a nest egg that might give them a new start. (A number of people left town before then.)

I buried Benny under a big cottonwood, in a polished wooden coffin with brass handles, and, surreptitiously, the night before the funeral, I added Solomon's bones in a padded silk bag I placed at her feet. There was a headstone. It just said her name and the dates, the second as near as I could get. Solomon would have to share that.

Mother Ames was buried outside the cemetery without a

headstone or marker and just as she'd been dug out of the stable rubble. Her bones still in the old sack they'd used. Funny
thing, but the locals didn't seem to think that she was so saint-
like any longer.

I got Mike a new dog, a terrier he called Jenkin, and three
months after Mother Ames died Emma had a son – and a
daughter. We christened our twins in the little church, naming
our son Andrew. Our daughter we named Benita. Yes, Emma
knows, I told her everything once I brought Mike home and
we put him to bed, and each year we take flowers to the grave,
then we both say a prayer in thanks, and in memory of Benny.

BEFORE ALL THIS MODERN STUFF

Jackson Mull was 80 in 1900 and he didn't like it one bit. When his father died, Jackson had cashed in every item of the estate and gone west. He'd found a nice little valley in Arizona, purchased the water holes, and been one of the first to fence in his land. He found a wife in the nearest town and settled in to breed cattle and children. Not that the cattle had always worked out – there was trouble two years before he brought Dora home.

"Indians?" He glared at his foreman, who stared back. Joe Green had been an Indian fighter, buffalo hunter, and at his age no kid who'd been ranching a handful of years was going to upset him, no matter how strong the glare.

"Yes, boss. They ran off half a dozen head of prime steers we had in the west paddock."

Jackson swore savagely. He'd had those animals cut out as samples. The army was starting to buy from cattlemen here and he planned to be one of those selling. "Take five men and go after them. Shoot the Indians and get those cattle back. An army buyer will be here tomorrow, bring the cattle back easy too. I don't want the fat run off them."

"Ah, boss?"

"What?"

"I think it was kids, not warriors, maybe with a woman or two."

"An' that makes it okay? You get the cattle back, shoot anyone with them, and that's an order. Get going!"

Joe Green headed out. He returned with the cattle, all but one and Jackson met him at the corral gate. "They took six steers," He said tersely. "You got five here?"

"They'd butchered one."

"Where's the meat?"

"Boss, they were starving. Two women an' four kids, littlest one was a baby. Steer was dead. I didn't see the point."

Jackson tried to stare him out and failed. He turned to walk back to the ranch house, tossing the words over his shoulder as he walked away. "Done's done. Tell Bill to come see me, I've got a job for him."

Jackson sprawled thinking, cup of coffee in his hand, on the big comfortable armchair that had been his father's and that he'd brought west with him. Joe was soft on Indians, said that this had been their land, that the white settlers had taken it illegally. Hell, hadn't Arizona become part of the United States in 1848 and wasn't he an American? He'd paid for the waterholes, bought and paid for the fences and overseen their building. He'd worked alongside his men to raise farmhouse and bunkhouse, barns and corrals. He'd spent every cent he had to bring in cattle, to cut hay in the meadows and make sure that his livestock wintered well. Was he supposed to hand over good beasts any time some ragged-ass bunch came begging?

Jackson snorted. He didn't think so. If the Indians wanted to eat let them raise their own beef, but they wouldn't, they were bone-idle thieves. He looked up as Bill Simons came in and studied the rat-faced man. He was nothing to look at, but Bill could track a fish upstream, and what he aimed at he hit. Bill didn't like any work he couldn't do on horseback, but he liked money and he had no conscience.

"I want you to track that bunch that took my cattle," Jackson said abruptly. "Joe let them walk off with a ton of good beef and you know what they are, they'll just come back for more once they've et that lot."

"An' you don't want them comin' back."

"Not ever," Jackson said, looking Bill in the eyes. "I don't want to see or hear from them again. I don't want trouble about it either. Can you handle that?"

"You care about any of the details?"

"No, just tell me when it's done. I want some sort of proof. You hand me that, I'll hand you a bonus. A month's extra wages suit you?"

From the gleam in Bill's eyes, it suited him very well. "How long I got to get the job done?"

"A week."

He knew that Bill would spend half of it idling given the opportunity, but he had a plan to cover that too. "Here," he handed over a couple of dollars. "Go to town and bring me back a bottle of whiskey, couple of loaves of fresh bread if Dora's baked. Talk to Rod at the livery stable an' tell him I'm in the market for a new saddle horse an' a pack mule." He was. He'd been considering the purchases for almost a year, now they'd make a good cover for Bill's absence. If Joe asks, I told you to circle over by Mannion's place to check the fences on the boundary first."

Bill's grin showed yellow teeth. "An' I don't need to?"

"Nope, I was over there two days ago."

They both understood the context of that. Mannion's was in the opposite direction to the way the cattle-thieves had gone. It would explain half of Bill's absence, and the errand in town would explain the other half. But the thieves had gone more-or-less in the direction of town, if they hadn't hidden their tracks very well, even slowed by having to track them, Bill would catch up in a couple of days at most – and in an area of rough broken land where bodies could lie hidden forever.

Jackson smiled to himself as he saw his man ride out. That would be one bunch of cattle-thieves that would keep away from his property in the future. His smirk widened. Let's see how Geronimo and his louse-ridden lot liked getting some of their own back.

Bill returned in a week. He slipped silently into the ranch house very early one morning, before even the cook started work, and roused his boss.

"Got something to show you – an' then you'll owe me thet bonus you promised."

Jackson nodded. There was no one in the house as yet. "Okay?"

Bill dug a small bundle out of his shirtfront, and let the bandanna unroll to dump its contents onto Jackson's quilt. Six left ears, two large, three small, and one very small. Jackson looked down feeling slightly sick. He couldn't show anything,

Bill had done what had been asked of him and he wouldn't respect a boss who couldn't handle that. He touched one, keeping his voice casual.

"Nice job. I'll get you your money." And, as he walked to the bureau he continued. "Did you have to go far?"

"Nope, they'd only moved on a few miles, they had a camp there in better cover; in case Joe came back I guess."

"How'd you get all of them without any getting away?"

"Got between them and the thickest cover, shot the two boys before they knew I was there. They hadn't no weapons bar knives. I got one of the women in the belly, an' the other in the back as she ran, kilt the baby she was carrying too. The girl kid I hunted." He leered at Jackson. "Reckon she was twelve or so, an' ran like a scared jackrabbit, but she wasn't fast enough. After I was done, I hauled them all into a hole I found. Caved in the sides a' that and tossed loose earth an' rocks all over, brushed over everything with a bunch of grass while I walked backwards out'a it. Sun will dry the earth out an' there'll be no sign left once it's rained or blown a time or two. Don't worry, boss. You said you didn't never want to see them cattle-stealers back, and there ain't no way they ever will be."

Jackson made himself nod graciously. "Good job, Bill. I knew I could count on you. Here's the bonus I promised and a little over."

Bill beamed at the money, picked up the ears and rolled them in the bandanna again. "Guess I should get rid of these, wouldn't like Joe to see them. Brought you a pocket piece though, boss." He handed over a deer's tooth that had been carved into a tiny coyote. It was beautiful work and Jackson accepted it, admiring the little wolf's stance and look.

"Thanks."

"Got it off the girl kid, typical injun work," Bill grunted. "Anyway, any time you got something special for me to do, boss, you just let me know."

Indian attacks on settlers and ranchers increased that year. There was a rumor that one of the chiefs had lost family, but the settlers didn't see why they should pay, there was no proof any of them had done anything. Not that the attacks bothered

Jackson, shooting troublemakers worked well in his estimation. It left fewer to breed.

Jackson bred himself three sons and a daughter over the next ten years, pausing for a double celebration when his daughter turned eighteen and the Chiricahua Reservation was abolished. He celebrated longer and harder seven years later when Geronimo surrendered to General Cook, and nodded in grudging approval when, much later, the war chief became a Christian and a farmer.

"Looks as if he's learned proper ways. Guess that's one Indian we won't have to worry about."

"That's right, pop," his oldest son endorsed. "Say, what's the time, I want to go into town and see Louisa if that's all right with you?"

Jackson hauled out his watch. He wore the coyote on the watch-chain his wife had given him to celebrate their tenth wedding anniversary, and a fleeting memory of Bill's words on how and where he'd acquired it came as he looked at the tiny beast on the gold links. He shrugged it off, Bill had died in the winter of '71 and the bodies of his victims had never been found. Besides, they were only Indian women and their brats. Plenty more where they came from – although, he thought, happily there were a lot fewer than there had been when he was a lad.

The ranch prospered as the years went by, Jackson bought a second ranch and put his oldest son in as foreman. Mannion's ranch on his boundary was offered for sale – all of the family but the son's widow had died and she wanted to go back east. Jackson bought the land, divided it, built a second ranch house and outbuildings, and put his other two sons in as foremen. All three of the boys understood that in time the ranches they ran would belong to them, if they did a good job. The home ranch would be his wife, Dora's, home forever, and once she died it would belong to his precious daughter, Gloria.

Some archaeologist started working in the rough broken lands between Jackson's ranch and the rapidly expanding town. There were rumors he'd found something – no one cared. An Apache woman, educated at an English University, came to see the archaeologist – locals were outraged. And Jackson had a stroke. He mostly recovered, but he couldn't ride his land any more, couldn't drive the buggy easily, and he didn't enjoy his food the way he always had.

When the archaeologist came calling, he let the man in. It should be entertainment if nothing else. "Martin Wilder, sir, pleased to meet you. I understand you're one of the earliest settlers in this area?"

Jackson shook the offered hand and sat back again. "That'd be about right."

"What do you remember about the Apaches of the time?"

Jackson decided to be cautious. "A good-enough people. Sly sometimes. Can stab you in the back, but warriors."

Martin Wilder leaned forward. "Do you know anything about their beliefs and superstitions?"

"Not really. Why?"

He listened to a tale of going back in time, of how one of the old medicine men was said to have learned to do that, and the place where it could be done. It wasn't until Martin added a final comment that Jackson took notice.

"The old man claimed that if you stepped through the cave mouth after the right ceremony, then you wouldn't just go back as you are, you'd go back to however old you'd have been then." Jackson showed nothing but within him, his mind came to attention. "I've made a note of everything he told me, all the ceremony, the place to step through, how to choose the time that you want to arrive in, all of it. It's a fascinating belief, a great legend. The paper will make my name at the university."

"Couldn't that Apache girl tell you anything?"

"Waterhawk? She's told me some of the stories. There's one that's right here. Her great-grandmother told her that there'd been a fight between an Apache family and the army, two women and four of their children got separated and were never seen again. They were related to a friend of Geronimo's and Waterhawk says that they looked for the missing ones all year. Do you remember anything?"

"When would that have been?"

"They went missing around 1855."

"Can tell you there was a lot of Indian trouble the next year, that's all."

"Oh," Martin Wilder looked disappointed and changed the subject. "That's a lovely little carving you have on your watch chain. It looks like Apache work?"

"No idea. It was a gift from a man that used to work for me." Yet he could feel something in the way the archaeologist looked at him, as if he wasn't certain that was the truth. How dare the man doubt his word. "Name of Bill..." he fumbled for the name and got it. "Yes, Bill Simons, died in '71. Good hand. Worked for me for twenty years."

"And he gave it to you? When would that have been?"

Jackson distanced himself as his daughter entered. "Maybe 1869, thereabouts."

Gloria giggled. "Pa, your memory's going. You put that on your watch chain when ma gave you the chain in '67 and I'd been playing with it for years before that."

He forced his face to betray nothing. "You say so? Maybe you're right, could have been 1859 I'm thinking of. Bill gave it to me an' I've never known where he got it, so what's it matter?" They assured him it didn't and the talk went in other directions.

It bothered Jackson Mull that the archaeologist stayed around working in that area where Bill had said he'd buried the bodies. He didn't like that Waterhawk being with him either. They said that she was descended from Geronimo's medicine man and one of the old warrior's war chief friends as well. There was something in the things he heard about her that he didn't like. Not that it mattered, he had other worries that winter when a heart attack caught him off-guard. The doctor was polite but clear.

"I can't do any more for you. To be honest with you, Mr. Jackson, I'm surprised you survived to this time."

Jackson peered at him. Damned eyesight was going too. "How much time have I got do you reckon?"

"A few months at best. And you should stay in bed as much as possible from now on."

Once the doctor was gone, Jackson considered his options. He could stay here, live his final humiliating months in bed, or he could gamble. The archaeologist was at his site just now but in ten days, he'd be gone from his site for a month and that

Waterhawk woman was said to be in Washington talking to the government. Jackson didn't believe in the superstitions of savages, but what did he have to lose? If he died trying to get to the place he'd been told about, he'd die on his own land under the Arizona sky. Archaeologists were always short of money. He'd use that as bait.

Martin Wilder came running at the offer. "Two thousand dollars towards the dig, that's incredibly generous, Mr. Jackson." With that amount he could work for a year without having to fund-raise elsewhere. He could even hire casual labor to dig as it was needed. "Yes, of course I'll show you everything, all my papers, translations of local stories, whatever you want."

All Jackson really wanted was information about the cave where a man might return to his youth. He wasn't foolish enough to say that however and he accepted everything. Delving, once Martin was gone, into the heap of books and papers until he found the one he required. That he copied with great care. Martin returned to collect everything for safekeeping before joining friends, humbly accepted the wad of bills wrapped in a bank strip, thanked his benefactor several times and left. Jackson retained his gracious smile until the young man was gone, when he felt safe to relax. The smile that curved his lips after that was quite different.

He could forget all this damned modern stuff if his plan worked. He could return to a time when the Indians were vermin and hunted as such. When a man was master in his own house, and an employee did as he was told if he wanted to keep his job. He'd be in the flush of his youth and strength again and wouldn't he make his ranch hum and his hands jump to it.

It took the ten days until Martin departed his excavation for Jackson to make all his plans. None of his children lived with him now. The house was run by a middle-aged Mexican woman who went to bed early and slept soundly. In ten nights, it would be full moon, providing enough light for a horse and buggy to travel after dark. He called the cook in and talked quietly. The old man agreed. If he obeyed his employer, he'd spend the rest of his days in the town, not having to work, and able to afford to live comfortably. And the story made sense to him, what man would wish to die lying in his own filth, fed like a baby by strangers? Better to die under the open sky on your own land, free to go as you wished.

He took messages to Jackson's lawyer, and to his banker. He gave Jackson's orders to the men, to make sure that they'd be working on the other side of the ranch. Jackson ate early, the Mexican woman retired, and Jackson waited impatiently for the moon to rise. After what felt like half a year, it did and the cook came in, helped his master out to the buggy, settled him into that, wrapped him in a blanket, and took the reins. The horse trotted towards the town, veering off before it on the thread of road that led to the excavation.

"Carry this." He handed his man the canvas pack with necessary items. "Help me walk." He was obeyed. They reached the shallow niche that was not so much a genuine cave as a hollow. If the Apache were right, Jackson thought, it was still the gateway. He had his old revolver and ammunition, and a large pouch of gold coins, double eagles. With that amount, he'd be able to buy far more land and better livestock once he was back. The cave was within walking distance of his ranch for a fit young man, a day and a half, maybe two days afoot.

"Come back for me in an hour. Here." He snapped the watch chain off his watch, handed the watch to his cook and dropped the chain into his pocket. The watch was a cheap one but the chain was valuable – and still more so where he was going. "Come back for me in an hour!"

The cook nodded as Jackson hid a smile. If this worked he'd never be found – not this side of the century. He'd be back in 1855, a ranch owner, and young again, fit and healthy, and with what he knew now of market trends and disasters of this time … He stepped into the doorway and began to chant softly as the cook's tramping footsteps faded. All that modern stuff, the man should have been glad to serve his employer for nothing. Jackson chuckled, a deep asthmatic sound. The cook might have some explaining to do when it was discovered that he'd lost his master. And once they saw how much he'd benefited – he could end on the gallows as a murderer. Jackson chuckled again.

Overhead the moon seemed to fade. A chill wind blew. Clouds raced across the sky as Jackson swayed on his feet. The moon faded suddenly. Daylight washed all around him and he fell, to lie gasping on the ground. His clothes were horribly uncomfortable, too tight in some places, flapping in others. His gun was there however, his gold coins, his watch chain and … he stared down at his hands. They were smooth on the backs, taut-skinned. He leaped to his feet and knew with that smooth unthinking movement that it had worked. He was young again, back in the days before he'd wed or slowed down – and maybe this time he'd take longer to marry.

He stared around, orientated himself by the rising sun and began to walk. Something nagged at him that he'd forgotten but it couldn't be important and he ignored it. He had a loaded gun, food, water, and his gold. He'd be fine.

The Apache came out of the rocks behind Jackson and he was in their hands before he knew they were there. They dragged him back to a shallow dip between two hummocks and when he saw what lay there he cried out. It was an opened grave, the bodies inside were still fresh enough that the marks of how they'd died were plain. Jackson shuddered, dear Lord, that was what he'd forgotten, he'd made a trip over here after Bill had told him, just to be sure no signs had been left. The man leading those who held him grunted before searching their prisoner's clothing. They found the tiny coyote on the watch chain and their cries were filled with feral triumph.

"No, no, it was Bill, Bill Simons. He gave that to me…"

A blow that split both lips silenced him. That night they gave him to the women once the moon rose, and he was silent no longer … not for a very long time. Doe-in-the-Meadow had loved her friend, and now she turned to the man who had killed her, killed her young cousins, her sister and her sister's baby, and she sought a vengeance that would exact full and complete payment.

Jackson lay shaking in fear. He eyed the woman's sweet face, the soft brown eyes, and relaxed slightly. She didn't look cruel, and what Indian had imagination? She'd probably have them beat him. Afterwards, he could pretend death, wait until they left, then escape. His wonderful future could still be his. Unobtrusively he watched as the young woman gathered a large handful of small smooth pebbles, each around the size of the end of her index finger. She walked to the still burning fire, turned briefly so that she obscured the flames and returned to a low tree. There she found a partly broken branch, took the bark from it and made a funnel. Jackson stared. What was she up to?

He was distracted when the warriors pounced, stripped him of his pants and bound his wrists together, then his knees, before they bound wrists to knees and dropped him in the dirt, where he lay chilled, uncomfortable and baffled. Doe-in-the-Meadow gave an order to the warriors and waited as Jackson was turned to crouch, his white buttocks in the air. Slowly, carefully, she inserted the bark funnel. He yelled, struggled, but he was easily controlled and she smiled.

Walking back to the fire she checked on the small pot half-filled with water that nestled in the flames, the little pebbles she'd placed in that were ready. Using two twigs as tongs, she lifted one pebble without allowing Jackson to see what she did. She paced back to him, and dropped the pebble accurately down the bark cone. There was a second's silence.

Jackson convulsed, his first scream brought birds from nearby trees, caused the horses to shift nervously, and about him copper-colored faces displayed rare smiles. Ay yah, truly it was said that if you wished to break an enemy, give him to the women. The white man squealed like a trapped gopher. They settled to their haunches to enjoy the sound and spectacle. Doe-in-the-Meadow waited until the screams died to gasping moans, before returning with a second pebble. This time Jackson's voice cracked on a high note, and his eyes bulged in his head as he rolled about, trying with all of his strength to expel the pebble.

He prayed for death, for release of some kind, for unconsciousness, for rescue, for anything that would prevent a third stone – no prayers were being answered today. Doe-in-the-Meadow allowed him to see and hear her approaching the next time and he thrashed so desperately that even the warriors were hard put to it to hold him in place.

His screams tore the lining of his throat and after that, his shrieks were hoarse groans rather than shouts of agony. His tormenters did not care.

Doe-in-the-Meadow brought more pebbles one by one. They had been carefully chosen, as had the method of their heating. They were hot enough to burn a small nest into the sensitive cringing tissue, not sufficiently hot to burn through into the stomach cavity and end this too soon. They were small, the heat died in minutes, but it cauterized the area where it lay so that it did not bleed. All there was, was pain, fire, blazing agony that went on and on while Jackson screamed until he had no voice and could only whimper as his mouth sagged open exhaustedly.

He'd come through to his old time and place to regain youth, health and strength, and he'd received them. Without blood-loss, without major injuries, he survived the long and terrible day. Now and again Doe-in-the-Meadow gave him water, it would not do to let him die from thirst. When he realized this and would not drink, they brought another funnel and forced that into his mouth. He lasted until sunset but by then they could wring little more from him than a vague twitching. They left him to lie through the night before the next act began.

Near where they had found the bodies of their kin and friends there was a crack in a rock shelf. It was perhaps four foot wide and seven or eight feet deep and it was at the bottom of that where they laid Jackson Mull, tossing his possessions – all but the revolver and ammunition – in beside his victims before they reburied them, chanting softly. Over Jackson, Doe-in-the-Meadow had them place branches in a heap an arm's length thick. Above the branches they stacked earth brought from a distance, and topped it with heavy rocks, cunningly placed to appear a natural heap of tumbled stones.

Then they rode away. At the bottom of the crack as time passed, Jackson recovered consciousness. Within was a burning ache, thirst tortured him, and he had been left bound. At first, he struggled, croaked for help, and tried to dig upwards with his tied hands. He was buried alive, his mind broke under the terror, and he struggled mindlessly for hours each time he came back to consciousness. Some while into the next day he died.

Time mends. A paradox can be paradoctored. In 1900 nearly five hundred acres of the land Jackson had owned became the property of Martin and Waterhawk Wilder, paid for with a pouch of gold coins he'd found in his excavation – laid along with a gold watch chain and a tiny coyote carved from a deer tooth – by the skeletons of two women and four children. The other skeleton that lay nearby – and deeper – he never found.

By now, almost no one remembered that there had ever been a Jackson Mull who had once owned the land. It had sold for back taxes, Dora married a deputy sheriff and their children were different. Much later, a museum was built on the site and dedicated to the Apache. The only thing that might have reminded anyone of Jackson was a local folk tale about a young man who'd gone into the broken land and never returned. But then in the middle years of the nineteenth century that had been a common enough tale. He was only one of very many, and no one cared that he'd vanished. Not then and not now.

FETCH ME DOWN
MY GUN

J edidiah Wilcox wasn't much impressed by the latest danger.
"Bright? What kind'a bright?"

"*Blight*, Granddaddy, it's crawling up the fields, killing
the grass, crops, anythin' in its path. If it keeps coming either
we leave or we starve."

And, reflected old Jed's granddaughter, that was all too
likely if nothing stopped the brown tide. Jed had been a smart
boy. When his folks arrived to homestead just outside of the
new, still wild and raw town, Jed had been fourteen. He'd tak-
en a job for two years at the nearest ranch and learned everything he could about crops, animals, building for the land here
and using the sense God gave a man. Then he'd homesteaded
on his own hundred and sixty acres and used his savings to
buy what he needed. He'd seen that what folks needed was
more diversity in their food and he'd catered to that.

He'd fenced in his acres before anyone else. He'd purchased sheep, pigs, hens and geese, and planted half a dozen
kinds of vegetables along with fruit trees. In five years, he was
making real money and he'd married. A girl who'd been seduced and betrayed by a drummer who'd run off as soon as he
knew she was pregnant. Jed had married Rosa in church, half-
killed one man who'd spoken against her, and she'd adored
him all the days of her life for his rescue. She'd born him a son
and another daughter and Jed had never discriminated against
the eldest girl – Dana's mother, Marie.

"Dana?"

"Yes, Granddaddy?"

"Tell me about this blight. Not the facts, tell me what people are saying. What stories are there about it?"

Dana shivered involuntarily. "They say it's sent from Hell. They say that devils come with it to take the soul of anyone who stays once the blight surrounds them. They say it sucks the life out of anyone who gets too close, and that it … hungers."

Jed nodded slowly, thoughtfully. "Who?"

"Who says?"

"Who died?"

"They say it was what killed Sammy Duncan. He wouldn't leave his house, he said if he gave up his land and home then his family would starve and better he died trying to save them."

"What do you think?"

"I think that Sammy weighed three hundred pounds and probably scared himself to death. John Keeley died too, I'd say that was alcohol poisoning, not the blight either."

Her grandfather grinned. "Sensible lass. In other words, we know thet blight kills plants. We don't know it kills people. Maybe we should see about thet. Whose farm is nearest?"

"Malcolm Spencer's."

"Take that black pig over there. It's weaned, but it's a runt, never likely to grow that big, but it's healthy enough. Take it over and ask if you kin kindly put it in his old sty. Make sure it's got food 'n water, bedding, an' such, but see it can't get out. Do thet now."

Dana obeyed. Blackie was settled into Malcolm's old sty, while Jed took his pony and rode up the hill that overlooked the Spencer ranch. The blight's brown tide was closing in, it'd be there the next day by his calculations, and he'd come back with first light.

Malcolm Spencer joined him where Jed sat his pony, trudging up the hill to talk. "You think t' learn something from the pig?"

"Aye, there's been a deal of talk about how it kills people. So far, all it's killed to my certain knowledge is plants. I want to see if it'll kill a beast, and if so mebbe I can learn something. Mebbe this talk of killing's all gossip alone and no truth to it."

"John and Sammy died?"

"From the drink, an' a heart attack most likely. No, I won't go by them. I want to see with my own eyes."

An hour after dawn the next day he was sitting on the hill

edge, the patient pony standing hipshot behind him when he saw. It was an hour after dawn, as the blight crept over the pigsty. Blackie kept moving back from the wilting edge until he couldn't back any further, then he screamed, a long horrible shriek, and collapsed convulsing. Jed watched several hours more as the blight passed the silent body, creeping on towards the house and barns, where Malcolm Spencer, his wife and sons moved out the last of the hay and livestock, everything salvageable from what had been their home.

Jed rose at last, swung into the saddle and walked the pony down the hill towards the blight's edge. Once close he followed it back towards the Keeley and Duncan farms and saw with deep interest that both were now clear of it. So? The blight was a finite thing. Certainly, the land it left behind was barren, no grass, trees dead and rotten, and it seemed that it would kill animals. But with it gone, grass would likely grow again, and trees could be replanted. That wasn't the problem.

He turned to the squirming sack at his saddlebow and lifted out a furious rat. It had been carefully tied so that it was in no great discomfort but it couldn't escape or bite. Silently, reluctantly, he rode back to the blight edge, flicked his knife across the rat's binding, and before it could realize what he'd done, with a wide-arm swing, he tossed the rat deep into the blight. It leaped for the green grass twenty feet away – and froze. It stood unmoving for a few seconds, and then it shivered, jerked violently, and died.

Jed nudged the pony with a heel and rode away from the small motionless victim. He'd been right so far as it went. He'd learned a few things. Now, he'd have to see if they'd be sufficient, and if his intuition too would tell him the rest of what he needed to know. He returned to the house he'd built with his hands fifty years earlier. There he sat in his old chair and called.

"Dana?"

"Yes, Granddaddy?"

"I want you to bring me a few things." He listed them and her eyes widened.

"Granddaddy, you aren't…?"

"No questions. Just git what I say an' tell the family to

move everything out from the house. Git the livestock away, an' anything else they can save. They're to stand back too."

He picked up his banjo and strummed idly. Dana recognized the tune, an old one that her grandmother had liked and often Jed's eyes had twinkled wickedly at his wife when he played the song.

It was all done a day later. The barns and corrals were empty. Every single piece of fruit that was close to ripe had been picked, the vegetables that were edible had been taken, and within the house, the only items of furniture remaining were in the old kitchen where Jed liked to sit. The rest of the family had gone ahead in two groups with the livestock and possessions. No one had realized that Dana was with neither.

From where she stood in the parlor behind the long curtains, Dana heard her grandfather as her aunt tried a final time to persuade him to leave with them.

"You'll die. You can't beat this blight. Better to run and live another day."

The banjo strings sounded that tune again and Dana whispered the words she knew so well. *"Before you start to running, you just fetch me down my gun, I was never much for fighting, but I'll die before I'll run."*

The aunt knew when she was beaten. Her footsteps sounded clearly as she left, muttering something about obstinate old fools.

Jed chuckled after her. "I'm an old man, if you lose my labor you don't lose much, just another mouth to feed. But I've seen things, been places, an' this here's mine, I make my stand here, and let what comes beware."

Dana waited. An hour ticked by, and another, and another. Jed's chair creaked softly as he rocked. Dana watched out from behind the lace curtain, saw the blight closing around the house, and somewhere about midday she knew that they were surrounded and there was no going back. Her Granddaddy's voice came to her then.

"Dana? Git me my gun, child."

She walked out of the parlor, strode across the kitchen and lifted down the old long gun that had pride of place over the kitchen mantle-piece. Wordlessly she loaded it with silver-dipped buckshot and salt, then handed it to Jed.

He said nothing, accepting it and laying it across his lap. In return, he picked up the flask of water that stood beside him, drank deeply, and handed it to Dana.

"Drink, girl, then lay out the salt."

He was so calm. "You knew I stayed?"

"I knew. Knew I couldn't change your mind an' don't have the time to try. Wouldn't ask anyone to drag you away. Live or die you'd never forgive me. Us two now, girl. Lay out the salt, git your stool and bide by me."

The girl reached down the bag of salt and laid it out carefully, a wide circle about their seats, then a second further out so that the whole room was double-ringed in an unbroken line of salt.

"Now the nails." He hauled out a box from behind his chair and pushed them across the floor to where she sat within the salt circle.

She laid them out as instructed – single unbroken circle just within the larger circle. They still had ample room within that to move about. There was food and drink within the protections. The fire burned, wood was stacked beside the hearth, and the banjo Jed treasured was by his chair. Dana moved the wooden three-legged stool, and looked at her grandfather as he sat in the ancient chair, long gun across his lap, her hand went out to the banjo and she plucked the strings singing softly. *"They've all gone and left us, I've given you the gun, I will stand beside you now, an' we'll die before we'll run."*

"Got no choice, child, blight's all around, be no running for us this day," Jed said, his face creasing in a wide half-resigned grin. "I allus thought the man that wrote that song might a' been in the same position. Well, guess we'll find out." His head turned sharply to look at the doorway. "Brace yourself. Here it comes."

The brown tide crawled slowly up the steps and through the doorway…

* * *

For those who had waited on the small hill outside and away from the blight's line of approach to see what became of their father and grandfather, nothing seemed to happen. There were no sounds, no cries, nothing to be heard. But after a time, they saw that the blight was withdrawing, not just from the house, but within itself, smaller and smaller, until it was a man-sized circle on the dead grass. It writhed, humped up into strange shapes, gave off what looked like wisps of smoke, and, condensed again until – abruptly – it was gone.

They returned very cautiously, but it was so. Jed rode out with Dana the next day and where they went or what they did was unknown. The blight never returned and old Jed refused to speak of it… or what else they had done. Dana too said nothing save that her grandfather had told her to be silent. And silent she was for all of a very long life, during which she wed, bore two sons, and inherited the family farm when Jed died. Her family prospered, spreading out, owning large ranches, with some running for office. The story of how Jed saved the farm from something evil was told and retold, a favorite story at family gatherings.

And in all that time children often wondered exactly what it was that old Jed and Grandma Dana had done to drive away the thing. They wondered too what it had been. It was her several times great-grandson who inherited a certain box that had belonged to her – a small locked box, made from camphor wood, and tin-lined. In it was a small deerskin sack containing an odd silvery dust, a sealed envelope, and a note to the one who inherited when certain conditions had been fulfilled. Tim poked at that with a forefinger. Probably the note or sealed letter would explain it. He picked up the note.

> *"My Dear Descendant,*
>
> *You'll have heard the family story of how Jed destroyed the blight that would have ruined us. You know that I always refused to speak of it and for that there was a reason. But being who and what you are, it's time that you heard the truth. I have, therefore, written the story, and left it with my lawyers to be given to one of my descendants when the time was right. My legatee had to be one who went*

*out beyond our own solar system, a star-farer who
explored and searched for other life. That you hold
my letter in your hand says that you are the one for
whom it waited. Go now, and do what is required
of you, and may the rest of your life be long and
joyous.*

Dana Wilcox Spencer.

Wondering what he'd find, Tim Wilcox opened the envelope. In spidery handwriting, in pale ink, it said only, "To a Wilcox." He grinned, a wicked smile that would have been familiar
to Dana had she been there to recognize it. Slowly, carefully,
he spread out the pages, peering at the faded writing. It started
the same way as the note.

My Dear Descendant,

*Only Jed and I knew what the blight was and
how and why it died, and we believed that it would
not be well that others should know as yet. Initially
my grandfather thought that the blight was something sent by the devil, and towards that we made
preparations. When it came, we had circles of salt
and iron to protect us. Jed believed that its touch
was poison, and if we could keep it from us then we
should survive and might drive it back somehow once
we could learn of it.*

*The salt was poison to the thing, and therefore
it halted and tried to attack us in a different way.
Into our minds it sent pictures, pain, and fear, so
that we were hard put to hold against the sending.
My grandfather was a strong man, he fought rarely
but when he did, he would take hold and never loosen
that grip so long as he lived. I stood with him and we
fought as one, and with that which was the two of us,
we somehow knew the blight so that it spoke and we
understood.*

*There had been a family, strange to our eyes,
different as anything could be from what we are, but
still people and kin to each other. There was an ac-*

cident and they came here. They died, unable to live in our air, or water, poisoned by the plants on which we live, on the salt in many things. One lived a little longer than the others, striving to survive, hoping to let their kin know what had become of them. Not a blight, but a terrified alien child doing what it must to survive and unaware of what its victims were.

They are both male and female in one and when the survivor touched people – who are not – it believed them still to be lower forms of life and used what life force it could take from them to stay alive. Until it touched us, not in body as it had with others, but in mind alone, and then it understood. We were intelligent beings, people whom it had killed by consuming their life essence, people whom it was leaving to starve and grieve in its wake. As it withdrew from us, we felt its pain and horror at what it had done, its grief for its family and its home, to be seen never again, the childish remorse and a terrible shame.

We reached out in thought then, and held it, offering forgiveness, soothing the weeping and the guilt. If only both sides had known, we might have been friends – although I knew that friendship was unlikely for anyone but my Granddaddy and I who had met the creature mind to mind.

It died willingly as its people can then, so that we might live, since it knew that if it continued it might become mad from the poisons here and thus continue to destroy us while no longer knowing what it did. My dear descendant, it died to atone for its actions, to save us further loss, and its last request was that we tell those who were its kin what happened to its family, where they lie, and if possible, take back to where it was birthed the dust that they had become, to lie in their own ground as is proper. We saw in the last picture it sent, where they lay and we went there, gathered up the dust of its family and brought it back to mingle with what we found on the spot where the blight died.

This task then is for you. Do what you can, for
we promised, and I would not be foresworn. Say that
a willing sacrifice paid for the deaths of our own kind,
and we hold no grudge. Tell them their ancestor died
with honor and courage and it may be that now you
know the story, the child can be remembered.
                                    Dana Wilcox Spencer.

Tim Wilcox, Captain of the First-in Survey Ship *Searcher*
– a member of the second generation of humanity to explore
beyond the solar system, a man who had landed on inhabited
planets and knew the strangeness of other-life – looked into
the deerskin bag, looked at the dust of a family gone astray in
the star lanes, lost and dying on an unfamiliar world. He knew,
from what Dana had written, from which planet they had to
have come, Elrishin-la, whose people were amorphous until
they matured at nine or ten of their years – at which time they
took on both shape and gender.

Yes, he'd go there, take the dust and tell them about a val-
iant little one of their people. He cradled the dust in his hands
and none to see. He wept for the child who had died alone so
that others not of her race or kind might survive. And as he left
the building he resolved that there should be a physical me-
morial to be seen and the story of it told. He smiled to himself.
He'd ask the child's people to place a large stone in some prom-
inent place, and on it he would ask them to engrave the child's
name and age, and below that they should place the words his
many times great-grandmother had added as a postscript.

"Greater Love." There would be no need for more. Those
two words said it all.

FIREDANCER

"**W**itch, witch! Firebringer!"
 The yells came first, then the stone. The girl dodged but the second struck hard. She'd come down from the mountains to trade the last of her father's furs for flour, salt, and perhaps a little tea or coffee. Another stone flew past and she hurried her steps. She reached the trading post, made her trade and threw the sack over her shoulder, slipping away by the back door.

"Witch, yah! Witch!"

They'd found her again. A stone grazed her cheek bringing blood. The girl had a sudden savage impulse to turn on them. She fought her anger but the spark burned. She was no different to them. The Olsens could make the crops grow. Everyone admired the way their corn and other crops were always better than anyone's. The dark-eyed Branlys made music to entrance. No one called *them* witches and threw stones.

But she … Her name was Tanda Summer and at this time and place she was just fourteen. She moved with a light swirling grace, and her fine-boned face was attractive with high cheekbones and storm-gray eyes. She was an odd mixture of races. Her mother had been Basque, that different secretive people whose origins even now, are uncertain.

Her father had called himself Martin Summer in jest. Western men sometimes asked if a name was a man's 'Summer' or 'Winter' name, indicating the possibility he'd changed it as he came West. Martin Summer *had* done so and taken the new name half-joking. Once he'd carried another but it told his homeland too clearly to those who knew. that was a place of rock isles and strange stories. The men from there were looked at sideways by the people of mainland Britain. Martin would rather it didn't happen here.

He'd wed an orphan girl and took her West with him to
live in the mountains, away from other settlers and the hot-
ter more settled lowlands. She was woods-crafty, knowing the
mountains and they were happy. The Comanche came rarely
and the Apache passed through but traded with a man who
knew both tongues and traded honestly. At least, it was so for
Martin Summer.

Tanda was born in solitude and trained to the ways of survival. Her mother had talked to her, taught her daughter to
read and write, told her the maxims of her people and their
stories, their beliefs. Her father had told her his and added his
own knowledge of the ways of the animals here; of hunting,
trapping, and their associated arts. Her mother had died of a
fever when Tanda was twelve and the girl still missed her. Her
father had died almost a year ago. He'd been ill too. A fever
caught from heaven only knows where. Ignored until it struck
so hard even her casual father must take to his bed.

He'd been asleep when Enright turned up. Tanda had gone
out to welcome the old prospector. Hearing her voice talking to
someone Martin Summer had tried to rise. He'd fallen back in a
faint but the jolt of his movements had knocked the lamp from
his bedside. It broke, flaming oil running across the old wood.
By the time Tanda and Enright realized the cabin was on fire,
the inside was already an inferno. Tanda had not hesitated,
she'd run into the roaring flames, dragging Martin from his bed
and out into the open. Then she'd tended him as much of what
they'd owned was reduced to ashes.

Enright had gaped as she emerged from the fire. Why, she
wasn't even scorched. Martin had needed hot food, a fire and
without thinking, Tanda reached for a length of flaming wood.
Her fingers closed over the burning portion but she was too
worried over her father to take notice. Nor did she see the old
man shy back from her, his eyes widening. She cared for her father all that night. He died with the sunrise and Enright helped
her dig the grave. His subsequent farewells were brief and un-
easy. When next she came down the mountains to trade alone,
she found the fruits of his chatter.

Tanda sighed bitterly. It hadn't helped that it had been
a long, hot, very dry summer after that. The prairie fires had

come more often from the heat lightning. Two farms had been burned out, their inhabitants escaping with no more than their wagon and horses and what they could carry. They'd remembered old Enright's talk and from that, the thing had spread. Most of the adults probably no more than half-believed it for the excitement. But their children made her rare visits down the mountains a misery.

She paused in the steep ascent to look back. Heat lightning danced on the plains. She reached the cave near the ruins of the cabin and dropped her sack. Her horse nickered to her and Tanda smiled. She entered her cave, laying away the various goods she brought back. At least she now had ammunition for her father's guns. Tanda prepared food and ate as she considered. She could go back to the lowlands permanently and find work as a servant, or a waitress. She could stay here and hunt as her father had done. There were no relatives to whom she could turn. Anywhere she went she would be alone.

She finished her food, banked the fire and slept – to be awakened by the clatter of hooves. Tanda came awake swiftly, sliding to the mouth of her cave, the primed and loaded gun ready in one hand. Enright's powerful black mule appeared, the old man urging her on. The mule stopped by the cave and Enright leaned over, his eyes guilty.

"I'm right sorry, girl. 'S all my fault. I'm an old fool who talks too much and I sure done it this time. Thet was the Olsen kid cut your face with a stone yesterday, wasn't it. Well, las' night lightning set their cabin afire. They all got out but the kid. He burned. They're coming fer you, girl. They'll bury the kid an' then they'll be a'comin' to burn you the way Joey Olsen burned. I'm sorry, girl, it's all my fault so I come to warn you."

Tanda thought quickly. Yes, they'd wait to bury the boy then they'd have a few drinks. By that time, it would be dark. They'd wait for daylight, but then they'd ride. If she left in the next hour or two, she'd have a good start. Already the Comanche were beginning to attack the farmers. In turn, the settlers stayed away from the inner tribal lands. If Tanda followed the mountain trails around back of the lower land, she'd end up behind Comanche territory where the settlers would hesitate to follow. If she could make them lose the trail before then they wouldn't even be sure where she'd gone. She was packing her gear even as her mind leapt from plan to plan. Enright sat his mule watching.

"I sure am sorry, girl. It was jest a tale fer the evenings. I didn't mean you no harm. Yer pa was allus a good friend to me."

Tanda nodded. "I know. There's some things I can't take. Why don't you pack them on the mule. It'd be a shame to see them wasted." She glanced at him, "An' I noticed Daisy's chipped a hoof. Let me clean that up while you pack. Just to show you there's no hard feelings."

She dug out the rasp and set to work while the old man scuttled about collecting her discards. Tanda hid a dangerous smile. None of that stupid bunch down there were hunters. Her hands worked busily first on one hoof, then on the others. Enright would have noticed but he was too busy scavenging. When she was done, she turned to helping the old man load the patient mule. She waved him away down the trail.

"I don't blame you for anything, but you'd best take the old trail along the ridge an' around. The ones who's coming might get nasty if they think you warned me."

He nodded and rode off, the scavenged gear clanking slightly as he went. Tanda looked after him. Like hell she didn't blame him. Her father had been Enright's friend. Martin had done the old drunkard many favors over the years and her mother had fed him often. As a return for food and kindness, he'd talked about Tanda until the settlers thought her the devil's own daughter. Now she'd be driven out of the only home she'd known just because the idiot liked to gossip.

She smiled again. He hadn't seen what she was doing to Daisy's feet. But with file and rasp she'd given them the look of shod hooves. It wouldn't last, just a day or so's riding, but the mule was heavily loaded and a large animal. Tanda would brush over the trail she and Buck made when they left. With good fortune the lynch party would follow Daisy and Enright. She'd sent him the long way home but it could easily be taken for an attempt to reach the road North. If the mob caught up with Enright, they'd likely hang him in frustration at losing her. Too bad!

She looked about the cave. Everything she could use was loaded on her mount. Tanda nodded to herself as she walked off leading the dun. Once she had him well away, she returned to cover their tracks. Back with him again, she continued to walk. She had time. The fresher he was the better he'd travel later if she needed to ride hard. She never did have that need. As she rode down the faint trail around the back of the plains a day later, old Enright was just dying. The lynch party had followed his trail in error, seen his scavenged gifts once they caught up. They hung him in a rage at being tricked and in the belief he'd done so deliberately. After that, they returned muttering to their homes.

Tanda plodded on. For the next year, she lived solitary, trapping and hunting until her more civilized supplies ran out. She sometimes saw riders but avoided them all. Finally, she was so hungered for salt, sugar, and a good cup of strong tea that she ventured down from her hideout. On Buck, she carried a small bundle of skins, all of them cured and tanned superbly. To the South there was a trading post. If she could make it there safely, make her trade, she would have supplies for a year maybe two if she was very frugal. She made it to the post without difficulty.

But the sight of a girl with skins of that quality, and the amount she was paid for them set men noticing. Two followed. Dregs from some city fetched up out West and she lost them easily enough but it made her twitchy. After that, she hid from humanity like one of the beasts she hunted. A year passed, and another. She must ride to the post again. By now, Tanda was almost eighteen. Her gift had matured and been refined in the long years of solitude.

She could call fire to burn sticks no matter how wet the wood. She could walk casually through the blaze of a grass fire unharmed. She'd found that did not apply to her clothing although worked deerskins burned less readily. And she could work the lightning. She'd found that the second year of her exile. A storm had brewed and lightning had begun to strike about her camp. Somehow, she found she was able to tell where each blow would fall. She saw then where the next would land and without thinking – she acted. Pulled aside from her horse, the lightning struck further away as Tanda stared at her achievement, sitting down abruptly.

All that summer she worked at training her new and older abilities. It was something to do, and it made her feel safe. The next trip to the far trading post was uneventful. In her buckskins and with her hair hidden Tanda looked no more than another young lad. The Comanche were out and no man was interested in some unknown boy. Only the storekeeper might have said different and he was a taciturn man who said little at any time.

But in the moonlit night after her return to her temporary home other things moved. The Comanche were shifting camp and in the high hills, a storm brewed. An end-of-summer storm, which would strike with a savagery peculiar to that season. It struck mid-morning while all were abroad. In the new Comanche camp, the adults were busy allowing the children to wander. Some had left for a patch of berry bushes below a bluff and unknowing of the camp's shift, Tanda rode quietly down a narrow trail above. It wound along a bluff and up into the high country where she would be safe once more.

The storm came swiftly and in silence. But she had seen and there was cover – a good deep cave which would take both she and her mount. She led Buck in and unsaddled him. He was too sensible to leave and stood three-legged, half-asleep as they waited. The storm struck in a bolt of lightning, which crashed into bushes below the cave. It had been a long dry summer. The impact was answered with a wall of flame. In seconds the outer circle of bushes was alight and the fire spreading. From behind the flames came screams of childish terror.

The wind blew lightly away from Tanda so that at first she heard nothing. Not so the Comanche. A mother was already searching for her daughter. She came running. Minutes after that many of the camp had come in answer to her cries but there was little they could do. The fire roared hungrily, catching hold of other dry brush – and behind that wall of fire three children cowered and shrieked for aid. It was the commotion that finally caught Tanda's ears. She crawled from the cave to look cautiously over the edge of the bluff. The brush had lit in a circle and as she watched the center space that had still been clear narrowed further in a new gout of flame.

The children crowded together too terrified to scream now, their faces lifted to the sky. She could hear the oldest boy raise a quavering chant as he stood, arms around a girl and a smaller boy. Tanda had heard that chant once. The child sang their death song as befitted a warrior. She looked at them then. The oldest no more than ten, the girl perhaps two years younger, the smallest boy only a toddler. The two oldest had pushed him between them, shielding him from flying sparks with their own bodies. But in a few minutes the fires would close in. Nothing would shield him then, nor those who tried to do so. The chant rose up, firming as the boy drew strength from it.

Above them, Tanda looked down on three children who would die a terrible death. She saw how, in the circle outside the fire, women wept. One tried to run into the flames, others held her back. Drawn as if by destiny Tanda stood. Slowly she walked down the steep slope. The fire raged but it obeyed when she reached it, parting to let her through. Beyond the fires, the Comanche fell silent, watching. From their medicine man, there came a soft whisper.

"Fire Dancer!"

Tanda stepped into the tiny space still left clear of the flames. The children ran to her as she reached out her hands.

"Come with me," she said softly in their tongue. "Keep close. Hold your heads down as near to me as you can." She gathered them in. As she turned, a puff of wind came. With a rush, the fire closed in on the tiny group. "Take a deep breath and hold it," Tanda ordered.

They obeyed as she marched forward. The heat was stifling, the air sucked away by the fire but safety was no more than ten steps away. Their clothing wisped into ash but the children's contact with Tanda held back the flames from their bodies. They walked from the fire unhurt still clutching at her waist and arms with all their strength. Mothers swooped, crying, weeping with joy and fear.

The old medicine man walked forward, his eyes searching the girl's face. With the wisdom both of his age and his power, he read much. His hands waved back any who would have approached.

"Bring the white buffalo-skin robe from my tent for the Fire Dancer. Let her come to us in honor. Let food be prepared that we may feast her." He took Tanda's hand. "Those of your blood are dead and you walk alone. Walk a little way with us. Ahead your path forks. Learn your choices that you may make them truly."

Drawn by the kindness in his voice and eyes she followed. A medicine robe was placed about her shoulders. Later she sat by a campfire and ate with her new friends. And somehow, without any definite decision made, she stayed. From Talks to Mountains she learned of her gift. It was not unknown to the Nemunuu, the People. Once, many generations ago, a medicine woman had the gift and the people had lived well and in greater safety because of it.

"There is an entrance to the land of the Gone-Before Ones," Talks to Mountains told her late one night. "It is empty and wide. All of the animals we have dwell there, all but the horse. Long ago, she who was Fire Dancer before you could open a path for us to that land. In bad winters, we sometimes stayed there for moons until the time of hunger was over because there the seasons are the opposite to those here. Yet always we returned. Our hearts cried for this land."

"How did she open the gate?"

"With the lightning. For a Fire Dancer who can call the lightning there is great power within that strike."

Tanda studied him. "I can't call it."

"Not yet. To learn takes many years, but I can teach, Fire Dancer." His hand came out to grip her arm, "If you will learn?"

Tanda sat in silence, Talks With Mountains letting her be to think. She remembered the hatred of the settlers. She was different, her gift a threat. She'd done nothing, never tried to hurt them. Just being different had been enough. They'd come riding in the end to murder her for being born with a gift they didn't have, had never seen before. In a daughter of two races, abilities had melded, shifted to something new to her lines. The Comanche had accepted her. To them the gift was a known thing and valuable to the people. Expressions passed over her face – grief, anger, joy – then slowly her face settled into lines of decision. She stirred, as her eyes met those of her teacher.

"I will learn all you will teach me. My people cast me out for my gift. Yours have taken me into their tents. Your people shall be mine from now on. When do I begin to learn?"

Talks With Mountains smiled. "Tomorrow, after you have rested. Yet it will not be I who teaches you always. I can show you the path, tell you of the signs by which you travel. You alone can walk that road, Fire Dancer. Yet I believe you will walk it well. Go now and sleep."

She went to her blankets but it was some time before she slept. Had she made the right decision? She slept then and with the morning came a cleared mind. This was her right choice, her true path.

The years passed as she walked the paths of learning. She learned to light the wettest stack of wood with a flick of her mind. Those first winters the people valued her greatly for that ability alone. Later she learned to divert all of the lightning in a storm away as if she held an umbrella over the camp. That saved the lives of many when in her tenth year in the camp, a storm struck at the area in which they cowered. Fifteen years after her arrival she mastered the last teachings. Lightning came at her call, and she could control the strikes, directing them as she wished.

But outside her clan, time had not stood still. The white man had swarmed into Comanche lands in their hundreds at first, then in their thousands. The Comanche killed until the grass ran red but still the settlers came, and there were always fewer of the people with each winter. Talks With Mountains had foreseen much. He and the chief had drawn their people back, far into the mountains. They were a small clan within the larger Nemunuu. Only twenty families and they could ill afford to lose lives.

Now, from the mountains, the warriors rode out to fight, but those who did not fight remained safe. Yet already settlers were moving towards the higher lands. Talks With Mountains waited. His dreams had spoken. At last, his adopted daughter mastered the final facets of her gift. After the first spring storm, she came to him laughing in pride.

"Did you see? I did it. I called the lightning. Then I made it strike at the cliff there."

"You did indeed, Fire Dancer. Now there is one more thing to learn. One more thing you must be able to do."

Tanda smiled. "I know. Open the road of the Gone Before Ones. Will it be a hard thing to learn?"

He shook his head. "No, but you must be further trained as a warrior. You command your mind, your gift. You must learn now to command your body past exhaustion. It must obey you though it die in the doing of your will. It will take all spring and much of the summer for this teaching."

"I will learn it," Tanda said quietly. "Then in the fall I will open the road for our people."

"It is well, daughter in power."

And it was. Tanda endured and learned. She grew lean and hard, and still she worked with her gift until it answered even as she thought. The children she had saved were adults. The men brought meat to her tent. The woman brought worked deerskins as gifts. Tanda lived alone but her tent was always pitched beside that of Talks With Mountains. As he aged, she took over more and more of his duties for the tribe. By the end of that summer, she was ready.

"There is a special place. We must go there taking certain things." He lifted a doeskin pack. "I have all we shall need, Fire Dancer. Are you ready?"

She nodded. They rode away, the people watching in prayerful silence. A day later they returned, Tanda drooping on her mount's back, in her exhaustion only half-aware that they were home again. She was helped down, fed, cared for and laid on her blankets to sleep. Beside her Talks With Mountains sat chanting softly. Triumph! The road had opened to the Fire Dancer's demand. Better still, she had not only lived, she was simply exhausted. In two or three days once she regained her strength, she could open the road again if she wished.

In a week, they left for the medicine place a second time and this time Tanda was able to open the road and walk away on her own feet. Both started their return rejoicing. They reached the camp to find it in turmoil.

"What is this?" Talks With Mountains' voice was suddenly fearful. Had his dreams come true so soon?

It was the chief who answered, his tones sad. "Word has

come from others of the People. The white men gather in great numbers with guns to attack us. If we go north or south the Apache will drive us back. Those lands are theirs. If we go deeper into the wild lands there is less food, the hunting is poorer. Where shall we go? What shall we do? Our tribe is less with each spring. Must we be as the snows that vanish with summer?"

Talks With Mountains waited. Beside him, Tanda stirred, then she walked forward to turn and look at her people. "I came to you as a stranger and you gave me honor. My own kind cast me out. Now they will move against you as they would have killed me – because I am different. Talks With Mountains taught me to cherish that difference and to use it. I had one last lesson to learn. It is learned. Listen to my father in heart."

The old man's voice was clear as he gave orders. The people ran to obey. Young boys fanned out on fast ponies to watch the trails. Women packed. Warriors gathered the horse herd. Overhead a great storm threatened. To the south, there was another where men rode, carrying guns to a killing. One by one, the scouts returned with word. The camp packed. Two days and a night. The men who hunted were almost to the camp. The chief mounted, signaled and rode out as the people followed in grieving silence, wrapped in the chill winds of fall. They were leaving their land forever, yet it was better to leave than to die, and for their children's children, the new land would be their heart.

Ahead in the medicine place, Tanda waited with her father in Power. About him, he wore a long woolen blanket so that only his head and hands showed. When all were assembled, she walked towards the rocks. Before them was a small grassy clearing. Tanda faced the clearing and opened her gift. Above her the storm came, bellowing its fury. In the abandoned camp, a day's ride away men sought angrily for the trail. The storm howled power. Tanda lifted her hands and the lightning came, flaming about her, striking closer and closer as she seized it with her gift. She lifted her head, her fingers thrust out, hands spread, calling with all she was.

The storm rose to madness and then – as the lightning flared to crash down into the clearing – there was a flowing, a warping of the air, as a road opened into a land that was soft with a coming spring. The chief swung onto his pony and led the people forward. Last came Tanda but Talks With Mountains waited still within the clearing. She turned.

"Come quickly, the door will close."

His smile was quietly accepting. "I cannot, daughter in power. For so many to cross when none plan to return, there must be a price. Power gathers against you. When the road shuts, it will strike. But if I remain here it is I who will die. The people will be free in their land and you shall walk with them."

Tanda stared, tears welling in her eyes. "NO!"

"Yes." He was adamant. "For all great power there is a payment to be made. I make it willingly. I am old and tired and my gifts fail me. You are young and those you have chosen as your people will need you in the days to come. The Great Spirit ride with you, Fire Dancer. Let the road close."

She looked into his spirit as he had taught her. It was true, all of it. She did not see what he still withheld. Long ago in the medicine dreams of his youth, he had seen the way this would be. He had seen the danger, the destruction of his people. He had seen the one who would come. If she were made welcome, trained in power, taught to love the people then she would be their gate to freedom. At first that was all she had been to him despite his kindness. But over time he had come to care. Once he had planned to let her die when the road shut. Now he had chosen again, knowing in his heart that it was right.

Into his last words, he put the dregs of his waning power. "Fire Dancer. You are Fire Dancer of the Nemunuu. Go into the land and make it your own."

Tanda bowed her head. Slowly she drew her mount backwards from the clearing. Step by step as she cleared the door she had created. Talks With Mountains took a rolled blanket from his pony, sending the mare after the others with a quick slap. He laid the soft length of wool out on the ground, stripped the other blanket from about his body as Tanda gasped. Beneath the wool, he wore the sacred white buffalo-skin clothing. Swiftly he bound eagle feathers about his head, placed bracelets and necklaces of rattlesnake rattles on neck, wrists and ankles. Then he lay down and began the death chant.

Behind Tanda the tribe was moving away. This was medicine business. She remained waiting, watching. Her skin crawled as power rose again. The chant was done. Across the clearing gray eyes met black ones in love and farewell. Lightning lit the clearing again and again to blue-white fury and – the road closed. Fire Dancer, medicine woman of the Comanche clan, claimed now and forever as her own, sat a moment before she turned to follow her people. Later those who hunted them came to the clearing. They found nothing there, only fire-scarred rocks and a drift of black ash whirling lightly on the chill wind.

THROUGH A
GLASS DARKLY

I am the fourth generation to live on the Graeme Ranch
on the outskirts of Bodie. Before that, it belonged to my
grandmother's father, who took the land by force in the
year 1865. He said the old man that lived there had fired upon
him without cause or warning, and for that, he shot him dead
and claimed the land which was not even legally homesteaded.
He was a hard man, but a fair judge of animals and he married
a woman who was better, as well as beautiful and wise, but also
frail, so that when he swept her into marriage, that lasted only
until she had born him a daughter, after which she lived five
years with no further child save two stillbirths, and died.

This story is not mine then, but hers, the small bereft daughter whom her mother had named Teleri from her mother's mother's home in Wales. Named Teli for short, she grew up without
much attention, disregarded by her father who blamed her that
his wife had died, and left him with a daughter of no use to a
man that had wanted a son. However, at that time a clerk had
been hired, a man from the east who missed his own wife and
children, assuaging that loss by continuing Teli's teaching so
that when he returned home two years later, she could read and
write well, which was good, since there was no teacher within a
day's ride. So in another three years Teli came to the age of ten –
and a month after that birthday everything changed.

Teli was up in the loft of the barn that had been the only
building on the place when her father took the land from the
old man who had been on the wrong side of the war. She
came there often to be away from her father and his men who
sneered at her for being a worthless girl and it was on that
bright day in May, when the new-captured horses and some

152

others her father had purchased were run into the corral, that she was at the back of the loft, the sunlight striking deep into the interior so, standing at that precise angle for the first time in all her forays there, she saw something high on a beam.

She reached it down, opened the worked leather case and stared at the contents. A pair of spectacles. Black tarnished wire rims, lenses of some sort of glass, and a long leather thong made to keep them safe about the wearer's neck. Teli grinned, and with the impulse of any child, she placed the thong about her neck, the spectacles on her nose and peered out at the milling horses. Then her breath caught. She'd seen the herd brought in. There was nothing there of anything but small value, but now as she leaned forward, studying each animal as it circled restlessly, she could see she had been wrong.

Amongst the dozen there was one that stood out, only a yearling, but she could see what the filly would be, and looking down at those men about the corral, as if something whispered in her ear, she knew too that the filly would die at their hands. Teli didn't think. She acted. Swinging down from the loft and racing across the dusty ground until she reached her father. He'd made her a promise last birthday, casually made, never really intended, now he should keep it, or stand foresworn before his men.

She took a deep breath as she reached out to touch his wrist, speaking clearly, so that all should hear. "Father, last birthday you said I might choose a pony for myself. I've chosen." She pointed at the filly. "I want that one."

Then she looked again at her choice and her heart fell. The filly was weedy and undersized, spindly legged, her coat a dingy shade that showed no particular color but which might have been a washed-out chestnut – had the filly been clean and her tufts of winter hair groomed out.

Michael Graeme snorted. "That! It isn't worth the dollar I paid."

At his side, unseen by him or anyone, Teli raised the spectacles to her face and looked again before dropping them down the front of her gingham dress. "You promised, father. You said I could have any horse I chose. It won't be any trouble. She will be a good horse, and I can break her myself."

One of the men laughed and said something she couldn't hear and her father scowled. "You don't have much of an eye for a beast, but," his smile was almost unpleasant. "If you're set on it, she's yours. You'll break her, handle her, train her, it's all on you."

"Yes, father."

He shouted an instruction and the filly was cut out, roped and dragged to the nearest stall in the barn, and there she was left, Teli understanding this was a lesson to her. She'd made a demand, embarrassed her father, now she was to pay.

And she did pay. She found buckets, fed and watered her new acquisition. It took time until the filly stopped panicking when the child approached. It took more time before the small halter she found could be placed on the wild-eyed head. It had been a mercy that the nearest stall had been a double stall at the end of the barn. By entering very slowly and quietly, the filly could be persuaded to move over so the stall could be cleaned, and Teli was in less danger from plunging hooves.

Days went by as the filly came to understand she wasn't being hurt, that the small figure brought food and water, that it scratched itches in the shedding coat, that its voice was always soft and gentle. Weeks, in which the filly, now named Sunny, found that while this creature was kind, it could also be firm. Months in which Sunny was slowly introduced to discipline, and more.

Michael Graeme had never thought about it, but his wife, frail or not, had understood horses. Not only that, she read, and had books about them, and Teli, finding the dusty stack dumped in the barn loft had whiled away many hours by reading about different breeds, training methods, and ways of teaching a horse without cruelty. And that was how she taught Sunny. Teli was small and slight for her age, and once the filly was two, Teli backed her, laying over the quivering soft skin, murmuring soft assurances, letting the horse know there was nothing to fear.

Michael Graeme was oblivious to all of it. He was often away from the ranch, buying or selling stock, visiting places in Bodie, and none of his men had any time for a child. Teli knew that, and, preferring her privacy anyhow, she would

take Sunny out from the far side of the barn, behind the building's bulk in a line through the trees behind and down along
a gully there. Well away from the sight of anyone she worked,
taught, and finally rode. She spent hours most days, talking to
her horse, sharing crusts as treats in return for work well-done,
and giving Sunny all the love she had since no one else seemed
to want it.

Then her father came home. It had been almost two years
since Teli had chosen her horse, and now, lounging in his big
armchair he looked over at his daughter as she read silently by
the oil lamp.

"Have you still got that ugly weedy runt you picked?"

"Yes, father."

"Riding it yet?"

"Yes, father."

Her heart pounded, waiting. "Right, then in the morning
after breakfast you bring it out. I want to see how bad it is. If
it's as useless as I thought when I saw it that time, I'll shoot the
damn thing and buy you something really fit for the daughter
of Michael Graeme."

She knew he meant it, and knew too that he wouldn't give
her that splendid other horse for love, but for his pride. And
as she walked to her room her father never saw the small curl
of her mouth. No one on the ranch had seen – or if they had,
they hadn't looked closely – and Teli had kept her mare camou-
flaged anyway. Now she got up early, went to the barn before
breakfast and groomed Sunny for the mare's life, stripping out
the dust and dirt that hid what she was.

She reached the breakfast table just ahead of her father
and was sitting meekly when he entered. He glanced at her.
"You ready?"

"As soon as we've eaten, father."

They ate, Michael Graeme heartily as always, calling for
seconds, and Teli lightly because she was nervous. Not that
Sunny would disgrace her, but that she might disgrace her
horse, or that her father would feel himself slighted and do
as he had threatened despite what he would see. At last, he
drained his coffee mug for the third time, sat back, and nodded.

"I'll be out front by the corral. Bring her there and show

me what she's got."

He may have felt a pang of compunction at his daughter's white face, if so he showed nothing, but strolled out of the door, across the yard and halted, leaning back against the corral rails. One of the men approached.

"Need me to do anything, boss?"

"Stick around. My daughter's going to show us what she's made of that disaster she insisted on having." The man guffawed and stayed. Three others drifted in to remain, all of them amused. It'd be a good show either way.

Michael Graeme called. "Teli, get out here, we're waiting." And unshod hooves sounded, soft on the dust, as child and horse came out of the barn, from darkness into the sunlight, posed for a moment, then moved on.

And by the corral the men fell silent. The horse was a pale bright chestnut, her mane and tail a flow of flaxen hair, in the sun she glimmered, her coat shining, the small hooves placed precisely at each step. Teli spoke softly, and the gait changed to a slow balanced canter, another word, and she was circling at a hard-gallop.

An unseen signal and she slowed, came to a halt, and Teli leaned forward. Quick movements stripped the light bridle from the proud head. Another word and they were away again, racing out across the flat land, to circle back, halt at a short distance, and turn left into a walk, ten paces, and turn to the right into a trot, ten paces and left again in a canter, each movement controlled by voice and the sway of the child's body. Then the halt, and Teli leaned forward, speaking into one backwards listening ear, before the filly reared, poised as was her rider clinging monkeylike to the warm back. Her hooves came to earth again and the filly advanced to halt before her owner's father.

"Her name is Sunny," Teli said, and waited.

For seconds it all hung in the balance, then Michael Graeme heard the soft admiring sounds from his men. "By God she's a true Graeme," he roared, laughing. "I can't believe you made that out of what you took, girl, what did you see in her?"

Wild with relief Teli answered without thinking as she stroked a hand down the filly's shoulder. "This, father. I saw what she could be."

She never saw how his eyes narrowed. His wife had been able to do that, if his daughter could, he'd make this ranch far more than it already was. And so he did. For the next ten years Teli went with him to buy horses, to buy cattle, to wild places filled with wild men, into outlaw country and even into the fringes of Indian land, but Michael Graeme prospered, and, surrounded by his men, no one dared speak to Teli other than very politely. Twice she saved him from disaster, once from a diseased herd, and again from horses that had eaten a deadly weed and would have died before they were got home. And he valued her for that – though little else.

Men came courting but her father sent them away, having found this treasure he had no intention of losing it while it was of use. Teli didn't care. She did care about the spectacles that hung inside her bodice. Whenever she looked, they showed her the truth of what she looked at, and once she was old enough she looked at the men too, and accepted her father's decisions.

She was thirty when he had a stroke. She nursed him devotedly, not because she loved him, but because it was still the eighteen hundreds and if he died, she might lose the ranch. The stroke turned him docile, kinder, but still coherent on most days, and when at last he died in 1914, his death went almost unnoticed. The people had other things to worry about – and the horses the Graeme Ranch produced were fine. The owner even donated a number of them to the government, and when the war was over officials were too weary and too busy to bother with a woman who paid her taxes, lived on an isolated ranch and had a child she'd taken in and Teli knew that so long as she drew no official attention she was safe.

Ceri, as she named the baby, had been born of a woman of the line who was passing through. She couldn't pay for a room, had walked out of town, found a hollow amid trees near a stream, and there, after the too-long walk, she found that she was in labor. Teli had come in time to look at them both through the spectacles, she took the child, leaving the mother to bleed out, and returned the next day to bury the body, after taking valuables and all identification.

To those that asked in later years, she said Ceri was her niece, sent by family back east who could not afford another child. She said it in such a way that they assumed the relatives had hoped the child would inherit, and in time, she did. She in turn when she was old enough to need an heir, found me.

I knew the stories. My grandmother had told Ceri how she had come to her, saying only that her mother had been buried in secret so that Ceri might not be taken away from her. She did *not* tell her that Ceri's mother had been left to die, that was my guessing, but I'm sure of it. I've worn the spectacles now and again and seen what they show. Not only what stock will grow into no matter what it looks like at the time, but other things, and it is my belief that Teli saw my mother's future, that she could use the spectacles too, that if she became a Graeme, the ranch would continue to prosper. It has. And when the time comes, I too will look for a girl whom the spectacles show to be suitable.

And one final thing. After the second war ended, I went looking for some explanation of the spectacles. When Teli found them, they had seemed to be of old glass and wire. Once cleaned she saw that the wire was silver, and very finely wrought. The glass had a tiny bubble here and there, showing that it was old, and it was her belief that they had been left by the old man from whom her father had taken the land and that was what she told Ceri, and Ceri told me.

But I went to school, I knew the glasses were older still, and I read, searched for stories, and I found a possibility. In Italy, two hundred years back, there was a man. They said that he was a saint who could look at any man and knew the truth of who and what he was and would be, and when, in his age he could no longer see well, a man of his town made him spectacles. The saint died, giving his spectacles back to the maker, who in turn gave them for luck to a son who gave them to his grandson when he set sail to come here. That was the man my great-grandfather killed, so they brought him little luck.

I may be wrong. Spectacles, no matter how old, do not come with a pedigree, but it is true that they show what is and can be for a living creature, and because of that the Graeme Ranch covers half a county and I am rich and will be richer yet. I *can* see that. There is only one thing I do not – chose not to – see. Because there is another story I found, that the saint's glasses were not made by a man of his town but by – another. Therefore, when my time comes they will pass to my daughter – whoever she is – and if you are she and reading this, be warned.

To look outward through them is to see clearly, but to look into a mirror is to see through a glass darkly and that could be – unwise.

Morwen Graeme.

CONTACT

It was, she thought, an uncivilized world, barren in places, and the inhabitants seemed to do little but breed, fight, and die. Nonetheless, it was the world she had been allocated. Here she was to land, to live and learn, and in the time listed, she was to produce a thesis that foretold whether, in time, the world would be worth approaching to be a member of the Star Civilization. (Although from what she could see, that day would be far off.)

Someone with a grudge must have arranged this disaster. However, if she wished to gain her qualification she must go, and so she left her cabin, prepared to make her shape-change, and choose the scenario to find a contact. At least she would be impervious to anything this world – or its denizens – could do to her. She hoped for a good contact. Her face twisted in what, on the world below, would be a smile. Impervious, and autonomous, a Grade Five world allowed her to do things she would never have been permitted had they been graded higher, and with that thought she prepared for descent.

* * *

He came around a bend of the long shower-dampened road with his mount reeling under him and pulled the exhausted animal to a halt.

"Whoa, Happy." He stared at the horse that stood in the center of the road, bridled, saddled, but alone. He'd made time on those who followed him. The men who pursued didn't know the mountains as he did. But there were four men behind him and they'd fanned out. They'd pick up his trail again sooner or later and then they'd cut him down.

160

He stepped down and approached the mare and the fallen rider, whispering softly as her ears went back. "Easy girl, I won't hurt him."

He hated what his flight was doing to the game little beast standing head down by the road but he had no choice. Harv Semple had put out the word that the O'Faiolin ranch was his. He'd claimed that before Pat's father had died in an accident that the boy was sure had been faked, that Michael O'Faiolin had bet his ranch and lost it to Harv.

Pat knew better, but Harv was a big man in the area since he'd arrived six years ago and he was the one people listened to. Pat O'Faiolin was seventeen, gun-handy, and still raw from his father's death. They caught him out in the open and told him to leave now. He'd lit a shuck all right, leaving two of Harv's men dead on the green grass, and two more packing lead. They'd lost his trail twice but they were still coming and without a rested horse, he had no hope of escaping.

"Whoa, girl. Yes, it's all right." He stepped a final pace towards the mare and she dropped her nose to him cautiously. "Yes, good girl."

She seemed to be considering him and he looked back. She wasn't a big animal, maybe fifteen hands, wearing an old, but well-cared-for saddle and a bitless bridle, a dark bay with good clean lines that told of speed, but the powerful muscles and deep chest also said 'endurance.'

Pat O'Faiolin waited, talking softly to the mare as she moved slowly closer. The drifting rain had stopped and a rainbow stood in the sky by the time she appeared to have fully accepted him. Finally, he lifted cupped hands as she dropped her nose into them and inhaled his scent. She seemed to sigh and relax. He stood a moment scratching along under her mane and talking to her while he thought. His own mount was exhausted but would recover if he were left here. He stepped over to the pony and unsaddled him, unbuckled the bridle and cached both items while transferring his rifle to the mare's saddle.

"You get gone, boy, don't let them catch you and I'll be back."

With a fresh horse, Pat could circle, elude his pursuers, and return to his cabin to pick up supplies. After that, he'd make a fight of it from the mountains behind his land. His father had built that cabin, the land was deeded in the O'Faiolin name and he wasn't of a mind to give it up. He'd been speaking aloud as he thought and now the mare nudged him, ears coming up alertly. He looked up to see a line of riders tiny in the distance as they dropped down from the last stretch of the mountain trail he'd used.

"Damn. Looks as if they're still coming an' I better go, okay, girl?" He took up the reins, swung lightly into the worn saddle and waited. The mare fiddle footed then moved out along the road. To see what she would do he allowed her free rein and to his surprise she walked to the left, dropped down into the bed of the dry stream and trotted lightly along below bank level.

Pat grinned. He didn't know where she'd come from but someone trained great horses. The mare had seen the riders first, now she was seeing that they weren't sky-lined. She seemed tireless too, he thought some hours later. She moved along easily, not straining as she climbed the trail, not sweating, just walking, trotting where she could, and always surefooted, hour after hour.

He made camp at last, deep into the mountains above his cabin. If he could just get down there to the cache where his father had hidden their papers. His smile was grim. Harv hadn't known one thing when he sent men to drive out a boy from his inheritance. It was why Pat had known their tale of his father's gambling away of their land to be untrue.

His mother had died when Pat was five and he had little memory of her save for two things. One was the photo in the locket that had been his great-grandmother's, and which hung on a leather thong about his neck. The other was the deed to the O'Faiolin home ranch. His father had staked and claimed that in his wife's name and her will bequeathed the land to Pat. Both papers were in the cache.

His father had good friends too. Pat had made his own will and hidden it, leaving the ranch to his uncle. If he lived and could get the papers to kin and friends, they'd see that whatever happened Harv couldn't claim that land. Pat grinned as he laid branches out in the small cave where he'd chosen to make camp. That'd be something for old Harv. Even if Pat were murdered like his father, Harv wouldn't be able to take over the O'Faiolin land.

He slept and in the morning he rode on again, winding his way along narrow mountain trails, some so dim that only one who'd ridden them all his life could have followed the path. He'd long since shaken off his pursuers but he knew that wasn't the end of it. He had to get the papers and get out, get to where he could send telegrams to his father's friends so that they'd know what was happening. His mother's family too should know.

He'd seen little of them since she died, but he remembered his uncle, her brother, who'd come to her funeral and later stopped over a couple of nights when Pat was twelve. Yarnell Duwarne was a slender black-eyed man with the gun-speed of a striking snake, and cold eyes. They'd warmed as he talked of his little sister though, and Pat thought he'd help. Last he'd heard of Yarnell he'd been down in Texas and it was there Pat had sent the telegram telling of his father's death and saying that he was worried about Harv Semple's claims. That'd been several months ago but likely the letter had to follow and it might be months more before Yarnell showed up if he was even still alive. It'd been near two years since they'd had word.

He'd ridden to Bodie to send the telegrams too. The people in Elmwood, the nearest town to O'Faiolin land, listened too well to Harv for Pat's liking and he believed that whatever he said would be known. But while he was sending word he'd written several of the flimsy forms, the others had gone to friends of his father's who should hear and know. His father had been a wild man in his younger days and not all of his friends had been upstanding citizens. But they'd been good friends.

Pat cantered down a last section of the trail and halted at the edge of a cliff. From up here he could see his cabin and much of the lands the O'Faiolin's had claimed. There was smoke rising from the cabin chimney and he scowled. Harv hadn't wasted time putting someone in there, likely more than one, and primed to make sure that the rightful owner didn't come back. Or if he did, that he stayed there, planted in the tiny cemetery back amongst the trees.

The mare moved restlessly and he laughed as he patted her sleek neck. "All right, Rosita, in a minute." The mare was a worker, always keen to be on the move and smart. There were times when Pat was surprised at her intelligence. He'd managed to retrieve his pony and gear once he'd evaded the hunters so that with two mounts he was almost safe from a straight pursuit. An ambush could still take him.

Leaving Happy, the pony, hobbled near his camp, Pat worked his way down the trail onto his land, watching all the time for signs of life. It was dusk when he reached it and he dismounted leaving Rosy to graze with her reins tied to the saddle while he crept up on the cabin. Inside two men sat at the lamplit table and drank while they talked. He couldn't hear their words but he knew them. Two of Harv Semple's men, they'd been there for some days. The room was a pigsty of unwashed dishes, cigarette ends, and rubbish in corners.

A nose touched his shoulder and he jumped. Rosy was interested in what was going on, it appeared.

"So, girl, what do you think? I guess if we don't make any noise they'll stay where they are and I can get those papers."

Rosy was still watching the men and he left her to it, moving off towards the trees and slipping through the slender trunks. Behind the line of trees was a broken low cliff filled with holes and crevices. Pat went to one, reached in cautiously with a stick and poked. Snakes sometimes picked such places to night over and he had no wish to find himself holding one rather than the small flat tin case that held the ranch's papers. No indignant reptile was evicted and he reached in to take the case.

Three weeks later, he was high in the mountains riding back to the telegraph office. He'd sent word he'd meet his uncle and his father's friends there. There'd been word waiting in return that they'd arrive in another week and Pat O'Faiolin rode back to his beloved mountains. His father had long since taught him patience and he would wait.

He passed the time by working with the mare. She was an unending delight; everything he'd ever wanted in a horse. Unlike many men of his time, he didn't wear spurs nor did he use a whip, his father had always said he'd give nothing for any mount that needed either to give of his best and Pat agreed. For the mare, there was no need anyway, and he'd not insult her.

When the week was past, he rode out, dropping slowly down the trail towards the small dusty township of Bodie. At the hotel, he dismounted, tossed the reins over the hitching rail, lifted his saddlebags free and entered the dim silence.

"Has anyone by the names of Duwarne, Abow, Critten, or Yost booked in here?"

The clerk shook his head. "Not yet, but I had telegrams yesterday. Duwarne's due tomorrow an' Critten's arriving the day after."

Pat looked at the register. There were empty rooms here. He had the coins a cheap single room would cost, and it would be a good idea to have a bath and wash his clothes. He wouldn't want those arriving to think him some idler who lived in his dirt.

"Give me a room," he said, laying his money on the counter. Wordlessly the clerk took it before handing him a key and turning the register towards him.

"Sign it, mister. Room twenny-seven. Top o' the stairs."

Pat signed, hauled his saddlebags into the tiny airless room and left them there, locking the door behind him. There was little enough to make it worth any thief's while anyhow. He took the mare to the livery stable, removed her gear and rubbed her down, saw to it that she had hay and a filled water bucket then turned to the ostler and spoke quietly.

"Give her corn but don't touch her otherwise. She doesn't like strangers an' don't shut the door on her."

The ostler stared. "An' suppose she lights a shuck?"

"She won't, an even if she did, I said it, I'll stand the bill."

The ostler shrugged philosophically. "Your horse, mister."

Pat nodded, and, moving back more quickly to the hotel, he dug out his only change of clean clothes and headed for the bathhouse and laundry.

In the dusk, there were few men to see as five men rode in only an hour apart. The five left their weary horses at the rail and went into the saloon. There they listened for almost two hours, dropping into casual conversation the occasional question before the four of them left quietly to talk by stables while the fifth vanished into the shadows in the direction of the ostler's room.

"No one here knows much."

"Not like Elmwood. There you can't hardly shut them up."

The third grinned. "Yes, useful that."

His friend snorted. "Yeah, but you do have to listen to a heap of shit to hear anything worth hearing."

The quartet behind them headed for the hotel. They came out again looking thoughtful and headed for the bathhouse.

The fifth man joined his friends again and they went silent as they saw his face in the glow of light from the lantern over the stable doorway.

"There's four riders came in right behind us. I know one of them from the ostler's description and he's trouble. They've had nearly a clear hour to do their work."

"There's been no shots?"

"Knives are quieter." The fifth man said softly. "Although the boy will be no pushover. They'll be hunting him an' hoping to keep it quiet. I reckon he's to disappear and that way there's no comeback."

* * *

In the stable, the mare listened. She smelled danger, the scents of death lying in wait, of cold metal and hot rage. Silently she drifted out of the stable and through the doorway. Unseen by any man she followed the trace of her friend in the wind.

In the bathhouse, Pat toweled himself off and dressed. He flipped the gun belt about his hips, took up his rifle and stepped out of the doorway into the street. Hands came out of nowhere and gripped him. A gun-butt slashed down. Pat staggered as a voice hissed at him.

"Make a noise and we'll shoot you where you stand. Come with us, sign over the O'Faiolin ranch and you get to live."

He knew that for a lie but he was giddy from the blow. Let them give him ten minutes to recover and he might make a try at getting free. The soft plop of hooves came then and he lifted his head. The mare wandered around the corner, halted by him and reached out to nuzzle his chest. A gun lifted.

One of his captors spoke quietly. "No. We don't need the noise an' that's some horse. She gets loose and comes to find the boy. You don't hurt her. I'll take her myself once we're done here."

They supported Pat as he staggered, guiding him towards the nearest alley. The mare came too, plodding silently along in the dust of the street, her nose out-stretched to the boy. Once they were within the shadow's shelter Pat halted.

"Where's the pen? I'll sign." They'd have no pen or paper but it might take them off guard if they thought he believed their offer. His head was clearing, and they'd taken his rifle but not his pistol. If only something would distract them, he could make his try. One of the men about him grunted amusement. Pat felt them close in a little.

The mare smelled the decision, the upsurge in the killing scent, and made her own choice. In the dusk, there was a whirl of motion, the sound of someone hitting a melon several times with a blunt ax. A scream, shouting, a shot, another, and then silence.

From the street five men came running, calling. "Pat? Pat? Is that you?"

Yarnell Duwarne slipped into the alley, eyes searching for an enemy. "They gone?"

And a youthful voice said, "Guess you could say that. Someone bring a lantern."

Mike Yost brought light and five men stared at the sight while Pat hugged the mare, crooning softly to her. In the lantern light her legs were splashed to hocks and knees in blood, there was blood on her muzzle and her eyes rolled wickedly white. At her feet, tossed aside like unwanted washing lay four dead men.

Critten stared. "What in God's name happened here?"

Pat looked at him. "They took me at the bathhouse door. They said I was to sign over the ranch and I could go but I knew they'd kill me. I was waiting my chance, praying that something would distract them when Rosy here came looking for me."

Abow looked at the bodies. The skulls of two had been shattered by kicks from a hind hoof. Another of them had died with his spine pulped as the mare jumped on him. The fourth man Pat had killed, wrenching his rifle from the dead man who had it and crushing his enemy's windpipe with the butt even as he shot. Abow's voice was serious when he spoke.

"I'd say maybe she was an answer to your prayers, lad. That was a distraction all right. Who shot?"

"One of them, he must have missed, there's no wounds on Rosy."

Yarnell stared. "At that range, in a narrow alley. It's a bloody miracle." He shrugged. "Well, let's get a meal and a bed. We've riding to do in the morning. There's a US Marshall on our heels heading for Elmwood to ask questions. I'd say you'll have your ranch back in a couple of days an' maybe Semple will be hitting the trail himself."

In all of which Yarnell Duwarne was right. In the years to come, Pat O'Faiolin's ranch grew larger as he bought some of the land abruptly deserted by Harv Semple. Pat wed, bred children and then grandchildren and all the time the mare had an honored place in his stables. In the year, he would be seventy-nine he had two episodes of pain and weakness and knew.

Late one night a week after the second attack, he went out into the starlit dark, called the mare and walked across his land with her at his heels. The ranch was empty of people. There was a dance on to celebrate the end of the Great War, and only Pat had stayed behind. At the big flat rock by the stream, he sat down feeling his breath shorten and a small growing ache in his chest.

"I heard the stories from Ireland an' from the Basque country from Pa an' my mother. No one's ever noticed how long I've had you," he told her softly. "It's never come to anyone that you've out-lived any horse that could be. No one ever really asked what happened to Semple either but I found the bones last fall. I saw how he died, the same way the men died who tried to kill me in that alleyway when I was a kid. I owe you a life, an' I've loved you for more'n sixty years, Rosita." He said her name softly and she came as always, dropping her soft nose into his cupped hands to breathe in his scent.

"I named my second daughter after you." He smiled. "My wife didn't mind, she knew I'd never have lived to meet her without you. But I've had notice to quit, two warnings and next time's the charm. The doc says it won't be far off. It's time you left. There's no knowing what some fool might try once I'm gone. I dunno what you really are or where you'll go or what you'll do an' I'm gonna miss you, but I reckon it's your choice to take and mine to offer it."

He fell silent, waiting. Over him swept a vast shadow. Out of it came a voice. Not a language he knew but somehow it was given to him to understand the words although they were not addressed to him.

"Come home. Your recording and learning are done and it is time. Come home with us, sister-kin."

The mare moved against him, thrusting her nose against his chest. He felt warmth there; a growing strength that roared through his body, and he rose to stand by her. Together they walked to the pale silver metal ramp that glimmered in the starlight. He hugged her neck.

"Gonna miss you." Her nose dropped into his cupped hands a last time before her hooves thudded very quietly up the metal. He found he was holding strands of her mane and he placed them in his pocket. There were those with her but his eyes blurred and he couldn't see them clearly, all his attention was on the mare. The shadow lifted, dwindled and was gone, and there was only an old man standing in the grass, tears crawling down his wrinkled cheeks.

He went back to the ranch house to die then – and lived. His doctor was confounded, his kin were pleased and only Pat grieved for the friend he'd lost. Now and again, he walked out into the meadow when the stars were exceptionally bright and looked up at them, wondering. He lived another twenty years and was laid in his coffin with the strands of the mare's mane hidden in his burial suit as he'd arranged.

And on the day he died with a rainbow overhead and the light rain misting on his coffin, one who had been Rosita knew, mourning the loss of a contact – and one who, as sometimes happened with students, had in fifty years, also become a friend.

THE SHEEP OF BODIE

Jalla Swansen had a problem, one in particular that was going to make the coming winter unhappy. Her sheep had had several accidents that year so she was going to be short of wool to spin and knit into sweaters to sell to the people of Bodie. It was her only source of income and she needed it. Part of the problem was that all the signs suggested winter would come early, stay late, and be more bitter than usual, and she needed money to deal with that. A voice from the bed in the loft distracted her.

"Jalla, love?"

"Yes, Bill?"

"Is the stone hot yet?"

Jalla moved to where the flat stone was soaking up heat and allowed her fingers to hover close enough to decide that it was. Carefully she wrapped a cloth about it, carried it to the bed, and inserted it by her husband's feet, removing the other, now chilled stone, as she did so. He sighed.

"Ah, that feels good. Thank you, love."

She bent and kissed his forehead gently. "My pleasure. See if you can get a little sleep, dinner should be ready when the children are home."

She watched as his eyelids dropped shut. She was better off than many. Bill had owned his land by the time he had that accident in the gold mine. He'd built a sturdy cabin, and it had all the amenities a woman could wish for with a large water tank that gathered not only water from the cabin roof, but also from the barn in which the sheep spent their nights. That was piped to a tank by the fire in the house which kept the water constantly warm, and could be used for washing and laundry.

Not that there'd be sufficient wool this year. If only there was some way to obtain more sheep. And, her mind added, as

170

Bill half-turned in the bed. If only he would get better. She was paying for things, or in some cases doing without, items that he had provided. Firewood was one of them, and watching the sheep was another. She opened the door, stepped outside where the cut wood was stacked, and sighed aloud.

The doctor had said that Bill wouldn't recover, in fact the last time he'd come he'd admitted that Bill's condition was slowly worsening, and in the doctor's opinion he wouldn't see out the winter. Jalla wasn't sure how long she could manage without him, but if she gave up, what would become of their son Harry, and his twin sisters Janet and Mary? They had a vegetable garden that Harry tended, while the girls helped her with sorting and carding the wool. Which reminded her, she went out and ran the small flock into the barn for the night, securing the door, and seeing the trough had clean water.

Bill had made her knitting needles, crochet hooks, and holding pins. She must ask for more so he didn't feel useless. She did that on her next trip to the loft and smiled at his pleased look. The children arrived back from school, ate, and the girls talked to their father while he worked on shaping a crochet hook. Harry lit the lantern and went out to check the sheep, bring in more wood, and see the strong, high fence around the garden was intact – it was amazing how high a hungry deer could leap. He came in to report and Jalla nodded. One more day without anything wrong, if only they could all be like that.

* * *

Winter was coming, Jalla thought a week later, and she needed to make preserves, and have Harry cut more firewood. The girls had the last shearing carded and she could knit. There was a quiet knock at the door.

"Ezra? Is there trouble?"

"No, marm, it's just that I was wondering if you'd do me a sweater for winter?"

Jalla allowed him to enter and made coffee from the kettle on the hob. "I can do that, did you want anything in particular?"

"Hood on it, like you did for Miss Powry, if that'd suit?"

Jalla nodded. That sweater for Lizzy had paid for a whole term of teaching the children, the hood had been Jalla's idea, it had a drawstring, and when that was used, it covered the head and all of the face, save the eyes. She settled to haggle and when the sheriff left both were happy with the bargain ... except, that it would take as much as a tenth of the wool she had left from the spring shearing.

Bill had slept through the sheriff's visit and now she checked he was still sleeping. She poured herself another cup of coffee, and sat at the table with paper and a pencil listing those she knew who would want some knitted garment for the cold. She looked down at the figures. She could cover those that would, but if there were more, then she'd have to refuse, and yet, she stared miserably at the results, those wouldn't command sufficient payment to take her family through the winter.

"What's wrong?"

The question slipped so quietly into her worrying that she answered without thinking. "We won't have enough money for winter." Then she bolted upright, staring up in horror at her husband's face where he had rolled to the edge of their bed and was watching her through the loft railing. She forced a small laugh. "But I do exaggerate, I'm sure we'll manage." Their gaze met and he shook his head slowly.

"I'm not a fool, love. While you had me to watch the sheep, cut wood, and bring in money, we were doing well. Now I can't do anything, and caring for me costs you time and money both." His jaw hardened. "Don't worry. I'll think of something." Before she could answer that, he changed the subject. "Isn't Frangi due back soon? I'd enjoy talking with that Martian critter when he gets here."

Jalla consulted the calendar and nodded. "Next week if he's on time – and he usually is. I'll watch out and tell him to come visit when he gets here."

She mentioned that to both Jed and Lizzy when delivering a knitted waistcoat to Feng Lee the next day, and returned to find the twins not yet home. Harry shrugged.

"I dunno, ma. They ran off, and I've been chopping wood. Mary said something about wool. They were giggling fit to beat the band and Janet had a sack."

Jalla started dinner and worried. It was almost dark. If they didn't come in, what was she to do? Harry had been up at five and working or at school ever since. She could go, but where? She had almost decided to leave Harry watching the meal while she searched, when there was a bang of the door opening, the twins crowded in laughing, and Janet thrust a filled sack at her.

"We found you some wool, ma. Look, isn't it pretty?"

Jalla's gaze fell on the sack's contents even as she opened her mouth to read her daughters a scolding. The wool was indeed pretty, she thought. It was more than pretty. It was lovely. It was a pale gray, all of it inches long, and her hand went out to touch it. She gasped. Soft! And so incredibly fine. She hefted the sack, it was full, but with wool that fine it would spin up to a considerable amount. A lot more if … her mind clicked through possibilities. If only it took dye?

She hugged the girls. "You're both wonderful." She added a light swat to each behind. "And not so wonderful. I was worried about you. Next time you do that let me know where you're going, and be back well before dark. Now, where did this come from?"

Janet shrugged. "We found it over towards the old mine."

"Oh, I see, on the bushes there?" The girls nodded. Jalla pondered. "Some sort of goat maybe, was there more?"

Mary giggled. "Some, we could go back tomorrow?"

"Yes, all right, now get your dinner, take this and go see your father."

It was a pleasant evening. Jalla had placed the sack by her chair and now and again her fingers strayed into the wool. She found herself twisting it, and studying the results. Yes, by itself, it would be too fine to spin easily. She got up quietly, picked out a handful of carded sheep wool, and twisted them together with about thirty percent of it sheep's wool. Yes, that would do very well.

In the loft, the girls were giggling at something Bill had said, while Harry was nodding into his empty plate. She sent him to bed, and walked to the spinning wheel in the corner by the fire. She sat down and spun, teasing the two wools together, allowing them to spin into thread and then pulling at the result. Strong, light too, and she thought it would be very warm.

Tomorrow she'd test another aspect of it. She saw her family to their beds, joined Bill, and fell asleep thinking. If only this wool the girls had brought her would do as she hoped, and they'd said there was more. If that was so there might be just sufficient and of good enough quality to keep them through the winter.

She could hardly wait once she woke the next morning. With the children off to school, Bill settled with coffee and a book, Jalla took the sack of wool and considered it. She spun until she had a skein, then she went to the cabinet Bill had made her, and which held bottles and small containers of assorted dyes.

For the morning, she was busy, fed Bill his lunch with a preoccupied air, and went back to the wool now drying on the line. Idamay had asked her for a dress, one knitted from the finest wool she could spin, and in a soft shade of apple green. With it being wool, it would be ideal for winter and for the times she trotted outside from bakery to saloon. A shawl of a darker green would go with it. Jalla brought in the damp wool, placed it on a rack near the fire and kept spinning, working out the amount of wool needed for the shawl. The skein of wool dried and she examined it.

Euphoria roared through her. Yes! The combination took the dye superbly. It was a rich moss green and from all she could see, it would take a lighter shade the same way. She hefted the sack in her hands, looked at the amount of the new wool that had gone into the skein, and smiled slowly. If she was right, there was sufficient in this sack to do Idamay's dress and shawl. If her daughters were right, and they could bring back another sack full.... The wool was better quality even in combination, she could ask more, and with this added, what she'd had from the spring shearing would go much further. They could manage, and they could make it through the winter. She sat, basking in relief. They'd make it after all, so long as the girls came home with one more sack of that wool.

* * *

Jalla was caught by surprise as the door opened; Harry stuck his head in and beamed at her. "I'm home, ma, girls said to tell you they're hunting more of that wool for you, but they'll be back before dark. I'll go see to the sheep."

Jalla nodded and let him leave without discussion. She could only be grateful they had a well even if it wasn't always reliable. But then most of Bodie had that problem. The original stream, while it ran much of the year, now and then stopped for several days at a time without warning and for no apparent reason. She began dinner, and was heartened when her daughters appeared, each carrying a sack that looked to be full.

"Is that all wool?"

"Yes, ma."

"That's wonderful. Put it by the spinning wheel and come for your dinner. Is there any more of the wool or was that the last of it?"

The girls looked at each other. Janet scowled. "I guess it depends."

"Yes, I see. You mean if the animal comes back or not." She dished up the food as they sat, and Harry collected his father's plate to take upstairs. Janet spoke again. "And, ma, sheriff said to tell you Frangi's back and he'll be by in a day or two."

Jalla smiled. She liked the creature, but Bill thought the world of him. A day of gossip, and talking about all sorts of daft ideas would set Bill up for weeks. She lay beside her husband that night, and knew that while Frangi would be a distraction, any other hope was unfounded. She'd started noticing her man's condition more and more and knew that he was fading – and what would they do when he was gone?

Frangi was there just after the children had gone to school, and she greeted him warmly. "Come in, you know where to find Bill, and I hope you don't mind if I go on spinning, I have orders I need to get done."

Frangi obeyed, glancing at the wool as he passed and pausing. "You get from where?"

Jalla told him the story, and ended with a chuckle. "Some sort of wild goat maybe. But it's wonderful wool."

Frangi made an odd gesture, and went on up the stairs to the loft. Jalla spun, only half-conscious of voices in the background. The children returned, and the girls went up to talk to their father and the visitor while Harry went out to dig

vegetables. Dinner was peaceful, and Frangi departed just before dark, pausing to assure Jalla he'd be back in the morning
if she didn't mind. She didn't.

The next day was a Saturday so they were all home when
Frangi arrived and to Jalla's surprise, her husband called them
all upstairs to join him and his friend. Bill looked at her. "There's
something you need to know." Jalla sat abruptly.

"The doctor said, I do know."

Bill grinned, his old carefree smile that she'd always loved.
"Not that, love. This is something else entirely. Now, girls, you
tell your mother where you really got the wool."

Jalla listened and was bewildered. Some strange animal in
the part of the stream that went underground, if they stroked
it, it shed the wool. They'd heard how worried she was about
money, so they'd taken the wool, and when she was happy
they'd gone back for more. She looked at Bill. "What animal?
What do you know about this?"

Frangi was the one who answered, the speaking mouth below his chin opening. "My animal. *Yaros*. We have in spacecraft,
it drinks all waste liquids, lets them out again clean. Sometime,
many years apart, it splits off a part of itself. It do last time I am
here, I put *yaros* underground to keep stream clean. But times
when there is very much it drinks all water, make another *yaros*.
Not here, here it drink and grow bigger, very big now."

That caught her attention. "Is it dangerous?"

"Not if you kind. Janet and Mary, they talk to it, stroke and
it shed wool for them. On world they come from, the people
there use that wool as you do. That how they gather it."

Mary cut in. "They do too have a baby, Lamb has one."

Frangi looked as startled as he was able. "Baby? You stroke
too?"

Janet giggled. "Yes, it purred."

Jalla observed their visitor relax and leaped to a conclusion.
"This creature – the girls seem to have christened it Lamb –
may not be normally dangerous, but what about when it has a
baby, or is it the baby that's dangerous?"

"Both, but not if it purr." He turned to the twins. "Lamb
purr for you?" They nodded. Frangi looked at Jalla and Bill.
"Then not dangerous," he said firmly.

It was then that Jalla had the idea. "On the world they come from they're like my sheep?" He nodded. "That's how they get the wool from them, stroke them?"

"Must like person who strokes. If they purr then they shed. Baby purr, that good. Lamb may have more babies, all purr, all shed. Give wool, keep water clean." And Jalla's idea bloomed into all its glory.

The New Year was 1881. The town rejoiced. It was a new year, and – Jalla was at the clothing shop talking to the mayor. "Yes, we have orders from the East. I talked to Short Bear and he's got some of the tribe's women knitting as well. The dresses and shawls are selling at high prices out east. Men are buying the vests."

Caron was sober. "I'm only sorry about Bill. He was a good man."

Jalla looked briefly sad. "He was, but he lived long enough to see this work out for us, and to know his family would do well. Just so long as everyone keeps their mouths shut we'll profit."

Caron grinned. "We're pulling the wool over Easterners' eyes."

Jalla laughed. "And so long as Lamb and the flock are happy that'll continue."

Caron's smile widened. "Yes, long live the sheep of Bodie, and may we never succumb to woolly thinking." The end of that conversation was Jalla's drawn-out groan, echoed very quietly from the underground section where Lamb and her kin lived contentedly. Honored, well-treated, and regularly stroked, they were now an integral part of Bodie … and anyone who thought differently could get the flock out of there.

LIKE A PITBULL

I left my small ranch near Bodie the year after the big drought. I needed money for improvements like spreader dams and solar power so that another drought wouldn't hit me as hard as this one had, and Ma Benson was taking her circus out to the stars again with contracts to set up the show on half a dozen planets. I could use a lariat pretty well. It wasn't the sort of thing most races had seen before and from experience with tourists here, I knew they'd cheer as I built a loop, spun the rope, and made the loop go up and down, before it went spinning out settling about some friend who pulled all sorts of antics trying to escape. I was using a rope of sixty-foot braided rawhide and as a kid, I'd got in a lot of practice so it impressed them some.

We were due to be gone almost a year and I sure as hell missed Duke, my pitbull. My neighbor was looking out for him and the ranch though, and old as she is, she knows her job and Duke loves her. I'd sold my cows down to the bare minimum of breeding stock, and with luck, I'd be home again a week or two before they started to calve.

Most races out here are good enough people, but now and then you get some that aren't too safe. We left Sirtis a jump ahead of a group of AnSirtians, and only found when we were in flight that one had come with us.

"What are you doing here?" Ma Benson was stern. "How old are you?"

"I am T'Voi, I'm an adult. The L'gai have a feud with my clan. My co-parent said I should get away in case we're wiped out. So long as I live, the clan lives."

Ma looked at me and I looked back. The second half of that sounded okay, but neither of us was sure he was an adult. Still, he didn't look to be far off it, and if we put back to the port and

178

dumped him, we could see him murdered in front of us, and anyhow, putting back wasn't an option. We had contracts on the next world, with harsh penalties for not appearing there on time. So we kept going, and the kid fitted right in. It turned out that he'd made a hobby of juggling, and with six limbs and a bit more practice he was soon doing okay as a fill-in act when needed.

Now and again, he talked; homesick, I guess. "The L-Gai live by hunting, a hunter is most valued, one that can kill the giant Esgartee with only a spear has great influence."

Huh? The AnSirtians weren't simple hunters, they had spaceships, and they traded – although there was a rumor that they only did that when they thought a world was too strong to be raided. And, of course, the Alliance didn't allow it officially. I'd heard they had some system where a race could appeal for permission though, sort of like a privateer sailing under letters of Marque.

"An Esgartee?"

"Big lizards."

I asked more questions and finally understood that the Esgartee were big and powerful, but from what T'Voi said, you could only kill one under certain conditions. In the mating season, the lizards would attack ferociously and it was then that hunters went out to take one out, one on one, with the hunter using only a ten-foot spear.

"A hunter must entice the Esgartee to charge, then he grounds his spear and the Esgartee runs onto the blade," T'Voi explained.

"What happens if he doesn't get the angle right?"

T'Voi showed his teeth. "Then he dies."

"He can't fight it off?"

He thought about that. "There is no law against it, but the Esgartee is bigger than any hunter. It has more teeth."

He kept talking and from what he said, it sounded as if he was right. A hunter that missed his strike, died. It was interesting and it shed a clearer light on T'Voi's people.

I also found that they boxed, well, sochata, their version of it. With two arms and two mid-limbs, they were more versatile, and they could strike a blow from odd angles. I'd learned to box from my uncle and T'Voi and I amused ourselves on quite a few nights by swapping techniques. The sparring kept me fit and T'Voi enjoyed being the teacher for once.

"No, Col. Watch for my right elo." I'd forgotten again that his mid-limbs could deal a hefty blow and I'd caught that one across the ear. "Look, I parry with my upper right, and while you watch my upper left, my right elo strikes."

After a while, I was getting the hang of it. With four limbs that they can use to punch, the AnSirtians tend to go for combinations. It's effective – if you aren't prepared. I didn't make it too obvious, but as time passed, I was starting to really catch on and if I'd wanted to, I could have beaten T'Voi most times. I didn't, he was a nice kid, a friend, and after some calculations I'd worked out that while I was twenty-seven he was just coming up to sixteen in Earth years. That made him almost an adult by his people's laws, but I wouldn't have felt right hammering a kid not much more than half my age.

We played a month on Ilashti, another on Farnow, and moved on to Vangse. They came for me the night after we touched down there.

"Col Martin, come with us."

They wore the uniforms of the Alliance peacekeepers and that made it official, but Ma walked in just then and asked questions.

"This man's my employee. Has he broken the law?"

"No, Vadasha Benson"

"Then why do you want him?"

They each turned all four eyes on her. "The AnSirtians say that you assisted an enemy to escape from Sirtis. They claim this as provocation and demand right of sackage against Earth." Ma cottoned on before I did.

"You mean that they say we sided with an enemy of theirs and that gives them the right to land on Earth and raid, and the Alliance will *sanction* that?"

"That is so, Vadasha."

"What do you want with Col?"

"He is test subject."

Eh? I wasn't any one's lab rat and if that was what they wanted, they could go climb a slippery pole before I trotted along with them meekly. Ma said something similar.

"You do not understand." That officer looked unhappy.

"Then explain it." Ma challenged him.

So they did, each in turn laying out the laws that governed the custom. It was fairly simple in the end. The AnSirtians had filed a legal grudge against Earth. However, the Alliance could insist on a form of trial by weaponless combat. A conveniently-to-hand Terran (me in this case) could be asked if he, she, or it, was prepared to fight on behalf of their world. The Alliance would withhold official approval if I won. If the AnSirtian chosen to fight me won, then they could legally land and plunder Earth all they liked. They had to keep the deaths to a minimum, but built in to that was a percentage.

Ma Benson stared at the officials. "You mean that they aren't allowed to murder more than a tenth of one percent of us?"

"Yes, Vadasha."

She nodded. "Must Vedesha Martin come with you at once now that you have explained, or does the law allow us time to discuss this and make decisions?"

"You may have two eluma if you state now that you will not leave this world and will appear when called upon." (That was around two weeks our time, and I knew that they'd take our word too. The Alliance is big on honor.)

Ma caught my gaze, raised an eyebrow. I nodded, and she turned to the one doing most of the talking. "We agree. Here and now I state that neither I nor Vedesha Martin will leave this world without permission and we will appear when called upon by an officer of the Alliance."

The officials bowed and walked away in silence as I turned to her. "Why you?"

She grinned. "Because someone has to see fair play. Apart from that, this is the seventeenth time I've been on this circuit, I know people here who'll talk to me. There may be some way out of this, and even if there isn't, there's things we need to know."

She spent most of the next five days off-site, connecting with friends, business associates, friends of friends, associates of friends, and some others who weren't all that friendly. When she came back, she had a lop-sided smile on her face. The sort of look you wear when you may have something, but you aren't sure how useful it'll be or where it'll take you.

"Col, you've been working out with T'Voi haven't you?"

"Yes, for most of the trip, just sparring for fun though, why?"

"But he's been teaching you sochata?"

T'Voi who'd been listening – he felt responsible for the trouble we were in – spoke up. "Col learns sochata well. He has only two arms but he is a good fighter."

Ma heaved a sigh. "Good, then there's a chance." She waved us down when we would have cut in to ask questions. "Sit tight and I'll do the talking. It comes down to this; the AnSirtians have stated that they will not accept the return of T'Voi as a reason to drop this demand. They say that we took him and cannot now change the event. One of us has to fight an AnSirtian in a form that they find acceptable." She sat down heavily and looked at us.

"If we win, then the Alliance will withdraw legal permission for any raids on earth. If we refuse to fight, the AnSirtians can raid at will with only the death percentage proviso. If someone fights and loses, the same applies. But if someone loses but fights *very* well, the Alliance may, at its discretion, annul permission for the death percentage. That would mean the AnSirtians couldn't kill more than a few hundred people and only those where they can show proof that they attacked them."

I snorted. "If they attack Earth they'll have all the proof of that that the Alliance could ask for. Earth wouldn't lie down under a bunch of aliens tearing up the place, stealing and murdering."

"No," Ma agreed. "But there's this too. With sackage permission withdrawn, if the AnSirtians attacked Earth after that we'd be free to hit them with everything we've got, and some of our allies would be happy to join in. I'd guess that the AnSirtians have wanted to try us for quite a while. This is an excuse to see how we stack up."

T'Voi chimed in. "The AnSirtians are not us, they are the city clans, they have held away from your world because you have not yet been made full members of the Alliance. If they attack a world seen as junior to them, they appear as bullies. They needed an excuse so they could appear in righteous wrath."

Ma nodded. "Makes sense. And there's another thing, Col. Officially you're the one challenged. You can name the form of hand-to-hand combat, so long as it's a form the AnSirtians know. I've had friends checking that, about the only thing we have in common is sochata. It's close enough to straight pro-boxing to pass on either side."

T'Voi looked at me and his triangular mouth turned down at all three corners. "They will choose a champion, Col my friend. Your world has you, they may choose from many clans and a hand of worlds."

Ma's grin was closer to a snarl. "I've petitioned the Alliance that a champion can only be selected from amongst the AnSirtians who were on this world when the challenge was made. They agreed and it's ratified."

And we had nine Terran days left.

I trained, sparred, worked out, and while I'd always been fit – working on a ranch doesn't allow you to get flabby – and being often on higher-grav worlds had put an edge on that, now I was aiming to be in better shape than I'd even been. I had a hole card I believed, but I'd have to play most of the game before it might come up to where I'd see what it was worth. Nine days went past almost unnoticed until the officials arrived at our campground again.

"Vedesha Col Martin, are you prepared?"

I knew to be formal. "I am prepared."

"Do you come with us of your own free will, to fight sochata against a champion of the AnSirtians, to win or lose as you stand?"

"I come of my own free will, and I am ready."

"Follow us."

I followed, and behind me came all the members of Ma Benson's circus with her at my shoulder. It seemed that it was going to be a public spectacle. I'd expected to be taken to a building, big maybe, but something under a roof. Instead, it was outside, in a sort of amphitheater, and all the seats that rose up tier upon tier around it were filled with people.

I was conducted down through a tunnel into the arena, Ma and T'Voi staying with me, the others being sent off to a block of empty seats that had been held for them.

Standing waiting by the arena was an AnSirtian. He was one of the biggest I'd ever seen. He wore a loincloth held up by a belt below his elo – his mid-limbs, and his hand-tentacles were encased in AnSirtian boxing gloves. My outfit was similar, although I wore boxing boots while he had nothing on the hard splayed pads of his feet.

The officials conducted us into the arena where they had placed a roped-off square. It was larger than the usual dimensions of a Terran boxing ring but that was okay. The AnSirtian had two witnesses. I had T'Voi and Ma, and the officials each took up a place at the other two corners. Someone made an announcement: "Vedesha Col Martin of Terra and AnSirti R'Val of Sirtis will now contend." And that was all that was said.

There was little more formality. I knew that there'd be no rounds. We'd fight until either we broke apart and couldn't fight on, or until one of us went down and stayed down. One official blew some kind of whistle and it was on.

R'Val didn't waste time. He came across the ring straight for me, and moved into a right, right, left combination. I swayed aside, parried, evaded the next blow and settled to work. For the first ten minutes or so, I let him think that I was trying desperately to evade his superior ability. Truthfully, he *was* the better fighter from a couple of points of view. He had a longer reach, four arms to my two, and he was heavier. I fought carefully, watching, learning how he fought, and noting possible weaknesses. He wanted it over with and he stepped up the speed.

I parried the next blow, briefly forgot about those damned elo and a mid-limb came out of nowhere and caught me so hard I saw stars. But I've been hit before; I paid off part of my ranch by boxing in a series of semi-legal street fights in Houston Space-Port. I shook off the stars and bored in punching hard in lefts and rights. That confused R'Val since their combinations are in triads. He adapted but before he did, I got in some solid punches to his trunk. I was trying for the area just between his elo and I was hitting home. He didn't like it and whipped a cross-handed right that smacked me in the belly. It hurt.

Then we were both at it, pounding each other, mostly in the body, with the occasional strike for the head. None of those hit home but I was feeling the body punches all right, and so was he. He went for another combination, right hook, left parry, left cross, and that last one got home – not as hard as it could have been. I was back peddling, but it stung. I answered it with a straight left to his mid-section that rocked him solidly and for the first time he gave back. Not much but enough to tell me that those punches were effective.

But then, so were his. We stood toe to toe and fought, I could hear the high-pitched whistles that were his fellows' encouragement, and the shrill rebel yell that was Ma. He was starting to tire but so was I and I didn't see it coming. I caught it hard, went down on one knee and rested there briefly. He stepped back as if waiting for me to fall down but I was up and handed him a right hook that jarred him to his pad-soles. He snarled, and attacked, punching in combinations that were coming so fast I lost track.

The punch came out of thin air, caught me moving in and I went down hard, rolling automatically, too dazed to know what I was doing, only that I had to get up on my feet again. I rolled, jack-knifed, and was facing him, and if my mouth was sagged open a bit, and my legs wobbled, I was on my feet. I was bleeding, the blood running down my face where the skin had ripped. Then I saw it, for a second as I came upright he stood flat-footed and gaped at me.

He came in cautiously, his eyes disbelieving, punched another combination while he waited for me to lie down, and I swayed to one side, and refused to parry the second blow as expected, instead I brought up a punch from the floor. It had everything I had left and all of my weight behind it. It took him square in the mid-section between elo and he went down in the way that tells you your opponent won't be getting up again for a while. I staggered back, resting my arms on the ringside and watched.

The officials moved in, checking R'Val. He was alive they agreed, and the fight had been legal. But he wouldn't be getting up to fight again any hour soon, and that meant I'd won. The AnSirtians were denied rights of sackage, and furthermore, I had fought so well against superior odds that – as was official right – they laid an edict on the AnSirtians. They were banned from earth for a period of no less than one generation. If any Emalti can look pleased, this pair did and I suddenly wondered if that had been what they hoped for all along. Had it been why they required this fight?

A couple of AnSirtians showed up and carried R'Val away; I was swamped in friends' congratulations and backslaps, and reeled off to celebrate before hitting the sack close to dawn. T'Voi was there with Big Tom, the circus strongman, when I woke.

"You should not have won, Col my friend. He was experienced, bigger, and stronger, he had a longer reach, and four arms to your two. You should not have won."

"No, not if that was all there was. But you told me that the city AnSirtians are ceremonial hunters."

He looked puzzled. "They are?"

"And they fight the Esgartee. If their strike is true, the Esgartee dies. If it isn't the hunter dies. Why doesn't he fight?" I asked, answering that myself. "Because no hunter can stand against an Esgartee, and when two AnSirtians sochata, if one gets home a winning punch, and the other goes down, what happens?"

"Then the one standing has won."

"What if his opponent gets up again – and again – what if he won't quit?"

Big Tom stared at me, speaking slowly. "As you did?"

"As I did. The AnSirtians – particular those from the city clans – give up if they're beaten. If a hunter fails to kill an Esgartee cleanly then he isn't good enough to fight the wounded maddened creature, nor is he fast enough to escape it, so he lets it kill him quickly. And over thousands of years, that attitude has become engrained, and in sochata as well. I was bleeding from a number of minor injuries, I fell, and to R'Val it was unbelievable I wouldn't accept that I was beaten. He saw me get up, he couldn't believe that I'd continue to fight, and for that second he was off guard. He was waiting for me to fall again, and when he relaxed, I was ready."

I could have added that Ma Benson had heard a few things about AnSirtian evolution too. They evolved without real predators on their world; it was only recently that there'd begun to be clashes between city and mountain clans. They've fought in groups, that they understand, but they'd never had to fight solo, as one person against another, get knocked down, pick themselves up and come back to fight again – and again. It's the difference between a lot of other dog breeds and Duke. They were bred to hunt other animals, while he was bred to fight other dogs.

He's a sweet-tempered dog, likes people in general, loves his human friends and his cat, Ed. He's amiable with other dogs and lets my neighbor's hens walk all over him. But once, when a big crossbred mutt cornered her bantam and the chicks and she went out to chase it off, the mutt turned on her. She yelled, a mix of fear and anger and Duke came running. The mutt was half again his size and would have out-weighed him by pounds. Duke hit that mutt hard enough to take its legs from under it, grabbed it by the throat and held it until she said he could let go. The mutt made for home on three legs squealing like a smacked puppy while Duke enjoyed the neighbor's pats and praise and the bantam came out from under the hayrack and joined in.

That's the difference I counted on. We're a friendly people, Terrans. Until we, or something or someone we care about, is threatened. Then, like a pitbull, we're prepared to fight, because we're used to fighting each other, bred for it over generations, and – like Duke – when the time comes there's no backing up and no quit in us either.

FLUFFY

I was sitting in the saloon when this rider came charging through the batwings, eyes popping out'a his head an' yelling. "Big explosion up the mountains. Like someone dropped a match in a keg 'a dynamite."

Half the cowboys in the saloon jumped up. "Where?"

"Back of the badlands. Must's a been a hell of a bang where it was, 'cause it looked to be miles off but it showed right up."

By now he'd arrived at my table, I looked up. "Is there anything out that way?"

He deflated a bit. "Nope, there ain't."

"So what do you think it could have been?" He looked blank. "I mean," I said. "Things don't just explode. You thought it'd be someone setting off dynamite, but why? Are there mines out there, a ranch blowing gullies deeper for a dam?"

He sat without asking – safe enough – and answered me slowly, thinking about it. "No mines an' the nearest town's a coupl'a day's ride."

"Anyone own land out there?"

Someone else answered. "No ranch out thataways. That's why we call it the badlands."

They weren't that bad, or that big, but I got the main idea; that there wasn't a ranch where he'd seen the explosion. Talk simmered on and off after that, and the rider got drunk on free booze as he told his tale over and over. I sat back, finishing my drink and thinking hard. I was on the drift, coming from a gun-hand job that had paid well, but more importantly, it had been all-found, so I hadn't had to spend a dime of what I'd been paid. I had a real wad of cash in my jeans, a good horse by the rail outside, and I was going no place.

I slept well, ate hearty next morning, and looked up the rider. He was getting old working for the nearest ranch, a small outfit that ran cattle, some of which had strayed into the badlands fringe. He'd been up a canyon, followed a steer onto the plateau above that and seen the explosion. I got the impression that he and the steer had come down and headed home at similar speeds. But without realizing and while sucking back more of my booze, he gave me a direction and a fair description of the area.

"Thanks, old timer. You take care, stay away from dynamite." I grinned. "If it's bank robbers they won't thank you to be walking in on them."

He shuddered, knocked back his drink and stood up. "Reckon not. Thanks, mister…"

"Jack Harris."

I saw from his eyes that he recognized the name. I grinned at him again, stepped out of the saloon and straddled my horse. Sandy's a dun and nondescript, nothing to remember about him – which can be useful – and I'm pretty much the same. Once I had a family but that was a very long time ago. I rode down the dusty street remembering.

* * *

Ma and pa came west before I was born. They settled on a piece of land, built a cabin and I was born there. Pa proved up on a second piece of land too. But ma died when I was near six, and the baby died with her. Three years after that a big man with a lot of cows and money, and a desire to own everything around him, moved in.

Pa owned his land but that made no never-mind to Mr. Carruthers. He suggested pa sell to him and leave while he was healthy but pa was a stubborn man. We stayed. One night our cabin burned down, and there was shots fired. Pa sent me away.

"Jackie boy, you go to the canyon, stay there, an' don't come back for five days. By that time, I'll have the cabin half rebuilt and we'll fort up. Here." He handed me filled saddlebags. "Take your pony and git going." I hadn't wanted to, but pa was adamant. "You go, boy. If anything happens to me, go to Aunt Mary."

I guess he knew. I came back after four days, to find him lying face down in the dirt, the new cabin's frame burnt again, an' all the livestock gone. I did as he told me and went to Aunt Mary. She was his aunt, my great-aunt, and already an old woman, but she took me in and sent me to school fulltime.

"Man needs a foundation, the more you learn, the better the foundation."

She died when I was fifteen and I was alone. But I'd learned – some of it things she hadn't paid for, because one of our teachers had been gun-handy. I learned from him, not just using a gun, but how to think before I did, and what to watch for. I was good with a gun, but his teaching made me careful too. By the time I was seventeen, I was making a living as a gun-smart cowhand, and while the pay isn't so good as what a straight-out gunfighter gets, it's a lot safer.

* * *

I swung Sandy off the trail at this point. That talk about an explosion interested me. There might be nothing there, but I was going to see. In the end, it took near two days riding. I was deep into the badlands and it was mid-morning when I found the valley. It was flat along the bottom and it looked as if something had torn up a strip of ground, the damage started midway, and stretched down around a bend and out of sight.

I followed the rimrock around the bend and there it was, some sort'a metal thing like a half-smashed giant can. There was the thread of a trail leading down and Sandy took that at my urging. I rode light, watching, I had no thought of what the thing could be but from the scorch marks on it and the earth around, this was what had made the explosion.

I swung Sandy past the tin can and there they were; a man and a little kid, a girl-child. She came running up to me and stood there, petting Sandy while he hung his head so she could reach an' all but purred. Fool horse! I was looking at the man. He was bad hurt, I saw that straight off, but he was hanging in, his gaze fixed on the kid, and I could see his fear for her. I swung down from my saddle, dropped Sandy's reins, and walked over to crouch by him.

"What can I do?"

His gaze met mine. "Nothing for me. But K'l'ion'a, please save her."

I blinked. The name had sounded like Cliona but with odd clicks within the word. "Cliona?" I asked.

"Close enough, will you help her?"

I looked at the kid picking bunches of grass to feed Sandy. "You from around here?"

He laughed, and then grunted in pain. "I'm from further away than you would believe. Will you save my co-daughter?"

"Mister, I've been here and there an' done this and that," I told him. "But I've never harmed a kid. What do you need me to do?"

"Get her away from here. I'm dying, and you can't save me. She needs a home, stability, someone to love her and teach her."

Well, that was a bit more than I'd bargained for, but I looked at the kid and just then she turned to look back. I fell into purple eyes and was lost. She was so small and fragile-looking, so sweet and her eyes on me were trusting. It was mad, but I couldn't say no.

"Guess I can do that. What about her gear, anything I should take for her?"

His hand came up and pointed shakily at a bag. "The bag itself. It's special. Keep it with her. Don't let them be separated." He was starting to fade and his gaze met mine imploringly. "Mister? I don't have enough strength to keep talking, but there's things you'll need to know. Let me touch you. I can put them in your memory. When times are right you'll remember what I tell you."

He was dying, I could see that. No wonder he wasn't making much sense, but he reached out and his face was so desperate that I took his hand in mine. He closed his fingers about mine, gripped – then they fell away and he was gone. The kid made a long whimpering noise and I turned to her. Something was there where she'd been. It was a soft powder blue, had six legs, long fine fluffy fur, and huge purple eyes. I shook my head and looked again. Gah, must be I was tired. The kid sat there, looking at me, her sweet blue eyes filled with tears.

I stood up and walked to her. "I'm very sorry, kid, but your daddy's gone. He asked me to look after you now, is that okay?"

She never spoke, but she went over to the bag, picked it up and came back, her small warm hand slid into mine and she nodded.

"Okay then. You go sit over there with your bag while I bury your daddy. Once that's done I'll put you up on Sandy and we'll get out of here."

I didn't waste around; I had a hole dug, her father laid out in it, and rocks piled over the raw earth in an hour. I would have looked through the tin can but somehow I couldn't get inside it. Oh well. I tied the bag to Sandy's saddle, picked the kid up, planted her in front and swung up behind her.

I started Sandy back up that thread of trail and when we topped out, I turned in the saddle to look back. The tin can was melting. I rubbed my eyes but it was still dissolving, and even as I looked, it soaked into the ground and was gone. Man, what didn't they think of these days? I guessed that Clio's daddy had been some sort of scientist like the men I'd heard about in school.

I talked as we rode. I explained what I was thinking about doing for a start. "My pa had land claims when I was a boy. I guess I won't be able to get back the land Mr. Carruthers stole…" She made a tiny questioning sound, so I explained about that. "But there was another piece of land. My pa called it Secret Canyon. There's about three ways into it, but you'd have to be real lucky to find any of them. I've still got the deed to the land. Pa built a cabin there. There's caves for storage, and when they killed pa and I rode out there was still half a dozen cows there. Could be if they've survived, we can go back and live in the cabin and I can start ranching again."

The noise this time was one of excited approval. That made me wonder. "Clio, can you say "daddy?" It was in my mind that it would be safer if people thought she was my daughter. She made a questioning sound but no matter how gently I encouraged her she didn't say a word. Shouldn't she be able to speak at her age? Come to think of it, how old *was* she? She looked around four or five to me but what did I know? Could also be that the shock of her pa dying and the crash of that whatever it was, had left her mute.

I shrugged, if it was shock that was keeping her from talking I guessed it'd wear off, and if she hadn't yet learned to talk, I'd talk to her and she'd get the idea soon enough. We rode all day until late afternoon when I made an early camp. She didn't seem tired but it'd been a long day for her. As far as we'd come would do.

And all the time I made camp I talked, explaining what I was doing, why, how things worked and having her taste the damper I cooked. She liked that and ate her full share.

It took nine days until we came to Secret Canyon. It's back of Bodie, and before we got to the canyon, I left Clio in camp and scouted around. Mr. Carruthers was still there, at least his Rocking C was on a heap of cattle, and the riders I saw were mostly astride horses with that brand too. I got back to Clio and she was giggling at something in the grass.

"What you got there, Fluffy honey?" (I'd started calling her Fluffy as a nickname. No idea where I got that but she liked it.) She showed me what she'd found and I took it from her hand. It was a fresh tooth. Human I thought, but there was no one in sight.

"How'd you find that?"

Her hand curled into mine as she led me around a patch of scrub and there was a saddled horse wearing the Rocking C. There was a rifle lying on the ground, and scattered about was clothing, a holstered pistol, and all sorts of odds and ends – the kind of things that any man might carry. I gaped. Odd thing though, there were faint signs of some minor scuffle, but no blood, and no clear tracks leading away.

I grinned. "Looks as if one of Carruther's men found trouble. What a shame. You're okay though?"

She nodded. "Good, we'll bury all the stuff someone could identify and let the horse go. You make us something to eat while I get the horse away from here."

Clio began to make damper while I got back on Sandy and led the horse off down the rim. Best to make things look like an accident. I knotted the reins then took them in my hands and yanked as hard as I could. By the left side of the bit the stitching was worn, it snapped and the rein came away, Good. I let the horse, now trailing a rein, go trotting off down the road and checking that I left no tracks, and kept moving until I was back at our camp. If anyone could follow that, he was the pure quill as a tracker.

Secret Canyon is a fair size as canyons go. I'd guess it to be close to half a land claim, around three hundred acres in total, the main part being something over half that, and there's several subsidiary canyons coming off it to make up the rest. Two of those run back into the mountains at different angles, and if you know where to find them, they can be ways in or out. The third way is a fine tread of trail that slips through a crack in the rock. Pa said that ma found it hunting blueberries, and being nosy.

He built a stout one-room cabin there that was still standing when we arrived, and I spent another month pulling off one side of that to build a second room. I built solid, using stone up to waist-high, and logs after that. While I was working on the cabin I made a trip to Bodie, buying careful, half at each store, and giving the impression that I was drifting through. Not that that would hold up if I kept coming into town.

But we settled in, had us a comfortable enough winter, since I'd been right, the cattle had bred, and in thirty-four years they'd learned how to survive. Clio counted them and reported the first week that we were there. (Yup, she'd come up talking, clear as day. She'd also shot up three inches over four-five days and looked to be eight now.)

"There are sixteen older bulls, thirty younger ones, fifty-seven cows, and forty-nine calves. And there are fifteen horses."

I was stunned. "Horses? How the ... heck ... could there be...?"

Then I remembered. My parents had come in over rough land on horseback, along with me in a riding cradle on their packhorse, a small, strong, fourteen-hand five-year-old mare named Nancy that was part carthorse. Pa planned to breed Nancy. I disremembered that he'd found a suitable stallion, but he had to have. Left in the canyon and in foal Nancy must have had a colt and bred back.

"What are they like, Fluffy honey?" Yup, from her report that was it all right. "Good, we'll break one in and you'll have a horse of your own."

"I want the one like Sandy."

I'd have refused. The one she wanted was a line-back dun, also about fourteen-hands, with a deep chest, well-muscled hindquarters, and he'd make a good mount, except for being a stallion. But Clio insisted, and it was true that he was incredibly gentle around her. So I killed a yearling bull, butchered him out, and all winter we feasted on steak, extended the cabin by another room, and broke in Dusty for Clio.

She came in four months later to tell me something. "Pa, the creek is thawing." I looked up. "You said we might go to town once we could get out of the canyon?"

I had said that, but I wasn't keen on Clio coming with me. On the other hand, if we went to a different town ... and I had an idea. "I'll go into Bodie in a couple of days on my own, then you can come next time and we'll go the other way to Leevining and stay a couple of days, but we've got work to do first."

I made a fast run into Bodie, arriving one evening after dusk. I bought from both general stores, and made certain no one could track me home. Then I started us on my plan. It was hard, dirty, and sometimes dangerous, work, but I knew what I was doing, and soon, so did Clio. Of the forty-six bulls, we selected the five best and ran them into a side canyon. To them we added the best of the cows and heifers. All the others we branded with the circle JH that had been my father's brand. His name had been John and it would serve as my brand as well.

It was around thirty miles to Leevining, and if we pushed them hard, we could be there in two days. The sheriff might ask questions, but I could say that I'd found the cattle back in the hills and that my little brother and I had rounded them up, branded them and brought them in to sell.

That was another thing. "Fluffy honey? Would it upset you to cut your hair, darken it, and wear boy's clothes? It'd be safer for you in town and if anyone in Bodie hears about us it should help throw them off the trail?"

Clio shook her head. "I don't mind, just so long as I can come with you."

"I need you," I said honestly, and she beamed.

We set out three days later, with Clio wearing jeans, a leather vest, and a check shirt I'd bought for her in Bodie. There'd been something else we'd done over winter too. The gear she'd found had included a holstered pistol. It was a good gun, but a common basic type. By the time we rode out with the small herd, Clio wasn't just wearing a gun, she knew how to use one.

There was no real trouble. I sold the herd, banked half the money I got for them and put Clio's name on the account too. I just said that she was my daughter and if anyone showed up with her name and showing my ring, then they could draw on the money. I don't wear my ring, but I'd taken it with us. It was pa's and his grandpa's before him. It was a seal ring and left a complicated design if it was inked.

I bought a good pack pony and we loaded that real heavy before we left town. Clio was talking as we left. "Did you see the lovely white tablecloth in the restaurant? She said it was linen when I asked. And I love the hairclips you bought." She giggled. "When you asked me to pick them out for my sister it was so funny."

I grinned at her. She'd picked up my cue like a professional – then, on behalf of the mythical sister, she'd wheedled several more pretty items out of me.

"I wonder what the fuss was as we were leaving?" I said thoughtfully. Someone had come past us leading a saddled horse and calling for the sheriff. Oh, well, it'd be some fool cowboy and nothing to do with us.

Whatever it was, no one came asking, and we made it home by dark. I did notice that Clio shot up again in the next few days. Now she looked to be twelve by the time her growth stopped and only the vest I'd bought her still fit. I guessed it was something to do with what her father had tried to tell me, poor man, a family trait of some sort maybe?

It was a good spring and summer. I cut hay in some of the canyons, built stables, and fitted planking and doors on the two largest caves and forked the hay into the driest so that the cows couldn't get that until I doled it out. In fall, I rode back to Leevining and bought schoolbooks. That winter I taught Clio to read and we were happy. I'd come to love the kid and now and again I worried that some kin would want her back.

I asked about that. "Fluffy, sweetheart, did your pa have any family? Do you recollect anyone, what about your mother?"

"I don't remember." She screwed her face up as she thought. "We were in a big ship and it went fast, then daddy called to me to hold on and it was all bumpy and bouncing. Daddy was hurt, and then you came. I don't remember anyone else." Ship? Oh, the tin can. Clio had gone to the door and was looking up at the stars. "He said we were having a holiday on a new world, that this one didn't know about us and I mustn't let anybody see me because it would upset them..." Her voice trailed off as she smiled at the stars.

I wasn't really listening. "So you were on holiday, maybe we'll have a break once the next lot of cows sell." She turned, shutting the door and beaming at me.

"Where could we go?"

"A city perhaps, some place we could see a play or two, eat out at good restaurants, and buy you some pretty dresses."

Two years later, we did that. We caught the stage from Bodie and came back there after ten days away, and that was my mistake. By that time, Carruthers had heard a story or two about a man and a boy who brought cattle into Leevining now and again. No one from the far side of the town where we sold them had ever seen us coming in from that direction. So he made a few guesses and decided we must have land out back of Bodie, someplace that could be cutting into his land, and maybe those were *his* cattle we were selling.

I didn't know it then, but in effect, he put a bounty on our heads. "You men keep an eye out. I'll pay six months wages to the man who finds where they're livin'."

One of his men decided that six months wages would fill his pockets just the way he'd like it to and began taking every opportunity to head in our direction, or into the area where he thought we could be. And in the way of things, he spotted Clio one day, riding Dusty out to look at a snare-line she planned to run for winter-white hares. I was in town for a final pack load of supplies before the real winter set in but I wasn't worried. Clio was used to spending a night alone now and again and Secret Canyon was so hidden away I doubted we'd ever be found.

I rode in, saw the horse outside the cabin, heard Clio scream, and then a man's shout – abruptly cut off. I came through the door with my gun lifting and shot as he staggered clear of Clio. And then there was a creature crouched over him, spreading like a skin to cover the body.

It hit like a thunderbolt; a memory of the blue-furred six-legged creature with purple eyes. And as my mind seemed to stretch for understanding, as my gun came up again, a voice spoke in my head.

"We are shapers. I could hold my shape past death because I clamped that command onto my body and the cells changed. K'l'ion'a is a child, sometimes she forgets, and also she needs … (a blurred sound I couldn't translate) to grow. But she will not harm friends, only those who attack her. Please do not be afraid. Love her as she loves you. Trust her as she has trusted you. Remember your promise!"

The blue thing was slowly contracting, and as it did, her prey's clothing was appearing beyond the blueness; clothing, the holstered gun, a pocket watch, boots … I lined up the gun, and then in my heart I saw Clio, her smile, her love, I could feel her lips on my cheek as she kissed me good night, her slender child's arms as she hugged me, hear her soft laughter. That first time the man must have come upon her by accident, maybe he'd grabbed some of our gear and frightened her. And at Leevining, that man leading a horse and calling for the sheriff? Had she gone for a ride while I was gone from the hotel and the missing rider attacked her? There was little doubt about this time. She'd been attacked but I was the one did the killing.

The blueness was Clio, Clio who proudly rode her pony by mine, who helped me gather the cattle, cook our food, build and repair buildings and fences on our ranch. Clio who called me "pa" and was the daughter of my heart … I holstered my gun and stepped forward to stroke the blue fur.

"When you're done, Fluffy honey, we'll take the horse down to the road and let it go." Oh, and now I knew from where that nickname had come. It had been the buried memory of what I'd seen by the tin can while her father gasped for breath and begged me to protect her, and died satisfied because

I'd given him my promise. No ifs, or buts, or conditions. Now I'd keep it.

I took the horse away and set it free the next day. I brushed out all traces of its trail, and once Clio had finished with her third growth spurt I went to Bodie, got myself a good lawyer, and had papers served on Carruthers to say that I was taking up my land claims. He didn't have a leg to stand on but I let him nudge me into allowing him to buy the claim my father had died for – so long as he ratified my claim to the Secret Canyon and promised in front of most of Bodie that it was mine, and Clio's after me and that if anyone tried to take it from us, he'd stand by me and mine.

Now he knew who I was and where I stood, we had no trouble from him. Clio started riding in to Bodie – and since she looked to be around sixteen – she was generating some interest. That worried me, I know men, and all it would take was some fool grabbing her and her reacting – where people could see. It was then that I remembered the bag her father had insisted that I take and keep with her.

I hauled it out of the old trunk and as I touched it, the voice was there. It gave instructions and I obeyed. *"They'll come to you now that's done. Be patient. Don't fear. They'll wear your shape, and remember this. Under law, Clio may make her own choices. But don't insist she be cut off from her kind, even if she agrees. Please, let her be free."*

And Clio is free. Her people came in the middle of the next winter, and listened to our stories. They said that by custom, law and love, we were father and daughter as long as we wished to be. That if Clio wanted to stay here, that was permitted providing that she never revealed herself. Our people, they said, weren't able to cope. (I politely refrained from pointing out that I'd coped perfectly well.)

In the end, we also compromised. Most winters a ship lands and leaves behind one, two or three of Clio's people. Some are sociologists, some xeno-anthropologists, but some are a father and daughter or mother and son, on what might be termed a school trip. We take them visiting cow towns, riding the rough lands, and down outlaw trails. And over the years it surprises many of those who live around here, how quiet the area has

become. Outlaws, thieves, and the rougher elements all seem
to be disappearing, and that, they feel, is all to the good. Since
I heartily agree, I continue to invite our friends, and I say nothing. Nor does Clio. But I have heard that they extol the benefits
of Earth, where a child may grow very quickly, and where the
wicked are always found – delectable!

SKUNKED

"**D**o I haf'ta?"

I glared at my ten-year-old son. "Yes, you do. I don't care that we live far from eastern civilization. It's 1865 not 1765. The schoolmaster arrives next week and as soon as he's settled in, you'll attend classes three days a week."

Matt glared rebelliously but I was adamant. "You'll not only attend class," I told him. "You'll work and learn. If the teacher reports that you have been lazy, rude or inattentive, your father will have something to say to you. Do you understand me?"

My son isn't a fool. He knew that his father wouldn't bother to reason. He'd just reach for his belt. So, unless Matt could think of some really convincing reason why he was unable to attend school, he'd go – and he would be polite to the new teacher and work hard.

After all, it was a miracle we'd found a teacher. The area is lawless still – and the Comanche are always with us – this part of Texas being still sparsely settled. But we'd built a schoolhouse, with a two-roomed school building beside it, three outdoor privies. There was a rainwater tank – that leaked constantly – providing a deep semi-liquid mud puddle beside it that was often abused by mischievous pupils. And we'd fenced everything in with a solid, high fence that sloped slightly outwards to stop any problems with roaming bulls. And at need, teacher and pupils could fort up and fight off an attack, until their kin could ride to the rescue.

I smiled as Matt trudged off. I'd had an excellent education and now his father (Jake Fletcher) and I wanted no less for my son. I'd been one of those to interview the new teacher and he had impressed me. I suspected that his enthusiasm would be imparted to his pupils as well.

"Matt? It's early. Are you leaving now?"

"Yes, Mr Patterson's telling us all about Romans."

I hid a smile. I'd been right. Mr Patterson did impart his own enthusiasm to his pupils and what was more they liked the man. It was infuriating therefore that a year later he had to take several months leave. His father in Fort Worth was gravely ill and there was no one else to care for him. But our neighbor had a solution of sorts.

"There's a man we could hire. He's an educated man, not a trained teacher, but he'd keep them from forgetting everything they've learned."

We hired Jonathon Weber on a month-by-month basis and found it a bad bargain. The girls were afraid of his sarcastic tongue and the boys hated him. Matt was increasingly reluctant to attend school, but I insisted. Until the day when he returned home in only the time it would have taken to ride there and back.

"Why are you home so early?"

"Skunk got into the school."

"A skunk?"

We had them in the area and it was true they often hid under buildings, but that was the idea of the fence. The gate could be barred from the inside and locked from the outside, and it was the custom to keep it secured at all times.

"How could a skunk get into the property?"

"Dunno, maybe Mr. Weber left the gate open."

It was possible. Meanwhile it would be several days before the schoolrooms were habitable again. Actually, it was longer than that. The smell faded to where Mr. Weber could teach within the building, and – a day later – another skunk made its presence felt.

This time Mr. Weber was certain he hadn't permitted the animal to sneak in. He yelled at the girls, believing, I think, that they could be more easily frightened into talking if they knew anything. Apparently, none of them did, or if they did, they weren't as scared of him as he hoped. He turned to threatening the boys, saying that he'd beat them all if no one confessed.

Matt's friend, Martin Lindsaw, promptly remembered an

earlier lesson and quoted the Magna Carta, the section about denying no man justice. Mr. Weber called him insolent and knocked him down. Martin stood up and left, mounting his horse, he rode for home where he reported events. His father, Colonel Lindsaw, is English, and as far as he could see, his son had been unjustly threatened, then assaulted for quoting a document the Colonel held in great respect. He went to the school and said that if Mr. Weber wanted to retain his job, he was on notice to do nothing to any pupil if he had no proof of wrongdoing and quoting the Magna Carta did not fall into that category!

* * *

The following day a skunk was again found under the school buildings.

Mr. Weber was angry and careless and this time it wasn't only the school that received a baptism when it was chased out. That did it. The temporary teacher wasn't going to be beaten by a group of children. He had a score to settle and if he could catch them bringing in a skunk, he could settle it on his terms.

He took to locking the school gate at all times, counting the children in and out, checking saddlebags and any bundle of clothing in case it held a black and white intruder. He was sure that the fence was too high and at the wrong angle to be climbed, but however the skunks were still appearing, every time the school became useable again, another skunk appeared to render it uninhabitable.

After three months Mr. Patterson was due back to teach from the following Monday and Mr. Weber had taught a bare handful of days over the period. But over the same time, I'd been listening, both to Mr. Weber and the children. As I say, I've had a good education, and that included tales of the Romans and their battles, also a popular topic with Mr. Patterson. Besides which, it's bad for children to believe their parents fools – even if their teacher is.

On the Friday, I gathered the Colonel, my husband, and several other parents and we rode to the school shortly before the children would finish their class for the day.

"Mr. Weber. I felt that it would be a good idea to discover how it is that the school is so infested with skunks."

There was a distinct sneer in his reply. "Of course, madam, if you believe you can do so."

I walked to the bookcase, reached down a book and opened it, showing the large hand-tinted plate to the Colonel.

"A ballista, by Jove. Do you think....?"

A neighbor peered at the picture, "What's a ballista?"

"A sort of catapult," the Colonel told him. "The Romans used them, you can toss huge rocks a long way with one of those."

He turned to look at me. "Where would it be?"

I smiled, having been watching both Matt and his best friend, Martin, and looking where they had glanced guiltily. I led everyone out of the school enclosure and up to a small copse of scrub oak at just the right angle nearby, I thrust bodily into that and, holding a bush aside showed them a small crude version of the ballista hidden under cut branches. Mr. Weber turned puce.

"Nonsense. Certainly, you could throw things over the school wall using such an engine. But a skunk would be badly injured when it landed on hard ground and none of the filthy little brutes ever showed much damage."

I saw light dawn on the Colonel and held my tongue. Let him be the person to explain.

"Of course not, man. Because as you said," here he laughed heartily, "they were filthy little brutes. Whoever used this machine made certain to drop the skunk in that large mud puddle by the water tank. That would cushion the impact. I'd expect the beast to have been fed a small amount of alcohol beforehand as well, so that, so long as it was neither hurt or frightened, it wouldn't react to being placed in the engine to be tossed over the fence. But speak the truth, wasn't each skunk that you saw, very muddy?"

The teacher nodded reluctantly. "I still don't believe it."

The Colonel snorted and then spoke that immortal line that none of us present that day have ever forgotten. He pointed decisively to the ballista.

"You're wrong, Weber, this is *exactly* how the pest was flung!"

ABOUT THE AUTHOR

Lyn McConchie started writing professionally in 1990, since then she has seen fifty of her books published and over three hundred short stories. She has written SF/F, but also true-life humor about her farm and animals (7 books known as the 'Daze' series), children's books, a YA quartet set in her own New Zealand, a western, a dozen Sherlock Holmes pastiches, half a dozen post-apocalyptics, and one non-fiction. Lyn says her imagination is related to the Energizer Bunny, and she hopes to be writing for many years to come.